LON

About the Author

Jo Whittemore has been captivated by fantasy since she was a child, dressing up as a fairy for Halloween (which also happens to be her birthday). She currently lives in Austin, Texas with her husband Roger, but longs to return to her California roots.

To Write to the Author

If you wish to contact the author or would like more information about this book, please write to the author in care of Llewellyn Worldwide and we will forward your request. Both the author and publisher appreciate hearing from you and learning of your enjoyment of this book and how it has helped you. Llewellyn Worldwide cannot guarantee that every letter written to the author can be answered, but all will be forwarded. Please write to:

Jo Whittemore
℅ Llewellyn Worldwide
2143 Wooddale Drive, Dept. 0-7387-0869-0
Woodbury, Minnesota 55125-2989, U.S.A.

Please enclose a self-addressed stamped envelope for reply,
or $1.00 to cover costs. If outside U.S.A., enclose
international postal reply coupon.

Many of Llewellyn's authors have websites with additional information and resources. For more information, please visit our website at
http://www.llewellyn.com

THE SILVERSKIN LEGACY

ESCAPE FROM ARYLON

Jo Whittemore

Llewellyn Publications
Woodbury, Minnesota

First Edition
First Printing, 2006

Cover design by Gavin Dayton Duffy
Editing by Rhiannon Ross
Image of figure on cover © Photodisc
Interior art by Gavin Dayton Duffy
Llewellyn is a registered trademark of Llewellyn Worldwide, Ltd.

Library of Congress Cataloging-in-Publication Data (Pending)
ISBN-13: 978-0-7387-0869-0
ISBN-10: 0-7387-0869-0

Llewellyn Publications
A Division of Llewellyn Worldwide, Ltd.
2143 Wooddale Drive, Dept. 0-7387-0869-0
Woodbury, Minnesota 55125-2989, U.S.A.
www.llewellyn.com

Printed in the United States of America

Ex-Friends

"Someone toss me another can of whipped cream!"

Ainsley Minks ducked to avoid a soda-soaked roll of toilet paper lobbed in his direction. "And that bag of bombs!" He pointed to a cardboard box filled with balloons painted to look like grenades, one of the many items the ninth grade boys had stocked for the Freshman Final.

Always popular with the students, never popular with the custodial staff, the Freshman Final at the end of the school year was the opportunity for the newcomers at Medmoy High School to celebrate the passage into their sophomore year.

By popular vote, Ainsley had been chosen to lead the guys onto the football field of battle. By practical vote, Megan Haney, one of the class's top athletes, commandeered the girls. When she wasn't dipping gym socks in buckets of egg yolk behind the dividing pylons, she ran among the girls shouting words of encouragement. And she, just as much as Ainsley, kept an eye on the other team's flag wrapped about the opposite goalpost.

They also kept an eye on each other.

When Megan decided to break for the guys' flag, Ainsley was ready for her. He dashed at her sideways, intercepting her spring across the field and yanking on the red flag clipped to the bottom of her T-shirt. Unfortunately, his fingers also grabbed a handful of her elastic gym shorts, and as he pulled downward on the flag, he exposed a leg of her bikini-cut underwear.

Another guy following Ainsley thought this was part of the plan and yanked down on the other side of Megan's shorts so that in a manner of seconds, everyone could see the four-leaf clovers patterning Megan's rear end. Those students closest to her catcalled and giggled while others drew nearer to see what had happened. Megan yanked up her shorts, glowering at Ainsley, face reddened by shame and the ketchup that had splattered her earlier.

"Oh Megan," he said, fighting back a laugh. "St. Patrick's Day has been over for months now. You can change your underwear any time."

Uproarious laughter rumbled across the field, louder than any football crowd the school had witnessed. Ainsley ran a hand through his perfectly styled hair and flashed Megan a smug smile. With a guttural screech, Megan drew back her hand and slapped Ainsley hard across the face. "Pervert."

A wave of silence washed over the earlier commotion, drowning all but a few gasps. Some students gave Megan disapproving looks, while others just stared, various food munitions dripping in their hands. Ainsley clutched his cheek, his lip curled in a vicious sneer.

"Don't flatter yourself." He looked her up and down disdainfully. "There is *no* part of you I would want."

"Yeah bitch!" yelled one of the guys in the crowd.

Megan's eyes narrowed and she glanced at the sea of faces. "Which one of you cowards said that?"

"Me." Ainsley stepped up to her so they were almost nose-to-nose. "I can throw my voice." The crowd rewarded him with snickers and clapping.

"Get out of my face, asshole." Megan shoved Ainsley in the chest, knocking him back a few paces. Ainsley jumped back where he had been, tilting his head from side to side mockingly. "Fine. Do you really want me to take you down, *Anal*-sley?" Megan opened her arms wide in invitation. "Because I can. Do you want to have your ass kicked by a girl?"

Ainsley glanced around at the other students who were hooting and catcalling, before fixing his icy gaze on

Megan. "Funny, I don't see any girls around here—just a freak," he said through clenched teeth.

Megan's eyes narrowed, and she raised her fists like a boxer. Ainsley tilted his head first to one side and then the other, his neck cracking ominously.

"Fight! Fight!" someone called.

"Ainsley! Megan!" Someone else was yelling, but it was an adult's voice. The crowd parted as a tall, gangly man with an oversized Adam's apple ran onto the field.

———

The man with the oversized Adam's apple, the principal at Medmoy, paced the carpet in his office, his wingtip shoes emitting the soft squeak of new leather. His hands were clasped behind his back as he bent over the two plush armchairs where Ainsley and Megan sat, clean and dressed in their regular school clothes.

"Your behavior was atrocious," he said. "I would have expected better from the president of the student council and the school's fencing champion." He glanced from Ainsley to Megan. "What would prompt you to come to blows before the entire freshman class?"

Megan cleared her throat, but she had scarcely parted her lips to speak when Ainsley interjected. "It wasn't her fault, sir."

Megan's eyebrows disappeared into her bangs. "It wasn't?"

The principal crossed his arms and leaned against his desk. "Are you saying *you* instigated this, Mister Minks?"

Ainsley looked at the principal, his eyes doleful. "No, sir. I think the real cause of the problem is her involvement in the fencing club. It's made her unnaturally aggressive."

"What?!?" Megan swiveled in her chair and fixed Ainsley with a fiery gaze. "You better take that back!"

Ainsley continued to look at the principal, feigning innocence. "See what I mean, sir? Maybe it's a good idea to remove her from that organization. The next thing you know, she'll be coming after other students with a *real* sword."

Elbows on his knees, Ainsley brought his clasped hands to his mouth with a grave expression. The principal couldn't see the smirk tugging at the corners of Ainsley's mouth, but Megan could.

"Sir," she began, rising from her seat, "after what happened today, I'm not sure if Ainsley is the best role model for his peers. As I'm sure you know, he is very popular with the students, and they look up to him. If they see him fighting, won't that send the message that violence is okay?"

Ainsley squeezed the arms of his chair, imagining Megan's neck in his grasp instead of the plush fabric. In the calmest voice he could muster, he said, "Sir, you know I'm not the aggressive type. I couldn't think clearly when Megan provoked me."

Megan whirled to face him. "Well—"

"That is more than enough from both of you!" snapped the principal. "*I* am in charge of this school and *I* will determine the appropriate punishment for each of you."

Ainsley and Megan settled back in their chairs to await their retribution, but not before shooting each other one last dagger-filled glance.

Other students would have been surprised to know that their relationship hadn't always been so embittered. They had been next-door neighbors since birth, and a friendship had blossomed from the comfort that accompanied their closeness. Ainsley had been protective of Megan, defending her from stray dogs and bullies, and Megan had consoled Ainsley whenever his father buried his nose in another dusty, weathered book instead of spending time with his son.

When they had reached the seventh grade, Ainsley had starred in a commercial and had been offered a modeling contract. The time he spent with Megan became shorter and shorter until she could only see glimpses of him between classes. Accusing Ainsley of becoming shallow and preoccupied with show business, she threatened to end their friendship if he didn't return to his normal life.

At his *father's* request, not Megan's, Ainsley declined the contract, but he never forgot the ultimatum that Megan had placed on their friendship. There had been many instances since when one or both of the ex-friends attempted to make amends, but unusual situations always prevented their reunion—such as the one they were in now.

After several minutes of silent contemplation, the principal came to his decision. "Mister Minks, I'm afraid I will have to place your presidency on probation pending the end of the school term next month. At that time, it will be determined if you are eligible for re-election the following school year."

Ainsley nodded and sat a bit straighter in his chair, attempting to smother a grin. Beside him, Megan crossed her arms and regarded the principal with a raised eyebrow.

"Miss Haney," he said, "since you were so keen to use your muscles to fight, perhaps you will be just as keen to use them to scrape gum from under the desks during today's afternoon break."

"All Ainsley has to do is go on probation over the summer when we don't even have school, and I get stuck with gum duty?" Megan's arms fell to her sides, and she leaned forward, her mouth twisted into a scowl. "Oh, that's fair!"

The principal mirrored her scowl. "Make it a *week* of scraping gum."

Megan clamped her mouth shut and nodded, snorting air from her nostrils like an enraged bull.

"I hope you both have drawn something from this experience," said the principal. He fished a key ring from his trouser pocket and unlocked a steel filing cabinet behind his desk. "Miss Haney, your cleaning materials." He held out a white, plastic bucket, a paint scraper, and a pair of yellow dishwashing gloves. "You're both free to go."

Nose wrinkled, Megan accepted the proffered items and exited the room with a smug Ainsley fairly dancing on her heels.

"It's a shame you have gum duty, Megan," he said in a voice devoid of any compassion. "Let me be the first to aid your cause." Ainsley reached into his mouth and withdrew a saliva-drenched blob of chewing gum with his thumb and forefinger. He released the piece, and it fell with a plunk to the bottom of the bucket, centered like a chewy pink bullseye.

Still outside the principal's office, there was nothing Megan could do except glare at Ainsley and walk away. As she turned to leave, however, a group of giggling girls appeared, blocking her path. Megan rolled her eyes, but behind her Ainsley grinned.

"What's going on?" He ran a hand through his hair and stood with his arms folded across his chest so that his biceps were more prominent.

One of the girls, a pony-tailed brunette, blushed. "Nothing, Adonis . . . I mean Ainsley!" She and the other girl dissolved into giggles again, and Megan mimed vomiting into her bucket. The girls quieted and stared at her.

"Do you have a problem?" The pony-tailed girl crossed her arms over her chest and stared down her nose at Megan.

"Nothing that a shovel and a body bag won't fix, Nicole," said Megan, fixing Ainsley with a saccharin-sweet smile.

He watched her disappear down the hall with the bucket banging against her legs and heard a door slam.

"Ugh. She's so disgusting." Nicole shuddered and waved her hands in the air as if shaking off the taint of being around Megan. "Why doesn't she join the rest of the dogs at the pound?" She snorted with laughter, and the other girls joined her.

Ainsley grinned. "Oh, come on, she's not that bad, is she?"

"Please." Nicole touched Ainsley's arm. "She's got that rat's nest of hair and those elephant feet . . . and those *ears*!"

"She's like Dumbo with an Afro!" exclaimed another girl. All the girls broke into peals of laughter, Nicole still clutching Ainsley's arm.

Ainsley frowned and pulled away. "Hey now, there's no need to tear her apart like that."

The girls stopped laughing and blinked at Nicole who just gaped at Ainsley, opening and closing her mouth. "We . . . we didn't mean—"

"Yeah . . . you did," Ainsley said, raising an eyebrow.

One of Nicole's cohorts stepped forward. "*You* were just making fun of her today."

"That's different. You don't know her like I do." Without offering an explanation, he walked off to look for Megan, leaving the group of girls staring after him.

He found her in the science laboratory under one of the desks, scraping the underside with as much force as she could muster. "Megan?"

She ignored him and kept dropping hardened bits of gum into her bucket.

Ainsley stooped beside her. "Uh . . . how's it going?"

Megan gritted her teeth as she fought a particularly stubborn wad of Dubble Bubble. "Like you care."

"Do you . . . do you need any help?"

"Not yours. Piss off." She returned to her task, purposefully ignoring the shocked look Ainsley now directed at her.

"Okay then." He straightened up, glaring at her back. "Since you obviously enjoy your grudges, I'll be going now. Make sure you scrub extra hard under the corner desk where I sit."

The Next-Door Neighbor

"Did your mail-order boyfriend arrive?" Ainsley asked Megan as the car that had dropped him off peeled away from the curb.

Megan slammed the mailbox lid shut. "Nope, but he received something of yours by mistake." She waved an envelope at him. "Looks like a bill from your plastic surgeon."

Of course, this wasn't true. Ainsley's breath was just as perfect as everything else about him. His hair was just the right cut and shade of blonde, and his eyes, a sapphire blue, always caught the sunlight so that they sparkled.

The sprinkling of freckles across his tanned face perfectly contrasted his gleaming, toothpaste-commercial smile, and the relentless hours he spent on martial arts had given him a build that even the seniors envied. He *was* the Adonis the other students made him out to be.

Ainsley snatched the letter from her. "It's probably my reward check for the Sasquatch I reported seeing in the house next to mine."

Megan glowered at him. True, she was no great beauty, but she certainly wasn't a Sasquatch either. Her auburn curls grew thick and wild, like a lion's mane, framing her heart-shaped face and constantly falling into eyes that looked like twin pools of coffee. She wasn't fond of her hair, as she could never part it properly because of the large cowlick on her widow's peak. Once, Ainsley had suggested that she pull it into a ponytail, but Megan had informed him this wasn't an option since her ears protruded from the side of her head like open doors on a sports car.

Megan's biggest complaint wasn't her corkscrew curls, however—it was her slightly bucktoothed smile. When she did smile, one side of her face raised up more than the other in a bizarre leer, which she dubbed her "lop face."

Ainsley thought her lopsided smile was endearing and liked the way her nose wrinkled up when she was especially pleased, but he would never admit that to someone who derided him for valuing physical beauty. Ainsley enjoyed the popularity that being attractive allowed, but Megan scoffed at such shallowness. She had opined, on more than occasion, that students who strove to fit in were nothing but sheep.

"Where's your fan club?" she asked, grabbing the handle of the garage door and yanking on it. "Meeting to decide whose underwear they should expose next?" She gave another tug on the handle, but the door wouldn't budge.

Ainsley bent down and flipped the locking latch. "You brought that on yourself, you know. If you weren't always regarding cool people as if they had the plague—"

"Cool people?" Megan interrupted him, jerking the door open with such force that a wire basket of racquetballs fell from the shelf above, pelting her like oversized hail before bouncing into the driveway. "Ugh!" Megan scooped up the basket and stormed from the garage with Ainsley still on her heels.

"Yes, cool people. You know . . . what you're *not*?" Ainsley leaned against the garage and watched Megan as she gathered up racquetballs. "I'm surprised they even allowed you in the fencing club. Someone must have been stupid to give *you* a weapon."

"A fencing foil isn't a weapon," said Megan witheringly, plucking the final racquetball from the pavement. "It doesn't even have a point . . . kind of like your mindless blathering."

Ainsley leaned forward and tipped the basket toward him, spilling several balls back onto the ground. "You missed a couple."

Megan gritted her teeth. "We can pick up where we left off on the football field, if you'd like."

Ainsley grinned maddeningly. "See? Always with the violence."

"Why don't you take this ball and——"

"Good afternoon, Megan, Ainsley," interjected a gravelly voice. They turned to see their elderly neighbor, Mr. Niksrevlis, uncoiling the hose he used for watering his lawn.

Mr. Niksrevlis, or Mr. Nik, as they affectionately called him, was a squat, balding man with a shaggy, gray beard and matching mustache, the latter of which fluttered when he talked. He wore his whitening fringe of hair tied back in a braid that reached all the way to his hefty waist and barely covered a small tattoo on the nape of his neck.

His potbelly jiggled when he laughed or sang, both of which he did often and with great exuberance. The ballads he intoned, though unfamiliar, still held fancy with Ainsley and Megan who enjoyed hearing of the make-believe world his lyrics brought to life. Ainsley's favorite, "The Ballad of Lodir," told of a young champion who performed many heroic feats for his people. Megan preferred "Onaj's Horn," a fast-paced tune about the struggle between a man and a unicorn.

"Hi, Mr. Nik!" Megan thrust the basket of balls at Ainsley and trotted to the wooden-railed fence that separated her yard from Mr. Nik's. "Are you going away for the weekend?" Mr. Nik typically did his yard work on Friday if he would be away.

Mr. Nik nodded happily as he turned on the faucet and began sprinkling water on his flower beds. "It's my grandson's birthday tomorrow."

"Cool. How old will he be?" asked Megan.

Ainsley, who had abandoned the racquetballs, joined them. "Why do you care? Looking for a boyfriend? I don't think Mr. Nik's grandson dates outside his species, Megan."

"Now, now . . ." Mr. Nik waggled a finger at Ainsley before answering Megan's question. "He'll be eighteen, which is a very special age in our family. We've planned quite a celebration, but nothing too—*OOF!*"

Mr. Nik doubled over, grasping his stomach. The water hose hit the grass, and its flow ricocheted, spraying Ainsley and Megan as they clambered over the railing to reach their neighbor.

"Are you okay, Mr. Nik?" asked Megan as Ainsley dragged the hose aside.

"I'm fine," he reassured her, looking down at his waist. "Just a bout of . . . indigestion." He cocked his head at different angles and shifted his belly from one side to the other before finally looking up at Megan, red faced.

"What color is my belt? I . . . can't see over my belly."

Megan balked. "Your belt?"

One of Mr. Nik's personal prides, apart from his meticulously manicured lawn, was the pewter belt buckle he always wore. Its surface was mesmerizing, a vibrant blue accented with wisps of white that seemed to drift across the blue background like clouds across a sky.

Today, however, his belt buckle appeared far less cheerful. Its background had shifted to a murky gray, and thin silver lines streaked diagonally across it like miniature bolts of lightning.

"It's gray!" said Megan. "How did it change colors like that? Is it a mood belt?"

Ainsley squinted and leaned forward. "If it is, you're in a towering temper, Mr. Nik. It looks like the sky before a storm."

"Are you sure?" asked Mr. Nik, removing the belt from his waist and studying it. There was an unusual edge to his voice that brought the teenagers' gazes from his belt to his face. "Oh dear," he said, twirling his mustache with one hand. "Dear, dear, dear."

For the first time in years, Megan and Ainsley exchanged a look that wasn't murderous. Megan touched her elderly neighbor's forearm.

"Mr. Nik, are you sure everything's all right?" she asked.

"Yes, I—I'm fine," said Mr. Nik absentmindedly, patting his arm several inches above where Megan's hand rested. "Thank you both for your concern. Good day." He hurried into his house then, leaving them to stare after him in bewilderment.

Megan waited to see if Mr. Nik might reappear to explain himself, but he didn't.

"What was *that* about?" asked Ainsley, crossing Mr. Nik's lawn to shut off the hose.

"I don't know," admitted Megan, hopping down to join him. "That belt buckle obviously upset him somehow, and I'm not sure I believe that part about his 'indigestion.'"

At the spigot under Mr. Nik's dining room window, Ainsley watched his neighbor yank open the drawers of a sideboard and paw through each one, not seeming to care about the items that fell to the floor in his haste.

"That's a strange place to keep the antacid tablets," Ainsley muttered to Megan who now crouched beside him.

"Looks like he found what he was looking for," she responded as Mr. Nik plucked a bottle of green liquid from among several other vessels and disappeared into his kitchen.

"What was that green stuff?" asked Ainsley.

"Maybe it really isn't anything more than a stomach ache." Megan sighed. "It must be some home remedy."

Mr. Nik emerged from his kitchen then, his mittened hands clutching a copper saucepan. Steam curled from its contents, but it was unusually dense, like woodsmoke. Contrary to Megan's assumption, he did not approach his dining room with the culinary concoction but turned and headed for his back porch.

"Let's see what he's up to," Megan whispered to Ainsley, tugging at his sleeve.

Ainsley pulled away with an imperious snort. "Forget it. I'm not so much of a loser that I have to resort to snooping for entertainment."

Megan's excited smile vanished, and her cheeks glowed pink. "I'm not a loser, and I'm not snooping! I'm just . . . checking to make sure Mr. Nik is feeling well."

Nevertheless, she hesitated. Ainsley knew she was torn between quibbling with him further and discovering the reason for Mr. Nik's secrecy. He guessed which choice she would make even before she darted from her spot under the window towards Mr. Nik's backyard. Smiling to himself, he returned to Megan's yard and bounced one of the racquetballs against the side of her garage, waiting to see what "mysteries" she unraveled.

A six-foot wooden fence bordered Mr. Nik's property, and as Megan drew close, she heard his sliding glass door glide across its runners. She listened as he stepped outside and poured the liquid from his copper pot into another container, but no unusual sounds reached her.

After a few moments of silence, broken by occasional mumbling from Mr. Nik, guilt tugged at Megan's conscience, and she turned to leave her elderly neighbor to his own affairs.

She paused, however, at the sound of an unfamiliar male voice. Mr. Nik never invited guests to his home, yet he was definitely speaking to someone in a rushed, anxious tone. Megan glanced at Ainsley, but he was now amusing himself by juggling several of the racquetballs, so she returned to the fence and listened.

"Yes, yes. I'll be leaving here in a few minutes," said Mr. Nik.

"We don't have much time, Bornias," urged the other man. "I cannot discuss the issue with you at length, but the family heirloom *must* be secured. The kingdom depends on this."

"I understand, Frieden," Mr. Nik told the other man, "but I need to gather a few things first."

Their conversation continued, but the words did little more than buzz in Megan's ears as she stumbled away.

"So what mysterious activities did you catch Mr. Nik doing?" asked Ainsley as she approached him. His eyes widened. "Was he . . . was he sitting on his porch swing?" He clapped a hand to his mouth in mock horror.

To his surprise, Megan grabbed him by the arm and dragged him into the garage.

"Something freaky is going on," she hissed. "Mr. Nik is talking about kingdoms and heirlooms to some stranger in his yard."

Ainsley stared at her, unblinkingly. "You're so weird. I'm going home."

"Wait!" she grabbed him by the back of his shirt. "I'm serious. He's leaving in just a few minutes."

"Bye," he said and walked away.

Megan peered around the wall of her garage, but Mr. Nik's front door remained shut. On the pretense of gathering the racquetballs, she dropped a few in her driveway and took her time placing them in the basket. After three minutes of puttering around in her driveway, however, she still saw no sign of Mr. Nik.

Wondering if he had changed his plans, she returned to his back fence. To her relief, she heard him on the opposite side, muttering to himself. Spotting a knothole in one of the boards, she peeked into her neighbor's yard to see what could possibly be delaying him.

What she saw almost made her laugh out loud.

Mr. Nik stood with his back to the fence, wearing ridiculously outdated knee-length pants sewn from a purple, velvety fabric. He wore a matching lace-up jerkin over a white ruffled shirt, the cuffs of which almost hid his beefy hands, and shiny leather boots that buckled across the arches of his feet. He reminded Megan of a performer she had seen once at a Renaissance fair.

Her eyes flitted from Mr. Nik's strange attire to a soft glow emitting from something before him. She noted with surprise that the glow was shifting in color from blue to purple to red. A low humming filled the air, and it piqued Megan's curiosity.

Inserting one sneakered foot into the knothole, she eased herself up so she could see over the fence. It had been poorly constructed, as if its maker had done nothing more than shove a row of boards into the ground, so she balanced herself precariously and peeked over the top.

Mr. Nik had stepped back into his house, and Megan noticed with curiosity that his friend was not in the yard. The "something" his body had been blocking appeared to be a porcelain birdbath. The light she had seen came from a silvery liquid that filled the basin.

"Too weird," she whispered.

Behind Megan, Ainsley watched in amusement as she dangled from Mr. Nik's fence like an inept cat burglar. He crept across the Haney's backyard and yanked on Megan's free foot. With a small squeak, she slipped from the fence, her right foot still caught in the knothole. He chuckled as she turned and punched him hard in the arm.

"You dummy!" she hissed. "You almost gave me a heart attack! Why are you here?"

"What you're doing is called invasion of privacy, you know," said Ainsley, rubbing his arm where Megan had pummeled him.

Megan shot him an irritated look and whirled back around. "It's a good thing Mr. Nik went inside," she said, sidestepping Ainsley's comment.

Ainsley peeked between two of the boards. "What's he doing that's got you scaling the fence, anyway?" he asked.

"I don't know," said Megan, climbing again. "He had his back to me the entire time, but there's a strange light coming from his yard, and it keeps changing colors."

Ainsley furrowed his eyebrows and looked up at Megan to see if she was serious. "What kind of—"

"Shhh. He's coming back," hissed Megan, lowering her head once more.

Ainsley returned to his spot at the fence, but the space between the boards was too narrow to offer him much of a view. "Megan," he tugged on her back pocket, "get down so I can see."

She kicked at him with her free leg. "There's that funny light again," she whispered down. "It's different now, though. It's stopped changing colors, and now it's . . . woah!"

The glowing light settled on a deep purple and began to encircle Mr. Nik.

Ainsley yanked harder on Megan's leg. "Megan, let me see!"

Megan didn't kick back at Ainsley this time. She was too busy staring openmouthed at the circle of light, which had now expanded to encompass the yard. Mr. Nik unconcernedly scratched the back of one leg with the opposite foot and plucked a piece of lint from his sleeve.

Grumbling, Ainsley backed away from the fence, and then sprinted towards it. His plan was to shimmy up the boards so he could pull himself to the top, but unfortunately, he was unaware of the fence's wobbly nature.

Megan glanced down in time to see him coming at her, and her eyes grew as large as dinner plates.

"Ainsley! Don't!" she whispered hoarsely.

It was too late. Ainsley hit the wood with the full weight of his body, and as he started to climb, the fence cracked sickeningly, toppling forward into Mr. Nik's yard.

Megan screamed, and Mr. Nik turned with a startled expression on his face, throwing up his arms to shield himself. Squeezing her eyes shut, Megan buried her head in her arms, preparing for the impact that would jolt through her body when the fence hit the ground.

The Brave New World

But it never did.

A veil of darkness enveloped them, torn by flashes of light that revealed nothing but the flimsy patch of fence and further darkness. Megan's screams intertwined with a howling wind that seemed to rush at them from all directions, jerking her and Ainsley about the strange void like a runaway roller coaster cart. She hugged the fence to her, feeling the splinters pierce her forearms. Beside her, Ainsley glanced around in confusion, the wind swishing through his hair and flapping his shirttails.

Then, as suddenly as the surges of air had occurred, they subsided, and the fence began to fall at a rapid pace.

Ainsley's stomach lurched into his throat, and Megan's screams lapsed into silence as she was left breathless by the sudden drop.

Ainsley was the first to notice the darkness around them lightening to a hazy blue, and with the enhanced visibility, he chanced a glimpse over the edge of the fence. A wavy green pattern loomed closer and closer, but he couldn't discern what it was. Then, he saw a bird settle onto the pattern, bobbing upon the waves, and his heart skipped a beat.

"Megan!" The bird fluttered away at the sound of Ainsley's voice, but Megan didn't need to see it to comprehend what was happening. Her chest tightened, as did her grip on the boards, but she was doing exactly the opposite of what Ainsley wanted her to do.

"Let go! We have to get off!"

But Megan refused to relinquish her stranglehold on the fence, and they were now much closer to crashing into the water. With an effort, Ainsley used his legs to push her towards the edge of their makeshift transport. Megan scrabbled at the planks, trying to hold on, but Ainsley was too strong for her, and she was forced from her one comfort. Helpless to do anything but free fall, she watched as Ainsley continued his rapid descent, still riding the fence.

He *tried* to leave it, but something hindered his movement. He glanced down in a panic and saw that the hem of his jeans had snagged on a stray nail, but no matter how he jerked and twisted, he couldn't free himself. In the next moment, the fence crumbled beneath him, and the icy water stung his skin. The board that held him prisoner released him, but it upended as it did so, banging him smartly on the forehead.

Megan hit the water seconds after he, and even though she anticipated it, the slap of water against her flesh caused her to cry out in pain. Unfortunately, it was at this same moment that she sank beneath the surface. Her lungs filled with fluid, causing her to choke and cough as she expelled enormous bubbles of precious air. Her arms and chest burned from impacting the water, but she still swam upwards, breathing in deep when she broke the surface to gulp mouthfuls of air.

They had landed, with luck, in the deeper end of a small lake. Megan wiped the damp from her face, a mixture of tears and water, and screamed for help. She hadn't even thought to look for Ainsley, who was now slowly sinking to the lake bottom, unconscious. She was, therefore, confused and somewhat peeved when she saw Mr. Nik standing on the nearest shore beside a hooded figure, waving at her with a pudgy hand but making no motion to rescue her.

Then Megan felt the water churn beneath her feet. Imagining all manner of lake creature surfacing to devour her, she screamed and kicked towards shore. After a minute's vigorous swimming, however, she realized that she was no closer to her goal. In fact, she had moved *upward* rather than forward until her body was no longer submerged, and she floated atop the water, as light as the leaves that drifted around her. To her left, the water continued to churn, and Megan eyed it apprehensively until Ainsley's limp form rose to the surface.

"Ainsley!" She grabbed him beneath his arms, but her assistance was unnecessary. An invisible force levitated her and Ainsley into the air and carried them ashore, depositing them onto the grass with a soft thump.

Leaping to her feet, Megan snatched up a splintered piece of wood that had drifted ashore and held it like a dagger, whirling left and right in search of danger.

"Put that down before you get a splinter," Mr. Nik chided her. "There is nothing here to hurt you." He dropped to his knees beside Ainsley and attempted to revive him while the hooded figure approached Megan, pulling back his cowl.

He peered at her through a curtain of chestnut hair that tumbled to his cloaked shoulders. His eyes were the color of creamy jade, and they conveyed wisdom beyond his years, which couldn't have been more than thirty.

"Are you alright?" he asked in a deep voice that sounded strangely familiar.

"Confused . . . and a little scared," she admitted, finally dropping the piece of wood. She glanced around, taking in the lake and a mountain range that loomed to the south, stretching in either direction for miles. On the north side of the lake where she stood, a vast prairie of knee-high grass bent to a wind that also bowed the tops of several pine trees lining the eastern shore. They grew parallel to the mountains and had enormous brown rocks piled beneath them. Nothing of the landscape was familiar to Megan, but she had to admit it was breathtaking. From the sun's position, it appeared to be close to noon, but the temperature was much cooler than she was used to.

"Where are we?" she asked. "Some national park?"

The man smiled, and it reached his eyes, settling pleasantly into the wrinkles at the corners. Megan found herself at ease in his company, as if he were some favored uncle rather than a stranger. "I . . . think it would be best if Bornias explained that to you," he said.

Megan remembered hearing Mr. Nik be addressed as Bornias just once before.

"You're Frieden, aren't you?" she asked. "The one Mr. Nik was talking to earlier."

He bowed before her. "I am. And you must be Megan. Bornias has told me stories about you and Ainsley."

At the mention of Ainsley's name, Megan glanced at his limp form and shuddered. Despite Mr. Nik's attempts to staunch the flow with his handkerchief, blood was spilling from an ugly gash on his forehead. "Will he be okay?"

"Once the wound clots, he should be fine," Frieden assured her, "but I should offer my assistance." He swept his cloak back and reached for a scabbard that hung across his right hip. From its casing he drew a sword, and the steel blade resonated in the cool morning air, glinting against the sunlight.

Megan regarded the weapon with an expression of reverence, for despite her position in the school's fencing club, she had never come across an actual sword.

With a swish of the blade, Frieden sliced a swath of fabric from his cloak and offered it to Mr. Nik who applied it to Ainsley's wound. As Frieden slid the sword back into its scabbard, Megan noticed an insignia on the gilt handle that mirrored the tattoo Mr. Nik wore.

"You like the sword," said Frieden with another smile. "Do you handle a blade?"

Megan puffed out her chest and raised her chin. "I'm the best in my class," she said, though she wasn't sure how similar fencing was to swordplay.

"Perhaps you and I will duel sometime." He winked at her before crouching to assist Mr. Nik.

Megan watched them for a moment, then spotted a thick tree stump and ambled towards it, almost tripping over a series of holes that were hidden by the tall, velvety grass.

"Stupid gophers," she muttered as she stepped into a particularly wide hole.

She extracted her foot and started to shake it clean, but blue pea-sized beads, not granules of dirt, dropped to the ground from her sneaker. Megan scooped up several of the beads and plopped down on the tree stump to study them, holding one up to the brightening sky.

"What is *this*?" The silhouette of a minute figure was outlined against the light. It shifted as she rolled it between her thumb and forefinger, as if repositioning itself. She examined several of the other beads, and they all appeared the same.

"Those are narshorn eggs," said Frieden, joining her.

"They're virtually impenetrable."

"I can believe it," said Megan, squeezing either side of the shell and feeling no give. "What's a narshorn?"

"A small rodent. You see this?" He pointed to a distinct triangular shape inside the egg that pointed skyward. "This is a barb on the underside of the narshorn's tail that it will use to penetrate the thick casing. It also helps the narshorn protect itself from predators."

"That must be a pretty sharp barb. Why is the shell so—"

"Are we enjoying our nature lecture?" asked Mr. Nik in a contemptuous tone. Megan and Frieden turned to see a livid expression forcing Mr. Nik's bushy eyebrows into a sharp V.

Megan smiled weakly and held out the egg she'd been studying. "It's a narsh . . ." She trailed off and jammed the egg in her pocket as Mr. Nik's face turned the color of tomato paste. His right hand tugged at his beard, an action reserved for when he was extremely upset, such as the time Ainsley had cut the buds off all his prize-winning roses and given them to a few girls at school.

When Mr. Nik's face reached a violent purple, he began chastising Megan and the unconscious Ainsley in shouts that sent spittle flying from his lips. He cut himself short several times, launching into a new sentence, as if his anger had chased away the old one. Megan cringed and glanced at Frieden for help, stammering an apology whenever she could slip in a word or two. Mr. Nik chose to ignore this, however, and his voice continued to echo off the mountains.

"What were you two doing? You could have been killed! What would your parents say? You're lucky you're all right! How am I supposed to get you home now?"

After five minutes of this diatribe, Megan burst into hysterical tears. Frieden alternated between comforting her and entreating Mr. Nik to calm himself.

"You are not improving the situation, Bornias," he said. "Ainsley and Megan have been torn from what was familiar to them because of an *accident*. I am sure their desire to be here is no greater than yours to have them here."

Mr. Nik grunted but looked sheepish, and the color in his face lightened from enraged purple to embarrassed pink. "It's not that I don't want them here, Frieden," he said. "I've longed to show them this world since they were old enough to comprehend their own, but this is not the best circumstance under which they could have arrived. On top of that, I lack the materials to create another portal to send them back."

Megan dried her eyes on the back of her hand, listening to the exchange of conversation. Several words in Mr. Nik's argument struck her as unusual. "What portal?" she ventured to ask. "Send us back where?"

Both men started and looked at her, unaware she had overheard their conversation.

"Portal? Who said anything about a portal?" Mr. Nik forced a laugh, but Frieden prodded him in the back.

"You might as well tell her, Bornias. She'll realize everything is different soon enough."

Mr. Nik sighed and nodded, fingering the laces of his jerkin. He twisted one of them around a water-pruned thumb and cleared his throat several times. "Well, as you know I often go away for the weekend to visit my family. This . . . this is where I go."

"And where is this place?" pressed Megan. "Are we still in North America?"

Mr. Nik made a funny sound in his throat, a cross between a whimper and a snort. "No, we're . . . we're not in North America . . . or on Earth." He suddenly became fascinated with a stain on his shirtfront.

Megan's eyes narrowed. "Excuse me? We're not on Earth?"

It was Mr. Nik's turn to look to Frieden for help now.

"You arrived here through an interdimensional portal," explained Frieden. "This is the continent of Arylon in the world of Sunil."

Megan backed away from the two men, not taking her eyes off them until she had reached Ainsley. She crouched beside him and, after ensuring that he was no longer bleeding, shook him by the shoulder.

He didn't respond at first, but Megan continued to jostle him until he groaned and opened his eyes.

"Megan, what are you doing?" Ainsley put his hand to his forehead and winced. "What's going on?"

He struggled to sit up, and Megan clenched a fistful of his shirt. She had meant to whisper, but the panic she felt caused her voice to come out in a high-pitched squeak.

"We have to get out of here. Mr. Nik has lost his mind."

"What?" Ainsley slapped Megan's hand away, squinting at everyone as he gathered his senses. "Mr. Nik lost . . . what?"

Mr. Nik stepped in front of Megan before she could speak further against him. "My name is not Mr. Nik or Mr. Niksrevlis. It is Bornias. I am a wizard, born of this world, and I am as sane as I have ever been."

Ainsley blinked slowly as Bornias's words sank in.

"You're right, Megan. He has lost his mind." Ainsley staggered to his feet, but the vertigo that spun the world around him caused him to stagger on the spot.

Frieden placed an arm around Ainsley's shoulders to steady him, but Ainsley pulled away, tumbling to the ground in an unceremonious heap. "Who's Mr. Touchy-feely?" he asked, rubbing his elbow.

Frieden kneeled beside him. "My name is Frieden Tybor, and I am governor of the Protectors of the Staff of Lexiam. I apologize if I have caused you discomfort, but you give the appearance of one who has drained the ale barrel."

He said this with such a straight face that Ainsley couldn't help but smile. His grin turned to a grimace quickly, however, when his head began reeling with pain. Clutching at it, he pulled off the makeshift bandage in the process, his laceration glistening with blood.

"We should get him to a healer," Frieden told Bornias. "He seems a bit delirious, and both of them should be examined to ensure they have no broken bones." He extended his hand to Ainsley, but Megan forced herself between them.

"We're not going anywhere," she announced. "Not until you tell us more about what's going on."

"We really don't have time for this," said Bornias, massaging his brow. "I have never, in all the years I have known either of you, given you any reason not to trust me." He placed his hands on Megan's shoulders and looked into her eyes. "I need you to trust me now. There are things in this world that defy all Earth reason and logic."

Megan looked to Ainsley, but he knew no better what they should do. "If you were borne of this world," Megan met Bornias's gaze, "why did you come to ours? What's wrong with this world?"

"I traveled to Earth on a personal matter and found it to my liking," said Bornias, releasing her. "There is nothing wrong with this world, but there will be if I do not attend to matters soon."

"Well, I'm sold," said Ainsley, though it was more the excruciating pain he was suffering than Bornias's logic that swayed him. He was able to stand alone this time but didn't refuse when Frieden ducked under his arm to support him.

"Well, Megan?" Mr. Nik extended his arms in invitation. "Would you care to accompany us, or would you rather wait here until nightfall when the shirkbeasts come out to hunt?"

"All right," she agreed. "I'll go with you, Mr. Nik . . . Bornias."

Bornias smiled. "I appreciate your cooperation."

Megan draped Ainsley's other arm over her shoulder, and the three of them followed Bornias along a worn footpath through the trees until the trail ended abruptly in the midst of the thicket.

Up close, the rocks scattered beneath the trees now looked more like huge seedpods. The ones that still hung from the branches caused them to sag and bend low to the ground.

"What are those?" asked Megan, nudging one with her foot. "Pine cones?"

"No, they're fire pine pods." Bornias piled several into his arms, but one of them slipped from his grasp and hit the ground with a heavy thud.

"What do you do with them?" asked Ainsley. He stooped to hand the fallen pod to Bornias, but it was as heavy as a shotput. "Use them as weapons?"

"Weapons?" Bornias simpered at him. "How primitive do you think we are?"

"We crack the pods in half and use the heat they generate to start fires," explained Frieden. "Or you can cook directly over them. The heat will last for a good few days."

"I'm sure we can use them in the kingdom galley," said Bornias. "We always need more."

"How much farther do we have to go until we reach the . . . er . . . kingdom?" asked Ainsley. The more he thought about all Bornias had told them, the more interested he became in exploring this enchanted world. He surveyed the area, expecting to see a castle or at least some sort of fortress, but to his disappointment, the tallest things for miles were the snow-capped peaks beside them.

"We're here. This is the entrance to the kingdom of Raklund," said Bornias, gesturing at the mountains, "built within these walls."

Ainsley exchanged a troubled glance with Megan as their elderly neighbor whistled a tune to the mountainside. After two verses, however, a furry, mouse-sized head popped out of a crevice in the rocks and started chattering madly at Bornias. Bornias imitated its tones, and the creature disappeared into the mountain.

"Chitwisps," he explained as Ainsley and Megan gaped at the place where the creature had just been. "They're similar to squirrels, but they nest in the mountains. They make very loyal pets and their language is easy enough to learn, but their heavy accents can be difficult to understand."

He said all of this matter-of-factly, as if talking to squirrels was nothing out of the ordinary.

"Bornias is an excellent linguist." Frieden told Ainsley and Megan with open admiration. "He's one of the few people who can communicate with unicorns."

"You're not serious," said Megan, turning to Bornias, wide-eyed. "Unicorns?"

Bornias nodded. "As I told you earlier, you'll find many things here that don't exist back on Earth. Chitwisps are actually one of the most normal creatures you'll come across."

"So, is that chitty thing going to let us inside the mountain or just leave us standing here?" asked Ainsley, trying to take all the strangeness in stride.

"He's gone to tell the guards to open the entrance," said Bornias patiently, shifting the weight of the pods in his arms.

Ainsley studied the stone wall in front of them, looking for cracks or seams that might indicate a doorway, but there were so many random fractures and rivets in the weathering rock that if there was an entrance, it was impossible to tell where it might be.

Then, there was a scraping, grinding sound of stone against stone, and a section of the rock wall opened inward to reveal a narrow passageway.

"Let's go," said Bornias, squeezing through the entrance and grunting. "I must get this passageway expanded . . . or lose some weight."

Megan regarded the doorway with unease. She was claustrophobic and none too eager to enter what could become her stony tomb.

"Go on, Megan," urged Frieden.

She took a deep breath and stepped into the passageway but backed out a second later, bumping into Frieden and Ainsley.

"I can't go in there," she said breathlessly. "It's too small."

"Nonsense," said Frieden, frowning. "If Bornias can fit in there, you certainly can."

"No, it's not that." Megan blushed, and Ainsley realized what was wrong.

"She's afraid!" he hooted, then put a hand to his head remembering his injury. "Don't worry, Megan," he said in mock sympathy. "If the tunnel collapses, we'll be sure to tell your parents that you died bravely."

"That will do, Ainsley," said Bornias from somewhere within the mountain. "Why don't you come in here?"

Ainsley shot Megan a demeaning look and pretended to cower in fear as he entered the passageway. He let loose a girlish scream from inside the tunnel. "Oh, help! The walls are caving in. I can't . . . ow!" His already bruised head smacked against a low hanging piece of rock.

Bornias rolled his eyes, and Megan giggled. Rubbing his head and blushing, Ainsley stepped out of the tunnel into an antechamber whose walls and ceilings were beset with foot-long spikes that pointed inward.

Bornias waited for him, fire pine pods now at his feet, flanked by several people in orange cloaks who regarded Ainsley as if he were a carnival sideshow. Ainsley's flush deepened, and he turned to watch Megan's progress.

Frieden extended a hand to her. "Close your eyes, and I shall lead you through."

Megan reached for it with hesitation and jammed her eyelids shut. Frieden pulled her forward, and after a few cautious steps, she no longer felt the sun's warmth upon her cheek. She could now sense the rock walls on either side of her and dug her heels into the ground, her heart pounding at a rabbit's pace.

Frieden tightened his grip. "Just a few more steps," he coaxed, but Megan leaned away from him like a mule pulling at the rope of its master.

Despite how ridiculous she looked, Ainsley couldn't help pitying her, and when he saw her lower lip tremble, he did the only thing he knew might help.

"I guess you *do* need someone to protect you, don't you Megan?" he jeered, leaning into the tunnel. "I never met a bigger *coward*."

Megan's eyes snapped open and locked on Ainsley's, ire lending them a cold edge that could have frozen water. Frieden noticed the change in Megan's disposition and had the good sense to tighten his grip as Megan now dragged him through the tunnel, her free arm outstretched to wring Ainsley's neck the moment her fingers were in grasping range.

As she stepped clear of the passageway, however, the people in orange cloaks shifted to either side of a set of spike-laden steel doors and pulled them open to reveal another, much larger room.

"Inside is the main hall of Raklund," said Bornias, gesturing to the open doors. "It's nothing fancy, but . . . we call it home."

He motioned Ainsley and Megan forward, but they both halted when they reached the entrance, shock melding their feet to the ground.

"Oh, my," was all Megan could think to say.

Ainsley was just as lost for words.

Exploring Raklund

To call the main hall "nothing fancy" was a bit of an understatement, and it took Ainsley and Megan several moments to recover from the aesthetic wonder that spread before them.

They were standing at one end of an enormous, oblong geode encrusted with crystals of all colors and sizes. Torches mounted in the larger formations caused the gems all around them to shimmer and sparkle. The crystals on the floor had been ground down by wear, but the ones on the ceiling resembled an elaborate chandelier, twinkling almost regally as the multi-faceted crystals caught the light from all angles.

"Pinch me," said Megan breathily as she looked around at the brilliant colors.

Ainsley was more than happy to slug her hard in the arm.

"Ow! I said 'pinch,' not punch!" She scowled at him and rubbed her sore arm, but Ainsley held a finger to his lips and gestured towards Bornias, Frieden, and the cloaked group.

The men and women in orange cloaks that had watched them enter were now speaking in low voices with Bornias, though several times their eyes shifted to Ainsley and Megan. The men held lethal-looking swords in their free hands and the women held orbs of electricity, which buzzed with white light.

"Well, where is Rayne now?" Bornias asked the group.

A stocky man with a belly paunchier than Bornias's answered. "He and a few of our Protectors went after the thief."

Bornias kicked at the floor with his boot and a loose piece of crystal skittered away. "I can't believe Rayne was foolish enough to remove the Staff of Lexiam from the security of the palace," he muttered. "Without binding it to himself, no less."

"Well, he was under the care of those inept Silvan Sentry," said the fat Protector. "You know if it had been the Protectors watching him, this never would have happened."

Frieden held up a hand. "Now, Stego, we mustn't start pointing fingers. The important thing is to retrieve the

Staff of Lexiam before its absence is noticed or before it falls into the wrong hands."

"I'd say it's a bit late for that," huffed Stego, crossing his sausage-like arms.

Bornias paced the floor, his boots crunching upon the broken crystals. "Frieden, we need to arrange a meeting this evening between the Protectors and Silvan Sentry. If we are to solve this problem, we must work together. I'll rejoin you as soon as I've taken these two to the hospital and ensured they're in good care."

Frieden nodded, beckoning to the Protectors, and, with a swish of their cloaks, they strode down the hall.

"Well," said Bornias, turning to Ainsley and Megan, "there isn't much else to see here, so I suppose we should be on our way. Just allow me a moment to rid myself of these things." He collected the fire pine pods he had dropped in the antechamber, and Megan closed the door behind him when he re-entered the room.

"Do you need help carrying those?" she asked.

"No, thank you, but if you would be so kind as to re-move that torch from its bracket." He nodded at one whose light seemed duller than the others.

Megan pulled it free, and the section of wall on which it had been mounted swung outward to reveal a small tun-nel in which a wooden cart rested. Bornias loaded the pods onto the cart and gave it a hearty push.

"That tunnel goes to the kitchens," he explained. "The chitwisps will see it on its way."

"So, this staff you guys were talking about must be pretty important, huh?" asked Ainsley as they started walking down the hallway.

The further they traveled, the smoother and more polished the floor underfoot became, so that soon the children's sneakers were squeaking loudly, while Bornias's boots clicked hollowly and importantly.

"The Staff of Lexiam is very important," answered Bornias. "It has the power to control the elements and has been in the care of the Silverskin family, my family, since it was created."

"Silverskin?" asked Megan. "Is that why you have that silver tattoo on your neck?"

"What silver tattoo?" asked Ainsley.

Bornias bent down and held up his braid so Ainsley and Megan could both see the back of his neck. The Silverskin tattoo looked like a wavy Greek cross with four different drawings emblazoned in the joints.

"What do the symbols mean?" asked Megan.

"They represent the four elements of life—earth, or land as we refer to it here, fire, water, and air," said Bornias. "There are other elements, of course, but those are the most crucial."

"Why does your family protect the Staff of Lexiam?" asked Ainsley.

Bornias straightened up and let his hair fall back into place. "Silverskins are the only people who can resist the draw of the staff's power."

"So, you use this staff to control the elements?" asked Ainsley with a frown.

"Oh my, no," said Bornias, shaking his head. "The Staff of Lexiam is used as little as possible. It's far too dangerous."

"Why don't you just destroy it then?"

Bornias smiled faintly. "Don't think we haven't thought of that. Generations of my family and hundreds of my followers have tried numerous methods, but the Staff of Lexiam always retaliates, and everyone who attempts to destroy it is vaporized. Since we couldn't do away with it, we formed the Protectors of the Staff, which Frieden currently governs. Their job is to ensure that the staff will never be usurped and put to foul use."

"But it's been stolen," Ainsley pointed out.

Bornias sighed, his brisk pace slowing to a pallbearer's march. "The Protectors have failed, and my world lies in peril. I know this." His shoulders slumped, as if he had been the one to fail, and Megan squeezed his hand.

"So, if the wrong kind of person got hold of this staff," began Ainsley, "are we talking, like, the end of the world?"

Bornias shook his head. "In the hands of the wrong person, the staff can cause great earthquakes, floods, destructive forest fires, tornados . . . anything that the elements can bring about. But without the Quatrys, the staff can fuel these events for just a short period of time."

"Without the what?" Ainsley and Megan asked together.

"The Quatrys." Bornias held up the fingers on one hand. "Four gemstones created from elements and very strong, very archaic magic. They can cause damage for a longer amount of time, but at a smaller degree."

"What happens when the staff and Quatrys are put together?" asked Megan, though she had a feeling she already knew.

Bornias's expression became grim. "Then we face destruction of apocalyptic proportions. The power of the staff is magnified a hundredfold, and it is no longer limited in size or duration." He paused at the expressions of alarm on Megan and Ainsley's faces. "But it gets worse."

"Worse than the end of civilization?" asked Ainsley dubiously.

"The joining of the Quatrys and staff creates a new form of magic that can be used to resurrect the dead and open a portal anywhere the wielder desires even, say, to Earth."

The hairs stiffened on the back of Megan's neck. "Earth?" Her mouth filled with saliva as it did when she was about to throw up.

Ainsley, too, was stunned. He hadn't found it difficult to discuss the problems of this world he barely knew but being informed that his own world might be in danger was an uncomfortable twist.

"The portal creation can be changed into potion form," continued Bornias, "which is how I manage to travel between the worlds, but I used my last potion for my trip here, not expecting to have any hitchhikers." He glanced pointedly at Ainsley and Megan.

"Where are the Quatrys? Are they safe?" asked Ainsley as they approached the end of the corridor. It intersected with another hallway, whose floors also shone like polished marble. The walls, however, were regular stone, though they were scarce for all the doors, statues, and tapestries that lined the hallways. Prismatic globes dangled from the ceiling, issuing vibrant beams of light that made it seem as if the sun was cutting through the bedrock and spilling across the floor.

People bustled back and forth, in and out of the many doors, clad in cloaks like the Protectors, but in different colors that ran the gamut from lime green to shimmery silver. Many curious glances were now being directed at Ainsley and Megan who were still wearing their Earth clothes.

"Why don't we drop this for now," said Bornias in a low voice. "These people don't know what has happened, and we don't want to create a panic."

Bornias pasted on his best smile and waved to a passerby, nodding occasionally. He was a popular figure in Raklund, as everyone seemed to know his name.

"If he's so well-known here, why does he keep coming back to Earth?" Ainsley asked Megan under his breath.

Megan rolled her eyes. "Not everyone revolves their life around popularity." To Bornias, she asked, "How is it so bright in here? You don't have electricity, do you?"

"We have something better," said Bornias. "Snow light."

"Those globes are made of snow?" Megan tilted her head back and stared at the ceiling.

"Filled with it," corrected Bornias. "In the mountains of northern Arylon, the snow absorbs sunlight rather than reflect it, so it's packaged and shipped across the country."

"How do they keep it from melting?" asked Ainsley.

"These globes are coated on the inside with Instant Ice, a special liquid that keeps them extremely cold for months at a time. The snow lights are far more efficient than the torches that were used to brighten the kingdom decades ago, mainly because they don't remove oxygen from the air."

"Why? Is there a limited amount of oxygen in here?" Megan glanced around in a panic for windows or vents of some sort.

"What's the matter, Megan?" asked Ainsley with a grin. "Air seeming a little thin all of a sudden?" He drew in a deep breath until it filled his chest. "Ahhh. I hope I don't use up all this wonderful oxygen."

"Shut up," said Megan, but she immediately began drawing shorter breaths.

"There is no real concern for lack of breathable air," said Bornias, "so take as many breaths as you want. Plants provide oxygen and take in toxic carbon dioxide. You may have noticed the plants hanging in the corners of the hallways and potted outside some of the doors."

"Yeah, but the amount of oxygen these give off can't be enough for all these people." Megan gestured around them.

"That would be true if these were Earth plants." Bornias smiled as he leaned in close. "But we're in my world now."

"Sooo, the plants provide you with oxygen, but how do they stay alive?" asked Ainsley. "I mean, you can water them, but they need sunlight, too."

"I would have thought that was obvious," said Bornias.

Megan grinned. "Snow lights! That's sunlight they're giving off, isn't it?"

Bornias nodded and gestured Ainsley and Megan close. "And now, perhaps, we should keep the questions to a minimum. These people know nothing of other dimensions, so they assume you're one of them. Best not to seem so unfamiliar with your 'own world.'"

They nodded and followed Bornias to the right along the crowded hallway. Megan heard the sound of several giggling voices issuing from a doorway to their right. She turned and saw three girls about her age dressed in white cloaks. They were huddled in a group, whispering and glancing up at Ainsley who was staring at the people who passed, totally oblivious to their attentions.

"Why do all these people wear different colored cloaks, Bornias?" he asked in a low voice.

"Well, the color of the cloak determines the career and ranking of the individual. Officials wear the richer, darker colors, while those of lesser status wear lighter, brighter colors."

As proof, he pointed at two military-looking men in yellow cloaks that were speaking with an important-looking man in maroon.

The three men continued down the hall, revealing a floor-to-ceiling mural on the wall behind where they had stood. It had been painted with the utmost attention to detail and appeared to be a story line with a man in a silver cloak as its focus.

The montage showed the man resting a foot on the arrow-ridden belly of a dragon, riding a cloud white unicorn, and standing with arms crossed triumphantly in the midst of a circle of beautiful dancing women.

Ainsley's face lit up when he realized who the subject of the mural was. "That's Lodir Novator, isn't it, Bornias?"

One of the giggling girls hissed to her friend, "He can be my Lodir any day," at which the other girls broke into peals of laughter. This time, Ainsley heard them and turned around. He flashed one of his thousand-watt smiles and ran his fingers through his hair so that the cut on his forehead was more noticeable.

"Ooh, he leads a life of danger," squealed one of the girls.

"If you consider banging your head on a fence dangerous," interjected Megan, unable to bear the thought of an Ainsley fan club in this world as well.

The girls stopped laughing and snorted indignantly before stalking away, noses upturned.

"You *have* noticed that you scare away normal people, haven't you?" Ainsley told Megan, slightly annoyed.

"Oh, whatever." Megan waved her hand as if swatting a pesky fly. "I'm sure there are plenty of other bimbos around here just as willing to worship you." She turned to the mural. "So this is the guy from that song, huh? I'm not impressed."

"Not impressed?" said Ainsley. "He's done all kinds of things nobody had ever done before—at least in this world." Ainsley began counting on his fingers. "He was the first to tame a dragon and ride a unicorn, *and* he was the first to resist the charms of the sirens. There's even a song about him." Ainsley pointed to a bronze plaque beside the mural upon which *The Ballad of Lodir* had been inscribed:

Hail to Lodir Novator, the hero of the day
   Hearken to his feats so grand and follow as you may
   The first tale is of Arastold, a dragon of great ire
   Her chilling gaze was snowy cold

Her gold blood burned like fire
   When Lodir spilt it on the ground
   It made an evil hissing sound
   The terror of the sky was gone
   Our nation praised its champion . . .

The ballad continued praising Lodir's exploits for several more verses.

"Was he a Silverskin?" Ainsley asked Bornias who stood behind them.

"No, but he did establish the Protectors. Some say he was a great man, but others found tremendous fault with him."

"Why?" asked Megan.

A trilling voice called out to Bornias before he could answer, and he glanced over his shoulder.

"Ah, here's Lady Maudred. I'll see if she can help you two from here. I need to get back with Frieden."

A bosomy, older woman approached them, beaming at Bornias. Her cloak was golden and her powdered, white hair was styled in an elaborate pompadour. Her posture and dress indicated that she was someone of importance, but to Ainsley and Megan's surprise, she curtsied gracefully to Bornias.

"Your Majesty," she said.

Megan and Ainsley exchanged surprised looks.

"Bornias is royalty?" whispered Megan.

"That explains why everyone knows him," answered Ainsley.

"Lady Maudred," Bornias returned the curtsy with a slight bow. "You know how much I hate that pompous genuflection. Nobody else bows to me."

Lady Maudred gave him a meaningful look. "Despite what you tell your followers, sire, I will continue to show you the proper respect I feel you are due."

Bornias sighed heavily. "You've always been a tenacious one, Cordelia."

"I'll take that as a compliment," said Lady Maudred with a wry smile.

"I knew you would," said Bornias. "You're actually just the woman I was looking for. I need you to take these two to the infirmary and then to get something to eat."

Lady Maudred looked down at Megan and Ainsley and jumped in surprise as if she were seeing specters rather than people. She nodded and smiled, but no warmth reached her eyes.

"They are Governor Frieden's niece and nephew," continued Bornias. "This is Ainsley and this is Megan. They are visiting from Pontsford."

"It is very nice to make your acquaintance," said Lady Maudred, offering her hand first to Ainsley who shook it hesitantly. "You remind me of my son when he was a boy," she said, peering down at him.

Ainsley stepped behind Megan, unsettled by Lady Maudred's scrutinous gaze. Megan, unsure of how to greet royalty, stepped forward and curtsied awkwardly, which won a genuine smile from Lady Maudred.

"This one has the potential to be quite a charmer," Lady Maudred said to Bornias.

Megan flushed with pleasure while Ainsley rolled his eyes.

"Will the two of you be staying long?" asked Lady Maudred.

"No more than a few weeks," spoke up Bornias. At his words, Megan and Ainsley exchanged another shocked look but didn't say anything. They hadn't been expecting to stay here for more than a few *hours*; they couldn't imagine what their parents would do if they didn't turn up soon.

Lady Maudred saw the look they exchanged, but mistook it for something else. "Bless their little hearts. They're so sad it's going to be such a short visit with their Uncle Frieden. Well, don't you worry. You can come back anytime!" She put out a hand to tousle their hair but paused mid-reach and looked Megan and Ainsley up and down.

"Your majesty, why are they dressed . . . so?" She plucked at Ainsley's shirtsleeve, and he and Megan also cast inquisitive looks at Bornias.

"Ainsley and Megan," began Bornias, glancing about him, as if hoping an excuse would materialize. "They're . . . performers in the traveling Carnival theater. These are their costumes. They brought them to show their uncle."

"Ah, that explains everything," said Lady Maudred with a nod. "We should still get you into some more suitable clothes for your stay here."

"I'll leave them in your care then, Lady Maudred," said Bornias, turning to leave.

"Rest assured you are leaving them in the best hands, your Majesty," said Lady Maudred with a bow.

Megan turned to Ainsley, who looked as if he would rather be tied to a moving truck, and then to Bornias. She gazed at him with her most doleful eyes, but he merely patted her on the shoulder.

"I'll be back for both of you this evening," he said. "Thank you for your aid, Cordelia."

Lady Maudred smiled and curtsied again as Bornias proceeded down the corridor and disappeared into the crowd. Then, she turned to Megan and Ainsley and clapped her hands together.

"Well, let's get started, shall we? Infirmary first, then clothes, and then lunch. We have quite a lot to do before the king returns to collect you."

In the Company of
Lady Maudred

The infirmary was situated at the end of the hallway behind a set of swinging double doors. Ainsley had never been overly fond of hospitals and hung back at the entrance until Lady Maudred bounced him through the doorway with her massive bosom.

They walked into a crude waiting room curtained off from the treatment area, furnished with a single row of wooden chairs and a receptionist's desk. The receptionist herself was a scrawny, bespectacled woman with her hair tied back in a messy braid. Her tortoise shell glasses were at least an inch thick, and she was reading a piece of parchment held inches from her nose. She took no notice of Lady Maudred or Ainsley and Megan until Lady Maudred forced a loud cough.

The receptionist dropped the parchment with a start and looked up at Lady Maudred with eyes magnified to the size of ping-pong balls behind her thick lenses.

"Goodness, I apologize. I was just reading up for my medical exam," she said. She tucked the parchment away and pushed a heavy ledger towards Lady Maudred.

"Sign in, please," she indicated a blank page and passed Lady Maudred a quill and inkwell. Lady Maudred scrawled her name, and the receptionist attempted to read it upside down, squinting as she did so.

"Ah, Lady Mulligan," she said, getting the name wrong, "How is that green rash on your chest coming along?"

Several people standing near Lady Maudred stepped away.

"I'm not Lady Mulligan. I am Lady Maudred. You must be thinking of someone else," she said haughtily, blushing.

The receptionist turned the ledger around so she could read it and laughed. "Oh, of course. How silly of me. Lady Mulligan is much younger, isn't she?"

Lady Maudred gave an indignant "Humph!" and steered Ainsley and Megan to the row of seats.

There were a few people waiting ahead of them to be seen, but Ainsley and Megan didn't mind. It allowed them time to observe the other patients and their fascinating maladies. One woman in a lime green cloak, a Protector-in-Training judging by the electric orb in her hand, looked as if she had just stuck her finger in a light socket. Her hair was frizzled and jutted from her scalp as if there were hundreds of staticky balloons holding it up. A Protector in an orange cloak patted the young woman's free hand reassuringly.

"It's all right, dear. You didn't know better. It's happened to all of us at one point or another. You just have to remember not to sneak up on your orb while it's resting."

The young woman nodded, her mouth opening and closing wordlessly as the Protector guided her toward an empty chair.

Behind the two Protectors, an old man sucked his thumb and tugged on the arm of a little boy who spoke to the receptionist in a deep voice well beyond his years. At one point, the boy grew tired of the old man yanking on him and snapped, "Not now, Padi. Grandpa's busy. I'll take you to buy some candy after the nice healer switches our bodies back."

"Candy!" the old man shrieked with delight, clapping his hands.

"Had a spot of trouble with a substitution solution, Amikri?" A man standing behind the little boy nudged him in the back and chuckled.

"Yes, and I'm out of the antidote," said the little boy. "What are you here for?"

Ainsley and Megan never got to hear what was wrong with the other man because a nurse appeared behind the curtained area and, glancing at the ledger, called Lady Maudred's name.

"It's actually these two who need to be seen," said Lady Maudred. She stood and beckoned for Ainsley and Megan to follow.

The treatment area had been partitioned into smaller rooms, each of which was also curtained off, so they were unable to see what was happening with the other patients. It was probably for the best, however, because they kept hearing strange, squishing sounds coming from behind several of the curtains, and at one point they heard a man screaming.

On one side of the hospital, a large set of black doors had been chained and locked. One of the doors bore an ominous sign that read, "Quarantined." Ainsley and Megan looked at each other, both wondering what lay beyond the black doors.

The nurse directed them behind a green curtain, where a short man with purple hair was washing his hands. He looked up from his scrubbing as they entered and smiled at them.

"Hello, I'm Healer Sterela," he said cheerily. His voice echoed as if he were in a cave. "What have we here?"

"The children need some medical attention," said Lady Maudred. "They may have some serious injuries."

Healer Sterela held Ainsley's jaw gently and inspected a bruise on his cheek. Ainsley looked at the echoing healer out of the corner of his eye and saw that Healer Sterela had violet eyes with silver pupils shaped like stars.

The starry eyes strayed up to the laceration on Ainsley's forehead, and he frowned at Ainsley in concern.

"How did this happen?" He touched the edge of the cut, and Ainsley winced.

"I fell off a fence," said Ainsley.

Healer Sterela didn't look as if he believed this. "Have a seat," he said, pulling a wooden chair away from the back wall.

Ainsley sat as Healer Sterela turned to the waiting nurse. "I need Majida." The nurse nodded and left the room.

Healer Sterela turned now to Megan and gave her a quick once-over as they waited for the nurse to return.

"You don't appear to be in bad shape. Did you fall off the same fence or a different one?" he asked, thumbing at Ainsley.

"Same," she said, doing her best not to laugh.

The curtain swished as the nurse returned carrying a gigantic, black spider in her arms. The spider was about the size of a housecat, and when Ainsley saw it, he jumped from his chair, knocking it over with a loud bang. Megan chose to hide behind Lady Maudred's massive backside.

"What is that thing?" asked Ainsley, righting his chair with a shudder.

"This is Majida," said Healer Sterela. "He's an anato-scopic arachnid. Hold still now. He's going to check your body for any signs of broken bones."

Lady Maudred forced Ainsley back into his seat as the nurse handed the wriggling spider to Healer Sterela.

"Mind the forehead, Majida," he said.

A sick feeling washed over Ainsley as the healer approached him and lifted the hairy-legged beast over his head. Its pincers clicked, and Ainsley was positive he saw hunger-induced drool at the corner of its mouth. He tried to jerk away, but Lady Maudred held him in a viselike grip.

As the spider was placed atop his head, Ainsley issued a rather feminine scream of terror. His heart raced, and his breath came in short sporadic gasps.

The spider probed his scalp with its long, hairy legs, and once or twice one of its limbs slipped from the top of Ainsley's head down to his eye level, where he could see it swinging in front of his nose if he crossed his eyes. The spider squeaked at Healer Sterela, who grunted in affirmation.

"Ainsley, Majida needs you to relax. Your vital signs are misleading, and it's making it difficult for him to notice any real problems."

Ainsley nodded and breathed deeply, trying to calm his nerves. A few minutes later, the spider squeaked again and Ainsley felt the weight of its body lifted from his skull. Lady Maudred relaxed her grip on his arms and he leapt out of the chair, rubbing at his head furiously and twitching.

Healer Sterela flashed him an encouraging smile. "Other than your superficial wounds, nothing seems to be amiss. You next, dear," he said to Megan as Lady Maudred forced her onto the chair. Megan had no time to protest before the healer placed Majida on her head.

Upon seeing that the spider hadn't devoured Ainsley whole, Megan remained much calmer than he had, and in a matter of moments, the spider squeaked again. Healer Sterela nodded in satisfaction, removed the spider, and handed it back to the nurse, who carried it out of the room.

"How does that thing work?" asked Ainsley, rubbing his hands on his jeans. He had managed to get his breath back, but his skin still felt clammy.

"What thing?" asked Healer Sterela as he scribbled on a scrap of parchment. "Majida? He reads your neural impulses—your brain waves, if you will, to check for any damage reports your body might be sending your brain. It took him a bit longer with you, mind, because your body was going into a 'fight or flight' mode and putting up a defensive front."

"There was a spider on my head!" squeaked Ainsley.

The healer was digging through a drawer now, not having heard Ainsley's argument. He found what he was looking for and turned back to Ainsley.

"Let's see to that laceration now, shall we?" He wiggled a tinted jar, and Ainsley covered his scar protectively.

"It's fine, really," Ainsley insisted, terrified that Healer Sterela might have some other creature inside the darkened jar that he wished to attach to Ainsley's face.

"Well, yes, it's clotting beautifully, but this salve will help it heal faster," said the healer. He handed the jar to Ainsley for his inspection.

The jar was labeled "Mossfur," and Ainsley removed the lid with trepidation. He relaxed when nothing jumped out at him but then wrinkled his nose. The mossfur was a clear gel with an overpowering stench, like a mixture of vinegar and wet dog.

"You see? Nothing to worry about." Healer Sterela took the jar back from Ainsley and dipped his index and middle finger into the smelly paste, rubbing it gently onto Ainsley's cut. It stung like rubbing alcohol, and the smell brought tears to Ainsley's eyes. The healer applied some to Ainsley's cheek for good measure before recapping the jar and handing it to him.

"Use this twice a day. Once when you get up in the morning and again before you go to bed. If you do so, that cut should clear up in a week's time."

"You mean I have to smell like this stuff for a week?" Ainsley wiped at a teary eye and rubbed his nose.

"You'll get used to the smell," the healer assured him. "Consider yourself lucky it wasn't infected. You don't want to know what you'd have to drink every morning."

———

As they exited the infirmary and rejoined the crowd in the hallway, Megan turned to Lady Maudred.

"What was behind those tall, black doors in the infirmary?" she asked.

Lady Maudred's mouth twitched, but she said nothing, instead leading the way to an unmarked door. It opened into a dark, vacant room, and she motioned for Ainsley and Megan to enter before her. After a backward glance at the crowded hallway, they stepped nervously through the doorway.

Lady Maudred followed and left the door ajar to allow a sliver of light to illuminate the room, eerie shadows playing upon her hardened features. She stared down at them with a stony expression, but when she spoke, her voice was soft.

"Since you are unfamiliar with our kingdom, I will entertain your question, but you are broaching a subject that is taboo in our land, and I shall ask you not to mention it again—especially around King Bornias."

Ainsley and Megan stared at her, mystified, but nodded.

"Those black doors lead to the Illness Room, and not a soul has crossed its threshold since the last of the afflicted were imprisoned there."

The hair on Megan's arms rose as her skin puckered with goosebumps. "The Illness? Was that . . . like a really bad cold or something?"

"It was far worse than any cold," said Lady Maudred. "It was a plague. It killed over a hundred people in Raklund alone and I'm sure many in other lands as well."

"Only a hundred?" Ainsley didn't bother to mask his disbelief. "In a kingdom this size that's not much of a plague, is it? Sounds more like a strong coincid—Ow! Megan!"

She had found his foot in the dim light and stomped upon it. "I think what Ainsley means is . . . don't plagues usually affect more people in an area as confined as this?"

"Does it matter how many people *should* have been affected? Even one person is enough when it's someone you love," said Lady Maudred. Her words held not malice but sorrow, and she reached into her sleeve for a handkerchief.

Ainsley lowered his eyes to the floor as Lady Maudred dabbed at her eyes with the tissue. "You're right. I'm sorry. It just seemed strange to me."

An awkward silence followed until Megan cleared her throat. "Why wasn't the disease more widespread?"

Lady Maudred composed herself and blew her nose with a genteel air. "The Illness wasn't contagious. It seemed to seek out certain people," she said, her words softened by her stopped-up nose.

"But . . . if it wasn't contagious," said Megan, "why were the people with the Illness quarantined?"

Lady Maudred folded her arms, the tissue crumpled in one fist. She sighed and looked at the ceiling as if selecting her words carefully. "The Illness caused . . . personality shifts in those it affected. The one thing that kept these changes bearable was the company of another who had the Illness. Anyone who didn't have it was regarded as an enemy . . . and promptly dispatched."

Megan tilted her head to one side. "And by dispatched you mean . . ."

"Killed," said Lady Maudred with an edge to her voice.

"Oh my." Megan held her hand to her mouth.

"It's over now, though, isn't it?" asked Ainsley nervously. Bringing a fatal illness home from this world wasn't his idea of a souvenir.

Lady Maudred nodded. "As silently and swiftly as the Illness arose, it vanished. There hasn't been a documented case of the Illness in over fifteen years—not since King Bornias's daughter-in-law succumbed to it."

"Bornias's poor son!" said Megan. "He must have been so upset."

Lady Maudred laughed then, but it was such an eerie, mirthless laugh that Megan backed a few steps from her.

"He didn't have time to grieve. Hers was a more aggressive Illness, and in two day's time she couldn't remember who he was. In her eyes, he became an enemy."

Ainsley's eyes widened. "She . . . she didn't kill him, did she?"

"She did, and King Bornias was deeply distraught . . . over both lost souls."

Neither Ainsley nor Megan said a word. The laughter and chatter from the other side of the door seemed to mock the solemnity within the darkened chamber.

"I don't mean to frighten you, but you must understand the gravity of this situation. Do you understand why you mustn't speak on this topic anymore?" asked Lady Maudred.

They nodded, and Lady Maudred held the door open, ushering them into the hall where life was waiting for them.

———

Lady Maudred spoke no more of the Illness as they started their shopping adventure, which led them into a wing of the hall they hadn't yet explored. Here, all the doors had images and writing burned into their wooden surfaces. Lady Maudred explained that the etchings upon the doors displayed the name of the merchant and his or her craft.

"So, this first floor is nothing but the infirmary and merchant shops?" asked Ainsley.

"*And* the royal kitchen, but that's in another wing of its own," said Lady Maudred.

They stopped before a door with the word "Sari" branded upon it beneath an image of a needle and spool. Lady Maudred rapped on the door, and a woman opened it, pins sticking out of her mouth as if she had kissed the wrong end of a porcupine.

"Good morning, Cordelia," she said. She smiled around the mouthful of pins.

"It is actually afternoon now, Sari." Lady Maudred pointed to a dingy window at the rear of the room where sunlight fought to get inside. "If you ever washed your windows you would know this."

"Perhaps if *someone* stopped coming by every day with a new request, I would have the chance."

She and Lady Maudred smiled at one another, and then something peculiar happened that seemed to confirm just how far Ainsley and Megan were from home.

Lady Maudred hummed a tune to herself, and as she reached her final note, the grimy window rattled. Ainsley and Megan turned their heads just in time to see the filth slide off the glass and onto the floor, settling into a dusty pile. Sunlight burst through the window, which now appeared as clean as if it had just been scrubbed.

Ainsley gaped at Megan. "Did you see—"

"How bright it is outside?" Megan interrupted him loudly. "I sure did!"

"Lower your voice to a suitable volume, please," said Lady Maudred as Ainsley frowned at Megan. "You see how easy it is to keep this place clean, Sari? Now, let me show you an easy way to get rid of the dust."

When Lady Maudred and Sari walked away, Megan flicked Ainsley's arm. "Don't say stuff like that!"

"Stuff like what?" asked Ainsley, rubbing his arm.

"We're supposed to be from this world, remember? We can't act amazed at everything we see."

"But she did magic, Megan!" Ainsley pointed excitedly at the window. "Didn't you see—"

Megan jerked Ainsley's hand down. "Yes, and it was incredible, but we could put ourselves in a lot of danger if people found out we were . . . aliens."

Lady Maudred and Sari walked within earshot again, so Megan could do nothing more than give Ainsley a warning look.

"So, what brings you to my shop today, Cordelia?" asked Sari. "I assume you're not shopping for yourself . . . for once."

Lady Maudred smiled at her. "No, the children need to be fitted for new clothes while they're visiting."

"Visiting, eh?" Sari circled Ainsley, looking him up and down. "These are interesting breeches the two of you are wearing. I've never seen a material to compare." She squatted between Ainsley and Megan and tugged at the leg of Megan's jeans. "It feels so durable! Where exactly are you visiting from?"

"We're from . . . um . . . ." Megan couldn't remember the town Bornias had mentioned to Lady Maudred, and she glanced at Ainsley for help.

"They're from Pontsford, but they're part of the traveling theater troupe," supplied Lady Maudred, eyeing Megan warily. "These are actually their costumes."

"Say no more." Sari sighed. "The material must have come from far away and probably cost more than my shop to import." She looked wistful for a moment, and then beamed at Lady Maudred. "Well, what did you have in mind for their outfits?"

"A royal three for the boy and a royal five for the girl," said Lady Maudred. She sounded as if she was ordering a combo meal at a drive-thru restaurant.

"I think, Cordelia," said Sari, now walking around Megan and taking in her mussed-up hair and grubby clothes, "the girl should wear breeches as well. I don't think she would be happy in a dress." She winked at Megan, who returned it. She hated dresses.

"Very well," Lady Maudred said, waving a manicured hand. "You know best of course, Sari."

"Let me see . . ." Sari tapped a finger against her chin. "I just received a shipment of spider's wool, and I also have some nice silk from Pontsford. Would you like me to sew something from those materials?"

She produced a swatch of silk for Lady Maudred to rub between her fingers. "The cloaks can be silk," agreed Lady Maudred, "but I'd prefer the tunics and breeches to be something other than spider's wool. It's too itchy for anyone their age to wear without complaining. Do you have any motley skin?"

Ainsley cringed, hoping motley was an animal, not a person. In response, Sari pulled out several fabric swatches that appeared similar to suede. She allowed him and Megan to choose their colors; Megan chose a rich plum for her tunic and a light tan for her breeches, and Ainsley chose a watery blue for his top with a dark brown for the pants.

"Excellent choices," said Sari, removing a roll of measuring tape from her dress pocket. While Sari took their measurements, Lady Maudred busied herself browsing the bolts of cloth that lined one of the shop walls.

Sari called out the numbers to her assistant who wrote them on separate slips of parchment. When she had finished, Sari rolled her measuring tape back up and gestured for Ainsley and Megan to have a seat.

"This should take about fifteen minutes," she said.

Megan wondered what kind of sewing machine Sari had that could produce two entire outfits in such a short amount of time. "Can we watch?" she asked.

"As long as you stay out from underfoot, I don't see it being a problem," said Sari with a smile.

Looking around, however, Megan couldn't see any sewing machines, just several men and women milling about long tables, talking quietly.

Sari approached the men and women with the two lists she had compiled as well as the fabrics they were to use. Megan's measurements were handed to the women and Ainsley's to the men. Each group huddled around their list before withdrawing to their different stations to work.

The people sewing the cloaks had the easiest job, pulling patterns onto their sections of silk. One of the cape makers opened a red velvet pouch hanging from her belt and measured a fine, silvery powder into a brass spoon.

The cape maker sprinkled the spoonful of powder over two pairs of scissors resting on the table, and they jumped to life, snipping furiously at the air, eager to begin their job. The cape maker laid each pair of scissors at opposite ends of the cape pattern and said, "Follow the lines."

The scissors quivered with excitement and began cutting the cape pattern out of the silk at a rapid pace, fairly eating through the fabric.

After watching the cape maker for a few moments, Ainsley and Megan wandered to another station where a tunic was being sewn. One man was instructing five enchanted needles on the stitching job he needed, while his partner surveyed the scissors' cutting job.

The enchanted needles and scissors performed their tasks much faster than any human could have, and as Sari had promised, the clothes were finished in fifteen minutes time. With a final nip and tuck, the scissors stopped clicking and the needles stopped moving.

"How do they know when to stop?" asked Ainsley as the men and women presented their completed garments to Sari.

"It depends on how much enchantment powder the tailors measure out," answered Sari. "That's what the measuring spoons are for. Would you like to try your clothes on?"

Megan looked around the room. "Um . . . where?"

"Against the wall should be fine," said Sari, holding Megan's tunic and breeches out to her.

Megan didn't reach for them. "I . . . um . . . I'm a little modest. Do you have a changing room or something?"

Sari nodded. "Stand against the wall, please."

Megan looked at the wall to see if a dressing room had magically materialized but saw only gray stone. "But—"

"Go on, dear. We haven't all day," said Lady Maudred. "You too, Ainsley."

Ainsley noticed that everyone was staring now, waiting for them to try on their new clothes. He wasn't as modest as Megan, but he did have a problem with a dozen people watching him disrobe.

"You know, I think I'll be fine in what I'm wearing," he said, backing towards the door.

"Nonsense!" Lady Maudred grabbed Ainsley with one hand and Megan with the other and steered them towards the blank wall.

Megan shrugged Lady Maudred off and dropped to the floor, her back propped against the wall and her arms crossed over her chest. "I'll wait here, but I'm not changing in front of all these people!"

Something swooshed overhead, and before she could react, a curtain hung on a silver, barrel-wide hoop descended from the ceiling, encircling Megan and hiding her from view.

"Well . . . this is convenient," was all she could think to say.

"We don't have much floor space," said Sari from the other side of the curtain, "so we raise these into the rafters until we need them." Her hand appeared through an opening in the drapery, clutching Megan's new clothes. "*Now* would you like to try these on?"

Megan got to her feet. "Of course."

"We travel so much, you know . . . with the Carnival," explained Ainsley, accepting his clothing before his own curtain descended upon him. "We've never seen anything like this."

"I should have guessed," said Sari. "I'm sure other places have more floor space than I do that they can devote entirely to changing areas. I've been thinking of opening a store in Pontsford, but I'll need to get the money together first."

"I told you I could give you what you needed," said Lady Maudred. "You wouldn't even need to repay me."

"I won't have your charity, Cordelia," said Sari, sounding a little offended.

"Accepting help when you need it isn't a sign of weakness," argued Lady Maudred.

Ainsley coughed twice then, and Megan could have sworn it sounded like "Listen . . . Megan."

"Well, how are we doing?" asked Sari. "Does everything fit?"

"So far, so good," said Ainsley. He had already put on the breeches, which were far more comfortable than his stiff blue jeans and didn't cling to his legs. He squatted experimentally, and the downy material stretched with him when he moved but didn't wrinkle when he straightened up. Pulling the tunic over his head, he breathed in the rich leathery scent, letting the fabric settle into place. He had worried that it might be baggy, but the material had been darted so the tunic silhouetted his frame.

"How do I look?" he asked, stepping through the curtain.

"Much better," said Lady Maudred with an approving nod.

"Very handsome," said Sari. She slid out a full-length mirror from behind one of the tables. "How does it suit you?"

"I like it," said Ainsley, turning from one side to the other.

Megan, too, was pleased with her own ensemble. The pants and tunic, though patterned for a boy, fit well and accented what little figure she had. When she stepped out and saw her reflection in Sari's mirror, she beamed.

"You do look pretty," said Lady Maudred, pulling Megan's hair back and fastening the cloak about her neck, "though I still think a dress would have been more appropriate."

Lady Maudred requested three more identical outfits for each of them to be delivered to her quarters and they bade goodbye to Sari.

"I thought it was really awesome how those scissors and needles were going all by themselves," said Ainsley as they re-entered the hallway.

Lady Maudred sniffed in disdain. "Please, my boy. I haven't seen magic that simple since the last Carnival. Anyone could have enchanted those objects."

"Really?" Ainsley stopped walking, eyes wide. "Even . . . someone like me?"

"How can someone who travels around the world know so little about it?" Lady Maudred sniffed again. "Of course you can. Magic is innate in everyone, you know."

Megan now looked up at Lady Maudred with interest as well. "It is?"

Lady Maudred frowned. "You can't seriously know nothing of magic." She regarded them through narrowed eyes. "What are you playing at?"

"Well, you see . . . the . . . um . . ." stammered Megan.

"The magicians we travel with refuse to teach us any-thing," interjected Ainsley. "They're afraid we might steal their jobs."

"And you probably could," agreed Lady Maudred. Megan was relieved to see she had dropped her accusatory tone. "But magicians perform nothing more than parlor tricks and sleight-of-hand illusions. They know nothing of real magic."

"But I . . . *they* could learn?"

"Everyone is born with the power to make magic happen," explained Lady Maudred, "but very few people possess what it takes to bring that magic out in themselves."

"Well, what *does* it take?" asked Ainsley. Megan saw a hungry look in his eyes that was slightly unsettling.

"Many things. A strong mind is key, but you must also possess the drive to learn and the persistence to continue, even if your efforts don't seem fruitful at first."

"Sari performed magic with powders," said Megan, gesturing back at the shop, "but you performed it by humming. Why?"

"What the wizard uses as his or her medium depends on the wizard. Some use words, some use wands, some use words *and* wands, some use gestures, and some even use music to summon their magic."

"So . . . how would someone learn the magic in the first place?" asked Ainsley.

Megan stifled a groan; she couldn't imagine anything worse than Ainsley with superpowers.

"By reading many books and finding a good teacher, someone who will allow you to be their apprentice," said Lady Maudred. "Then, of course, you practice, practice, practice."

"Oh," said Ainsley, looking crestfallen. "It sounds like a lot of hard work."

"It is," agreed Lady Maudred, "but it makes the reward that much more valuable in the end."

"Who was *your* teacher, Lady Maudred?" asked Megan.

"King Bornias taught me himself," said Lady Maudred, revealing one of her rare smiles. "But even *my* powers are nothing compared to the king's. He is probably the greatest wizard of our time."

She steered them farther down the hall from Sari's shop to a doorway with a picture of a boot on it. She didn't knock on this door but opened it and walked inside.

This room resembled more of a typical store back on Earth. The walls of the store were lined with shelves, which were laden with boxes. There were a few customers in the store trying on pairs of shoes, but nobody was taking measurements or making product like at Sari's.

The shoe shopping wasn't anywhere as interesting as the visit to the tailor had been, though they did see a man with three feet. He was arguing with a salesperson because he didn't want to pay full price for two pairs of shoes.

"Are there a lot of . . . odd people in Raklund?" asked Ainsley as they left the shoe shop.

He and Megan now carried their sneakers under their arms in addition to their bundles of Earth clothing.

"I assume you're referring to the man with three feet," said Lady Maudred. "There are a few other races that reside in Raklund, dwarves mainly, but they tend to keep to themselves."

"Dwarves? Really?"

"Of course! They were the founders of Raklund, and some of them continue to live here out of an allegiance to their ancestors."

Lady Maudred led them up a staircase at the end of the hall. As they passed the second floor, which appeared to be mainly classrooms and offices, Lady Maudred pointed out the Raklund library.

"If you two are really that interested in the Silverskin history, we have an extensive archive section that could explain much more about the city than I ever could, including its founding."

They continued up to the third floor where Lady Maudred lived, and she explained that the wealthier families lived on the floors closest to the main level. Ainsley couldn't help but pity the poorer families, who probably had to live on the mountain's peak.

Lady Maudred stopped at a door where two men wearing helms and breastplates barred the entrance. The guards held large axes, and as they saw Lady Maudred approach, they lowered their weapons and stepped to either side of the doorway. She nodded at them in acknowledgement and nudged the children into her front hallway.

"*This* is where you live?" asked Megan incredulously.

For someone with such a self-important persona, Lady Maudred's home was surprisingly plain. There were no golden chandeliers or red velvet carpets. The floors were bare, and the walls were decorated with a few simple paintings. The furniture was sparse: a cushioned wooden couch and a distressed coffee table.

"Welcome to my home," said Lady Maudred, gesturing around the foyer. "Make yourselves comfortable, but don't touch anything," she added in warning. "Wait here while I speak to the guards and get you something to eat."

She walked away and returned a few minutes later carrying a large tray loaded with sausages, a loaf of bread, a block of cheese, and an oversized pitcher, along with two clay mugs.

"Now, if you will please excuse me," she said, setting the tray on the coffee table. "I have an important meeting which I am chairing and must attend. You will wait here until King Bornias comes for you this evening. That food and water should be enough to keep you satisfied until he arrives. If you do need anything, however, let one of the guards know, and they will oblige you if they can."

She turned and strode out the front door before Ainsley or Megan could even speak.

"I thought she was supposed to stay and watch us until Bornias got back," said Megan.

Ainsley shrugged and grabbed one of the sausages, biting an end off with a snap. "Personally, I like it better without her," he said. "She creeps me out. Plus, now we can really do some exploring."

He turned out to be wrong, however. Lady Maudred had been gone no longer than five minutes when the two guards at the front door entered the room, and two more guards took their place at the entrance. The guards who had entered the room stood in front of Megan and Ainsley, axes in hand.

Ainsley raised an eyebrow at Megan.

"Somehow, I get the feeling we're more Lady Maudred's prisoners than her guests," he said.

The Lost

"Can we help you?" Ainsley asked the two guards.

"Lady Maudred has given us orders to make sure you remain in this room," said one of the guards brusquely.

"You're kidding," said Ainsley. He stood and walked towards Lord Maudred's quarters. The guard walked beside him like a shadow. When Ainsley got too close to the blue silk curtain, the guard stepped in front of him, blocking his path.

Ainsley curled his lip at the guard and then turned, heading for the front door. The guard followed alongside him once more, and when Ainsley was less than a yard away from the entrance, the two guards there turned to face him, blocking out the doorway with their bodies. Feeling defeated, Ainsley returned to the divan.

"This is ridiculous," he muttered to Megan.

"Well, what can we do? They've got axes, and there are four of them and two of us—not to mention their size," Megan pointed out. "Besides, I thought you didn't care whether we stayed here or not."

"I do now that someone's actually trying to stop me," he scowled.

Megan sat quietly for a moment, nibbling on a piece of cheese. "All right, I've got an idea. Follow me with the pitcher."

She picked up the tray of food, smiled charmingly at the guard who had been shadowing Ainsley, and strode to the front door. The two guards in the foyer followed her and Ainsley to the doorway where the other two guards turned to watch them.

"Hello," said Megan in a sugary sweet voice that Ainsley was all too familiar with. "I was just wondering if you might like something to eat or drink. I'm sure this must be a hard job, and I just wanted to apologize for any problems my friend here might have caused." She leaned towards one of the guards confidentially. "He can be such a pest."

Ainsley frowned at Megan, not comprehending the path of her plan. One of the guards at the door smiled, though it looked as if it pained him to do so. "No thank you, my lady. We are not permitted to eat on duty."

He and the other guard turned their backs, leaving Ainsley and Megan in the hands of the foyer guards.

"Oh, well. Just thought I'd offer." Megan shrugged and turned, smiling at the two guards in the foyer who had been standing behind her. Then, without warning, she tossed the tray of food to them. On reflex, both guards attempted to catch the flying tray before it hit them, dropping their axes in the process.

When the heavy axes clanged to the ground, the two remaining sentry whirled around to see what had caused the commotion. Ainsley threw the water from the pitcher at them and they flinched instinctively as it doused them, giving him and Megan time to try and break past.

He managed to get through the doorway, but Megan was seized around the arm by one of the dripping wet sentry. She screamed and kicked out, catching him in the shin. Ainsley hammered down hard on the man's forearm with his fist, and the sentry let go with a yowl of pain.

Grabbing Megan's sleeve, Ainsley pulled her down the hall where the two of them rapidly descended the stone stairs, every step in sync with the beat of their racing hearts. A shrill whistle pierced the air, accompanied by shouting voices that drew closer and closer. They could hear numerous pairs of footsteps thundering down the stairs after them, and Ainsley began taking the steps two at a time, Megan following his lead.

"Where . . . do you think Bornias . . . and Frieden are?" she asked somewhat breathlessly.

"I don't know, but let's worry about losing these guards first," replied Ainsley. As they passed the second floor, a feminine voice joined the sentries' shouts.

"Great. Now Lady Maudred is after us," moaned Megan.

When they reached the ground floor, Ainsley opened the first door they came to and pulled Megan inside. He had hoped to blend in with the shoppers in whatever store this might be, but he and Megan were greeted by darkness.

"Brilliant idea, Ainsley," hissed Megan. "Now we're trapped like rats."

The heavily booted footsteps of the guards sounded just outside the door.

"Check all the rooms," said Lady Maudred. "I can smell that boy from here."

While Ainsley groped around for something with which to jam the door, Megan looked for a place to hide. She bumped into a waist-high counter and pulled Ainsley behind it just as the door to the room opened, spilling light into the darkness.

Ainsley and Megan measured their breathing as best they could, but their jaunt down five flights of stairs made this difficult.

Then, a raspy voice spoke from directly beside them, almost startling them out of silence.

"Who's there?"

Megan opened her mouth to respond, but Ainsley clapped a hand over it, refusing to let go, even when she sank her teeth into his finger. He shook his head vigorously and gestured toward the open door.

As if on cue, a timid voice spoke from the doorway. "Just the Silvan Sentry, Sir Inish. Have you seen anyone come in here?"

"See? How can I see, you idiot? I'm blind!" The hoarse voice of Sir Inish snapped, and Ainsley and Megan jumped.

"Of-of course. Th-that's not what I meant, sir," stammered the sentry. "I only meant—"

"I know what you meant, you half-wit, and no, I haven't noticed anything unusual except how incredibly brainless the Silvan Sentry has become in recent years."

They could hear nervous shuffling from the doorway. "Y-yes, sir. Sorry to trouble you. I will be sure and register your complaint with—"

"Just go," barked Sir Inish.

The sentry squeaked and the door slammed shut. Ainsley let out a shaky breath and started to lower his hand from Megan's mouth but then Sir Inish shifted in his seat.

"Of course I know you're here," said Sir Inish quietly. "You two must be pretty important to have the Silvan Sentry after you."

There was a tinkling sound, and the room was illuminated to reveal an elderly dwarf with a massive gray beard. He glanced down vaguely with his blue sightless eyes at

Ainsley and Megan who had hidden next to the stool he was perched upon.

The tinkling sound came from a set of crystals he was holding up to an oil lamp. Every time the crystals knocked into each other, they produced a blue spark. After lighting the lamp, Sir Inish used one of these blue sparks to light the tobacco in a pipe he placed to his dry lips. He puffed furiously on the pipe, trying to get the fire to take, and was rewarded with a wisp of smoke that curled from his lips, which he wet before speaking again.

"Tell me, you two, why Lady Maudred and the Silvan Sentry are interested in your whereabouts."

Ainsley opened and closed his mouth a few times and glanced at Megan, not sure how much of the story to tell.

"We came here with our Uncle Frieden and King Bornias, but they left us with Lady Maudred, and we wanted to find them," said Megan.

"Frieden doesn't have any brothers or sisters." The old man sat in silence for a moment, puffing his pipe. "You're not from around here, are you?"

"Why do you say that?" asked Ainsley, skirting the question.

Mr. Inish shook his pipe at them. "Your accent's different, and you smell unusual—not like the mountains."

"Well, we're from Pontsford," explained Ainsley.

Sir Inish shook his head. "No, you don't smell like Pontsford either. In fact, you haven't the scent of anything I'm familiar with."

Ainsley stared at Sir Inish. "You can tell all that just by smelling us?"

"So, I'm right, eh?" Sir Inish grinned, revealing tar-stained teeth. "Well, when you lose one sense, the others gain in strength, and I've been blind for about eighteen years, so I've had plenty of time to develop them."

"I'm sorry," said Ainsley. "How did it happen?"

"Ainsley—" Megan nudged him, but Sir Inish laughed.

"It's all right," he said, settling back on one elbow. "I used to be the captain of the Silvan Sentry. At that time, they still worked alongside the Protectors for the commonwealth. The Governor of the Protectors back then was Kaelin Warnik.

"He had lost his nephew, Losen, in the Swamp of Sheiran and he beseeched the aid of the Silvan Sentry to find him. We agreed to help and sent a search party looking for Losen. Kaelin is a friend of mine, so naturally I had volunteered to lead the search."

Sir Inish paused to relight his pipe before continuing. "It was raining the morning we went into Sheiran and the ground was much softer than usual, making it more difficult to maneuver. We waded into the mire and called for Losen, foolishly allowing our weapons to hang by our sides.

"We never expected that someone might be waiting in the marsh grass, and we walked right into an ambush. I never saw our attackers, but they killed everyone in the party and blinded me with black magic. I barely managed to escape and stumbled back to Raklund, blind as a newborn chitwisp."

"That's terrible," said Megan. She placed a comforting hand on Sir Inish's arm. He smiled and patted it with his own calloused one.

"It took me over a month to reach the kingdom, and by then it was far too late to reverse the magic that had taken my sight. Nevertheless, I moved on with my life."

"So what happened to Losen?" asked Ainsley.

"I tried to gather another search party to return to the marsh for him, but Kaelin himself adamantly opposed the idea. He was very upset that so many had lost their lives to rescue his nephew, and he wasn't willing to be the cause of any more death. He felt that whoever had killed my men would have obviously felt no remorse over killing an innocent boy and gave up on finding his nephew."

"What? I can't believe he quit so easily," said Ainsley. "Did they ever figure out what happened in the swamp?"

"Well, rumors have been floating around ever since that a dark wizard who dwelled in those swamps, a man named Farris, killed Losen and turned the Sentry soldiers into an army of zombies."

"That is so creepy," said Megan with a shudder.

"Kaelin must have thought so as well; shortly thereafter, he resigned from his post as Governor."

"So, Frieden took over Kaelin's position?" asked Ainsley.

"Not directly," said Sir Inish. "There were a few governors in between, but they didn't last long."

"How is it that you're no longer in charge of the Silvan Sentry?" asked Megan. "Did they fire you?"

Sir Inish barked a laugh that turned into a heavy fit of coughing. When at last he could speak again, he said, "Without my eyesight, I was considered more of a hindrance than a help to the Silvan Sentry, so before they could ask me to turn in my uniform, I resigned. My second in command, a man named Kyviel, took over, and the Silvan Sentry has never been the same."

"What do you mean?"

"The death of the Silvan-search-party members created a rift in the relationship between the Silvan Sentry and the Protectors. The Silvan Sentry placed blame on the Protectors for the loss of their forces, and the Protectors blamed the Silvan Sentry for Kaelin's resignation."

Sir Inish paused and took a long draw from his pipe, which threatened to die out again.

"So, what are you doing now?" asked Megan. "I mean, what kind of business do you run?"

"I lecture the new sentry on military tactics and combat maneuvers, but lately, it seems like I'm just talking into a bottomless pit. The caliber of men and women has been going down over the years. I wish they'd let me handle the recruiting, but I'm told I'm not a good enough judge of character for that sort of thing." He said these last words somewhat bitterly, then waved them away with his hand.

"I've probably bored you by now, so I'll send you on your way. Your 'uncle' and Bornias are outside the city walls inspecting the grounds where the attack took place."

"What attack?" Ainsley asked in what he hoped was a nonchalant way.

Sir Inish smiled again. "The one where the Staff of Lexiam was stolen. I may be blind, but I've got ears, my boy."

"Who do *you* think took the staff?" asked Megan. Sir Inish chewed on his pipe for a moment.

"From the snippets of conversation I've managed to catch, I'd say it could be a wizard named Evren, but he doesn't typically do his own dirty work. Mind you, he's a very powerful wizard, but he's also very concerned about his image. Especially when it comes to what the Community of Amdor thinks of him."

"Community of Amdor? What's that?" All these names swirling around in Ainsley's brain were beginning to overwhelm him.

Sir Inish didn't respond. Instead, he put a finger to his lips and tilted his head to one side.

"Get down," he whispered.

Ainsley and Megan crouched behind the counter once more as a sharp knock sounded at the door.

"Come in," said Sir Inish in a loud voice.

The door creaked and a stiff voice boomed from the doorway. "Good afternoon, Barsley. I need you to come with me to the training grounds. We've just got some new guards to replace the ones we fired over the . . . issue."

Sir Inish grunted. "Hopefully, this lot will be more adept than your previous choices, Kyviel. They couldn't even figure out which end of the sword to hold. Give me a moment and I'll join you."

"Very well," said Kyviel, and the door closed with a click.

Sir Inish looked in Ainsley and Megan's direction as they got to their feet. "Give me a moment to make sure the area is clear of sentry. When you hear me say the name 'Dexi,' count to five and open the door. Do you remember the way out of the kingdom?"

"Yes," said Ainsley. "But what do we do if someone is guarding the front hall?"

"They won't be. They monitor entrances into the palace, not exits. If you do run into any trouble, though, tell them Barsley Inish pulled you from studies to run a favor for him."

He rose from his stool, and Megan reached out and grabbed his hand. "Thank you for keeping our secret," she said earnestly.

Sir Inish's wrinkled and weather-beaten face softened into a different, more somber, smile than those before. "I don't know who you are or where you're from, but something tells me to be thankful you've come to us."

Sir Inish snuffed the candle, and the room was plunged into darkness once more. It took their eyes a moment to adjust to the dark, but Ainsley and Megan could hear Sir Inish shuffling towards the exit. They waited in the dark, and moments later they heard Sir Inish bellow, "Let's discuss Dexi's training, Kyviel."

Ainsley whispered a five-count and reached out for Megan. She grabbed his sleeve and they slinked to the door. Inching it open, they listened for heavy footsteps, but there was nothing beyond the normal chatter of people in the hall.

Ainsley peeked around the door. "The coast is clear."

He and Megan casually strolled out of Sir Inish's office and down the corridor to the intersection with the front hall, all the while scanning the crowd for Lady Maudred's telltale hairdo.

They had just rounded the corner when they saw Bornias and Frieden rushing towards them with a sobbing Lady Maudred close behind. Bornias did not look happy.

Megan sighed. "Looks like we've been busted."

7

A Call to Action

Bornias must have spent hours practicing reprimanding at home. After he saw Ainsley and Megan wandering the halls alone, he dragged them into Sir Inish's office and chastised them for fifteen minutes, constantly gesturing to "poor Lady Maudred." He made them both apologize to her and forbade them to leave his sight for the rest of the day. Unbeknownst to him, they found this more a relief than a punishment, preferring his company to that of Lady Maudred's.

That evening, they helped him and Frieden prepare for the meeting between the Protectors and Silvan Sentry officials. Sir Inish had allowed them the use of his office to hold the conference and, upon Bornias's request, had also agreed to stay on as mediator.

They brought snow lights and plants into the room, which, once illuminated, turned out to be as spacious as Lady Maudred's foyer—except there were far more interesting things to be found here. The back wall was covered with bookshelves and the bookshelves were lined with rows of dusty tomes and battered wooden boxes.

Ainsley pulled out one of the volumes, a large red leather-bound book with faded gilt lettering on the cover, and carried it to the counter. He read the title aloud. "*Analysis of the Enemy*. Did you write this book, Sir Inish?"

Sir Inish, who was helping Megan spread a linen cloth over a long, sectional table, gazed in Ainsley's direction.

"Actually, no. It was a gift from an old dwarf friend named Lirktog. In fact, many of these books are donations from military friends, and a few of them I stole from enemies."

Ainsley lifted the cover, and the book's spine crackled in protest. The pages were yellowed with age, and a musty odor wafted to his nostrils.

Analysis of the Enemy was divided into sections based on the particular race of the adversary. Several races listed in the table of contents Ainsley had never heard of, but he was familiar with trolls, so he flipped to page forty, which showed a detailed drawing of the grisly, scowling troll.

Sketches of troll weaponry filled the following pages, along with the maneuvers most used in combat, some of which looked gruesome. The captions under each drawing were scrawled in a language Ainsley couldn't understand.

"What's this writing?" he asked Frieden. He pointed to one of the pages, which had a picture of a troll cave.

Frieden cocked his head to one side. "It's Dwarvish. It says, 'For the most part, trolls prefer to live in solitude, making their homes in caves or beneath the ground. One can tell where a troll dwells by the strong stench of fish which seems to constantly surround it.'"

Ainsley looked down at the writing as Frieden translated. "Awesome. Do you know any other languages?"

"A few," said Frieden with a nod. "Elvish, Ponzipoon, Human, of course, and Icish."

"What's Icish?" asked Megan, joining them at the counter.

"It's the language of the Icyll who live in northern Arylon," said Frieden. He pointed to a spot on one of Sir Inish's maps. "They're similar to humans but have hair all over their bodies that's so white it's almost blinding. It helps them blend in with the snow that covers their land.

"How come some of the cities on this map have little initials stamped by them?" Megan traced the imprints with a finger. "What do they say . . . K.C.?"

"Yes, it stands for Kingdom Coalition," said Bornias. "All kingdoms with that mark are part of an alliance that is headquartered in Pontsford."

"But I don't see a K.C. by Pontsford," said Megan, leaning close to the map.

"And you never will," said Sir Inish. "Pontsford considers itself one of the few neutral territories in Arylon, even though they won't allow some of the more evil races into the city."

"So what does the Kingdom Coalition do?" asked Ainsley.

"Each kingdom on the coalition council fulfills a specific duty," said Bornias, arranging the plants beneath the snow lights. "Raklund, of course, is in charge of defense. Most of the feuding nations don't attack any members of the Kingdom Coalition because they fear retribution by Raklund."

"Is there anyone in charge of magic?" asked Ainsley.

"That would be the fay kingdom of Hylark where the elves and fairies reside," said Frieden.

"Do they live nearby? Maybe we could visit them."

"I don't think so," said Megan, studying the map. "Hylark is up north in . . . what looks like a big flower." She turned to Bornias. "It's not though, is it?"

"It certainly is," said Bornias. He pulled a thin blue book from a shelf and thumbed through it. "The flower itself is actually called an enchanted hylark, and there's one that grows on every continent. The fay care for it, and it in turn cares for them." He lay the book on the table opened to a picture of a mammoth white flower with five long petals. "The citizens live here." He pointed to the center of the flower, which appeared not yellow, as was typical, but a cucumber green. There was no stem proper, the hylark budding straight from the ground. "The actual living area for a full-grown hylark is 2 miles in diameter, so you can imagine how far the petals reach."

"That's one big, bland flower," commented Ainsley. "What does it do for the people who take care of it?"

"If there is ever a danger to its inhabitants, the petals will fold up and encase the kingdom, like drawbridges of a castle, but far less penetrable."

Megan leafed through the book that Ainsley had abandoned and lifted the front cover from the table. "If this is called *Analysis of the Enemy,* then that means Icyll and dwarves are enemies?"

"They loathe each other," Bornias spoke up as he placed a brass candelabra in the center of the table.

"Why?"

"Nobody really knows. It's a sore subject between the two races, and if you attempt to bring it up in front of a dwarf, he'll punch you in the stomach more often than not. Personally, I think it's because the dwarves are jealous that the Icyll have so much more hair."

Bornias dropped a wooden crate on the table and sifted aside a layer of dried grass that sheltered the contents beneath.

"What's in there?" asked Megan as Bornias lifted out eight candles that appeared to be made of styrofoam and inserted them into the candelabra.

"Enchanted candles," he said, draping heavy veils over the snow lights so that the room was almost dark again. "Watch." Fire erupted from the tip of his staff and flitted to the wicks of the candles. They sputtered before lighting, but when they did, their flames flickered into various shapes, silhouetted upon the wall like shadow puppets. Bornias held a white card up to one of the flames. "It says here that this is the 'Astral' collection," he said as all eight flames shaped themselves into stars.

"They're incredible," said Megan, watching the shadows transform into miniature, ringed planets. "Where do you get them?"

"A store in Pontsford. They sell candles with dancing flames, too. Sometimes, when dinner conversation gets too dull, I lose myself in their hypnotic movement." Bornias sighed. "Pity I don't have some for tonight."

———

Officials from both parties began to arrive shortly thereafter, greeting Bornias with a slight bow and Frieden with a firm handshake. Dinner was to be served prior to the meeting, so the officials situated themselves around the table, talking on issues other than the missing staff.

"The new recruits are coming along fine," Captain Kyviel boasted to Sir Inish who appeared unimpressed.

"The trick to keeping the slug flesh tender is to peel the skin away last," a Silvan Sentry official demonstrated with his hands to a queasy-looking Protector.

"Someone told me that Lady Maudred went to the infirmary today for a green rash on her chest," one Protector told another.

Megan and Ainsley looked at each other and laughed at this last comment. They had been allowed to stay for the dinner after they had promised they would behave and not make any mention of their world or question the lifestyle of Sunil. Bornias had decided this would be safer than having them run amok in the kingdom.

"When will the food be here?" demanded Stego, tucking his napkin under his double chin. "I haven't eaten since lunch!"

Sir Inish, who was sitting to Stego's right, lifted his head and sniffed at the air. "The food is on its way," he said, at which Stego licked his lips and began drumming his fingers on the table.

Soon, everyone in the room could smell the delicious aromas wafting down the hall, as several men and women pushed silver carts laden with baskets of food into Sir Inish's office.

There were appreciative murmurs around the table as the baskets were emptied and the table was covered with sumptuous roasts glistening with their juices. Dishes of savory greens followed, along with a platter containing buttery ears of corn on the cob. Two large tureens of thick, brown gravy were placed in the center of the table and several smaller baskets of freshly baked bread rolls were handed around.

Conversation halted as slices of roast and spoonfuls of greens were dished onto plates, and the room became almost silent as everyone began to enjoy the banquet.

Midmeal, there was a knock at the door, and it opened before anyone rose to answer it. A handsome dark-haired boy, who couldn't have been older than eighteen, peeked his head around the corner and flashed a wide grin at Bornias.

"Hello, Grandfather!" he said. His brown eyes sparkled as he moved across the room to hug Bornias.

"Look at you, Rayne!" exclaimed Bornias, rising from his seat. "You've grown so much since I last saw you." He clapped Rayne heartily on the back.

"My crest came in the other day," Rayne told him. He turned around and pointed to a shiny silver tattoo on the nape of his neck that mimicked Bornias's.

"So it did," said Bornias, examining the mark. "It looks exactly like your father's did at your age."

Rayne beamed and stepped away from his grandfather. He walked around the table, shaking hands with everyone, but paused when he reached Megan and Ainsley.

"You're rather young to be on the council, aren't you?" he said with a grin that revealed a slight gap in his front teeth.

"That is my nephew, Ainsley, and my niece, Megan," Frieden said from his seat at the table. "They came down from Pontsford for the birthday celebration."

"Ah," said Rayne. He shook both their hands, his smile drooping. "I'm afraid you may have come all this way for nothing."

"Were you able to find anything out about our thief?" asked Bornias, placing a hand on Rayne's shoulder. Everyone at the table turned to look at him.

Rayne shook his head. "We tracked him into Guevan, but we lost him after that. We suspect he was headed for Pontsford. I'm still finding it hard to believe that the staff was stolen in the first place."

Several of the officials nodded, giving him sympathetic looks, but Captain Kyviel leaned forward expectantly.

"Your Highness, if you don't mind me asking, how was the thief able to get to the staff in the first place? Is it not protected in the Halls of Staves?"

There were murmurs from around the table, and Rayne looked sheepishly at the floor.

"It was all my fault, really. We were rehearsing for the coronation ceremony, and I decided to put aside the practice staff and use the real one. One of the guards convinced me that we might as well rehearse outdoors, since that is where the actual ceremony would take place, so I carried the staff outside the kingdom walls."

Kyviel grunted in satisfaction and leaned back in his chair. "I wonder if we should be entrusting such an important article to such a careless boy?" he asked.

"Kyviel, that is not the issue we are here to discuss this evening," said Bornias with a slight scowl. "Granted, it

was not wise for Rayne to take the staff out of the kingdom, especially without better protection, but what we
are here to discuss are plans for retrieving the staff."

Bornias looked around the table from Protector to Silvan Sentry. "As I am sure you are all aware by now, the
Staff of Lexiam has been stolen. From conversations with
the guards in Rayne's company at the time of the attack,
we have narrowed our suspects down to two men who at
one time worked within Raklund."

The table buzzed with conversation, and Bornias raised
his voice to be heard over the din. "These men would probably not have taken the staff themselves. Rather, they had a
collaborator within the palace who actually took it for
them."

"And who are these alleged ringleaders?" asked Stego,
drenching a slice of meat in gravy.

Bornias nodded to him and held up a finger. "Bear in
mind that these names we provide you are no reflection on
the integrity of the party to which they were allied. However, the two men that we feel would have had the most
motive and opportunity to take the Staff of Lexiam are
Kaelin Warnik, ex-governor of the Protectors, and Evren
Sandor, former lieutenant commander of the Silvan Sentry."

No sound could be heard following this comment except the tinkling of Sir Inish's crystals as he lit his after-
dinner pipe.

At last, Stego, looking haughty, dropped his napkin on his plate and said, "Well, it's obviously not Kaelin, so I guess that narrows down the list."

The other Protectors nodded in agreement, causing uproar from the Silvan Sentry.

"Excuse me?" said a Silvan Sentry officer, who was almost as large as Stego. "I don't recall *Evren* ever resigning from office under strained circumstances. Sounds a bit suspicious to me."

"Besides," added Captain Kyviel, "Evren has no interest in the Staff of Lexiam. I know for a fact that he has been devoting his time to planning an expedition up north. What has Kaelin been doing with *his* spare time?"

"I'm sure he hasn't been wasting it licking the Master Mage's boots, unlike someone else I could mention," a female Protector sneered.

Voices elevated around the table as Silvan Sentry united against Protector. There was a great deal of finger-pointing, fist waving, and rude gestures, as each party came to the defense of their alleged thief. The outsized Silvan Sentry member and the equally stout Stego were now standing belly to belly, yelling in each other's faces, each trying to force the other back with a thrust of his paunchy stomach.

Bornias clapped his hands together and waved his arms above his head in a vain attempt to regain control of the situation. He tried shouting as well, but his voice mingled with those of the angry crowd.

Sir Inish laid a hand on Bornias's arm. "I'll handle this," he said, reaching into his pocket.

Extracting an egg, Sir Inish set it on the table. He felt around for his dessert plate and brought it down hard on the shell, which gave a muffled crack. When he lifted the plate, bits of eggshell stuck to its bottom and a gooey string connected it to the table. A moment later, the room filled with the noxious odor of rotten egg.

"Ugh! What is that *smell*?" asked one of the Silvan Sentry officials, holding his nose.

"It smells like raw sewage!" chimed in Stego.

"Are you sure it's not coming from you, Stego?" asked Kyviel. He placed a napkin over his own nose.

The two parties stopped arguing as the overpowering stench hit their nostrils, and they began holding their hands to their faces. One of the Silvan Sentry finally came to his senses, threw open the office door, and rushed out into the hallway. The wooden door frame was soon moaning and creaking as everyone, except Sir Inish, tried to fight their way free of the smell.

Sir Inish grinned to himself as he scooped the shattered remnants of the egg onto a plate using his napkin. Reaching into his pocket once more, he pulled out a leather pouch and poured a glittery purple powder into his cupped hand.

Sir Inish blew gently into his palm, sending some of the fine particles flitting into the air. He walked around the room and repeated this process at the other end of the table, then paused and breathed in the air. With a satisfied smile, he placed the leather bag back and wiped his powdery hands on his shirt.

Bornias, who had been watching from the door, motioned for the others to follow, and they all filed back into the office. The nauseating odor of rotten egg was gone, but Sir Inish was holding two more eggs in his hand.

"I have two rotten doo-dah eggs left, and I'm almost out of neutralizing powder," he growled threateningly. "Now, sit down and be civil or I'll lock the door and smash the other two eggs with all of you trapped in the room."

The Silvan Sentry and Protectors grumbled but took their seats.

"Well, I really don't think *that* was necessary," the skinny Protector woman said to a Sentry, who nodded his assent.

"Thank you, Barsley," said Bornias before returning his attention to the Silvan Sentry and Protectors. "Now, my intention in naming Evren and Kaelin was not to cause bedlam, but merely to state the facts. I, personally, am remaining neutral on the issue, though I am familiar with the character of both men."

"Tell me, Your Highness," said Kyviel, "what makes you so sure it has to be one of those men? Could it not be just as likely that it was someone in this room?"

"The Staff of Lexiam is far too powerful of a magic to be controlled by any mere man or creature, and those who know anything about the staff know that if the wizard who attempts to wield it cannot control it, it will devour his soul." Bornias paused for emphasis. "I cannot imagine any wizard foolish enough to try and wield a power beyond his expertise. It always yields negative consequences. I, therefore, am forced to consider those who would consider themselves powerful enough to control the Staff of Lexiam and those who would be interested in using that power."

"So, what are we planning to do about this? Without the staff, our people, and anyone else in the Kingdom Coalition for that matter, are vulnerable to attack," said Kyviel. There were several murmurs of agreement.

"This is where I shall depend on all of you," said Bornias. "Naturally, everyone here is expected to keep this information confidential. We don't want to start a panic among the citizens, nor do we need our enemies to know we are weakened. Kyviel, I'm going to need you to increase and strengthen your forces. We're going to need extra protection on the grounds in case word does leak out, or if our thief decides to come after the Quatrys."

Kyviel nodded, and Stego spoke up. "Where *are* the Quatrys, your Majesty?"

"They are safe, and that is all anyone needs to know. I am going to need the Protectors to work side by side with the Silvan Sentry. We still don't know who the thief is, so I will need all of you to do some investigating to see what you can discover. Barsley, can you help Kyviel with recruiting?"

Kyviel glanced up quickly and Sir Inish's eyebrows rose, but he nodded.

"I will be going to Guevan to find clues, and hopefully, our thief," continued Bornias.

"You'll be going alone?" asked Captain Kyviel incredulously. "Sire, I do not think that is wise."

"I will not be going alone," Bornias assured him. "Rayne and Frieden will accompany me."

Several of the Silvan Sentry and a few Protectors frowned in disapproval, as did Ainsley and Megan. Then, the protests began.

"Two companions? That's preposterous . . . and dangerous!"

"Bornias, you can't leave us here! Lady Maudred's a nightmare!"

"You're going to take the boy who lost the staff and a *Protector*? Isn't this a job for the Silvan Sentry?"

"Honestly, King Bornias, I expected you of all people to take this seriously," said Captain Kyviel with a patronizing chuckle.

As the arguments grew louder, Bornias became redder and redder in the face until it looked as though his head might explode. When Bornias reached for his beard, Ainsley and Megan covered their ears with their hands.

"Enough!" Bornias pounded the table with his fist, causing the cups to dance in their saucers, clinking angrily. The candles on the table flickered, and the maps on the walls fluttered as though a gust of wind had swept through the room.

Everyone quieted at Bornias's outburst, and several people exchanged frightened looks.

"And you were all afraid Bornias might not be able to take care of himself," scoffed Sir Inish, breaking the silence.

"This is not a matter up for discussion," said Bornias in a calmer voice. "I wish I could take a larger party, but in the interest of remaining inconspicuous, we must keep our numbers small."

Captain Kyviel pushed his chair away from the table. "If you'll excuse me, then, I have some issues that need my attention. I can see my opinion matters not," he huffed. "Clearly, the decisions, though rather poor, have all been made."

He stormed around the table, but Sir Inish reached out and grabbed his arm tightly as he passed. Captain Kyviel tried to jerk free of the old man's grasp, but Sir Inish refused to let go.

"Don't you speak to your king that way, you duplicitous ingrate!" Sir Inish barked, spit flying from his lips as he slammed his pipe upon the table.

Captain Kyviel flushed and looked down his nose at Sir Inish. "Kindly call off your dog, King Bornias," he said coldly. "He's soiling my uniform with his slobber."

For an old man, Sir Inish was quite spry. Still holding Kyviel's right arm in his left hand, Sir Inish balled his right hand into a fist and punched Captain Kyviel hard in the stomach. Captain Kyviel let out a "Woomph!" of air and doubled over, clutching his midsection. Sir Inish chopped him sharply on the back of the neck with his hand, and Captain Kyviel hit the floor.

"Apologize for your rude behavior this evening," demanded Sir Inish.

"It's all right, Barsley." Bornias rested a hand on his shoulder.

Captain Kyviel said nothing as everyone stared down at him. Scrambling to his feet, he brushed off his uniform and nodded to the remaining Silvan Sentry before turning to Bornias.

"King Bornias," he said curtly. Further words seemed to fail him, and he left the room, slamming the door behind him.

There was an uncomfortable silence, broken by a cough or two, until Bornias said, with a rather forced smile, "Any other objections?"

Like Prison

The meeting ended shortly after the scuffle. Sir Inish apologized to Ainsley and Megan for his outburst, but Ainsley told him he didn't mind and even complimented Sir Inish on his attack while Bornias looked on disapprovingly.

"I think it's time for you two to go to sleep," he said. "You've had an eventful day."

"I don't want to stay with Lady Maudred," said Megan quickly.

"Me neither," said Ainsley.

"That's fine. You may stay in my quarters." Bornias turned to Frieden. "Frieden, would you meet me in my study in fifteen minutes?"

"Of course." Frieden nodded. "Barsley and I have a few things to discuss first. I'll be up soon."

Ainsley and Megan bade them goodnight and followed Bornias into the hallway. All the shop doors now had "CLOSED" signs hanging from their knobs and every snow light had been shaded except for two at the intersection with the main hall, towards which they headed.

"Sir Inish isn't going to be in trouble, is he?" asked Megan in concern. Her voice echoed in the almost empty hallway.

"No, he realizes he shouldn't have responded to Kyviel like that," said Bornias. "They're just going to have to get over their differences and work together."

He stopped in front of the mural of Lodir. "Each of you grab a sleeve," he told them, holding his arms away from his sides.

Ainsley and Megan consented with hesitation, and as Bornias stepped forward, Ainsley saw his foot disappear into the mural. "Um, are you sure this is safe?"

"Come along," urged Bornias. The three of them walked through the mural into another hall as if they had done nothing more than pass through an open doorway. Ainsley and Megan looked around in confusion.

"Did we just walk through that wall?" asked Ainsley. He felt his body to make sure he hadn't left anything behind.

"It's my secret palace entrance—a shortcut, really," said Bornias. "I'm the only one who can pass through the doorway. Everyone else encounters a stone wall."

The passage they had entered was lined with red carpeting and was as dimly lit as the front hall. Every few feet stood a stone figure, brandishing some form of wicked-looking weapon.

"Not much protection around here, is there?" asked Ainsley, looking at one of the stone figures that held a flail. He reached up to feel the spikes, and Bornias called to him.

"Don't—"

But Ainsley had already touched the statue.

The stone figure came to life, jerking away from Ainsley and swinging the flail over its head. Ainsley gasped and backed away as several other figures nearby stretched their stony muscles and advanced towards him, weapons raised.

"*Breknal e va shrem*. Return to your posts, please. Everything is all right," said Bornias, loudly enough for all the stone men to hear him.

The mobile statues lowered their weapons and bowed to Bornias, their mighty stone bodies grinding with the effort. They returned to their stations, and the stone figure that had been holding the flail lowered his arms to stand like a pillar once more.

Megan exhaled a shaky breath. "What were those things, Bornias?"

"Stone golems. The best protection a king could have." He patted one of them fondly on the shoulder, and it shifted in response. "They never need sleep, they never need food, and they're practically indestructible. They're devoted to my family because we have taken care of them through the centuries and treated them as equals."

"Where did they come from?" asked Ainsley. He circled the flail-wielding golem again but kept his hands behind his back.

"They were created from an ancient Druid magic and have lived in these mountains since long before the dwarves made Raklund their home."

Ainsley and Megan followed Bornias along the narrow stretch of carpet to a set of transparent double doors composed of thousands of tiny clear cubes, each about the size of a quarter.

"Is this glass?" asked Megan, running her fingers over one of the doors.

"No, it's diamond," said Bornias, opening the other door and passing into a smaller circular room.

Megan looked at the doors in amazement as she followed him through, but Ainsley lingered in the hallway staring at the gems.

"Diamonds? Hundreds and thousands of diamonds? Bornias, these doors must be worth the entire kingdom!"

Bornias chuckled and pulled Ainsley inside. "I assure you, diamonds do not have quite the same value here as they do on Earth. All the diamonds in this door wouldn't buy you more than a cord of wood here."

Ainsley wasn't disappointed by this fact. "If they're so cheap, maybe you can let me take some home with me."

Bornias laughed again and gestured toward one of the many colorful bejeweled doors in the smaller room. "My sleeping chambers are in here."

He held it open and Megan gasped as they stepped inside. "I would *kill* to have a place like this."

The bedroom situated on the edge of a flat overhang that jutted out from the mountain's face, overlooking an immense valley dotted with hundreds of cottages. There was no ceiling proper, so Ainsley and Megan received a breathtaking view of the velvety black night sky, sprinkled with thousands of shining, white stars. A stream flowed through the center of the room and cascaded down the overhang to the valley below.

"Where's this water coming from, Bornias?" asked Ainsley, dipping his fingers in its icy depths.

Bornias lit a torch by the door. "There's snow atop the mountains, and when it melts, I have my own little river. It used to spill everywhere, but I've fixed it now so that it's restricted to one path."

"Who lives down there?" asked Megan, pointing to the valley below. "I thought everyone lived in the mountains."

Bornias joined her at the cliff's edge. "Well, the farmers like to be close to their crops and animals, so they choose to live in the valley. It's a very secure area because the mountains are the only way in and out."

"All those hundreds of houses can't belong to farmers," said Ainsley, counting the number of chimneys he saw.

"No, there are others who choose to live in the valley, humans and elves mainly, because they prefer to be closer to nature. Now, let's get you bedded down."

Bornias stripped sheets off of a sleigh bed against the wall and bundled them in his arms. Aside from the bed, the only other furniture on the close side of the stream were a rolltop desk and a straight-backed wooden chair.

Bornias carried the bundle across a footbridge that straddled the stream; Ainsley started to follow him, but Bornias turned and blocked his path.

"I'd prefer it if you didn't cross the bridge. I've got some highly sensitive ingredients over here that I'd rather not have touched."

"But there's just a birdbath and a wardrobe over there," Ainsley complained. "I'll keep my hands to myself."

"No, Ainsley," said Bornias, opening the wardrobe door.

Ainsley paced at the edge of the stream, trying to see over Bornias's shoulder into the wardrobe. Hooded cloaks hung on a rack inside, and a box labeled "Knacks" rested on a high shelf.

"What's a 'knack'?" asked Ainsley.

"An elemental potion," said Bornias, pulling open an empty drawer and stuffing the bundle of sheets inside.

"There aren't many spells that don't involve a knack of one form or another." He opened another drawer and pulled out a neatly folded pile of sheets, along with a quilt.

"So, you mix your knacks in that birdbath?" asked Ainsley, indicating the stone basin resting on the pedestal.

"No, I use that basin for just one purpose. Mixing anything else in it would destroy its magical properties."

"And what do you use it for?" asked Ainsley.

Bornias smiled at him but didn't answer his question. "I haven't slept in this bed for quite some time," he said, crossing the bridge once more, "so I thought it would be best if we changed the sheets. Megan, could I get your help?"

But Megan had scarcely heard any of the conversation, so enraptured was she by the cozy cottages that were spread below. She imagined the laughter of children as they caught fireflies and the scolding voices of their parents urging them inside for supper. Perhaps, she mused, the younger children were already being tucked in for the night, content and unaware of any danger facing their peaceful kingdom, let alone their world.

Exhaling a shaky sigh, she pressed her lips together, determined to keep her emotions at bay. Thoughts of families reminded her that her own was literally worlds away, and even though there were times she would rather admit she didn't know them, her parents had always supported her. She may have been a loner in her world, but she had never felt as *alone* as she did now.

Footsteps shuffled toward her, and she turned to see Bornias smiling sympathetically. "You know, I'm very lucky to have two homes," he said, placing a hand on her shoulder and gazing down at the valley, "so I feel comfortable in either world. I suppose the transition isn't as easy for someone so young."

Megan couldn't bring herself to answer.

Bornias cleared his throat. "I don't know if it helps you to know, but if you miss your family . . . I've always considered myself to have . . . three grandchildren."

Megan's lower lip trembled and she hugged Bornias around his plump waist.

"What say we make this room more comfortable for the two of you?" he said as she sniffled into his sleeve.

"I know what would make *me* more comfortable," Ainsley called to them. "If you'd let me see what was on the other side of the bridge."

"Nice try," said Bornias, grinning.

Megan wiped her nose and helped Bornias unfold the sheets and spread them over the bed. "What will we do if it rains or something?" she asked, smoothing out the wrinkles.

"You'll be fine. I've cast a dome of obstruction over the area," Bornias gestured at the sky, "so that rain and snow slide down the sides, completely bypassing the room."

"It's cool how you guys have magic here," said Ainsley. He watched from the chair as Megan and Bornias tucked in the corners of the linens. "I don't understand why you don't use it more often, though. Wouldn't it have been easier to make the bed?"

"I only use magic when it's absolutely necessary," said Bornias, fluffing a pillow. "I find that if you start relying on magic for everything, you get quite lazy."

"You used magic to get Ainsley and me out of the lake, didn't you?" asked Megan.

"I did," said Bornias. "It was the quickest means of saving your lives. I may look buoyant, but I'm not the best swimmer."

"Can you teach me?" asked Ainsley. "Please? I'm a quick learner."

Bornias smiled at him. "Very few mages can learn overnight, Ainsley. However, I need to cast one more spell before I leave, so you can try and learn from that." He pulled his staff from beneath his cloak and waved it at the door.

Ainsley and Megan stared, expecting it to burst into flame or vanish, but they were startled when the door detached itself from the wall, and the empty hole it had left behind sealed shut. The door shuddered and hopped before transforming into a massive black bear, which rose onto its hindquarters and roared, displaying long yellow fangs.

"Did you catch that, quick learner?" asked Bornias, grinning at Ainsley.

"Change it back," said Megan quickly.

"Not to worry," said Bornias. "The bear won't hurt you. It's just a warding spell."

"Warding?" Ainsley's eyes narrowed. "Like a guard?"

Bornias looked evenly at Ainsley. "Yes, that's right. I don't want the two of you wandering off alone again."

"Couldn't you have turned the door into a rabbit or hamster or something . . . less likely to tear our heads from our bodies?" asked Megan, hiding behind her pillow.

Bornias rolled his eyes and waved his staff at the hulking bear, which now paced against the wall.

The bear began to diminish in size, its body to narrow. The length of its fur shrank and lightened until it had become a white coat of short, bristly hair. The weighty paws became golden hooves, and the bear's short, stubby tail elongated and split into hundreds of strands of silvery, silken hair. Its face narrowed and a golden horn sprouted from the center of its forehead. Instead of growling, it now whickered and tossed its mane.

"A unicorn!" Megan slid off the bed and crept toward it. "It's beautiful."

Bornias stroked the unicorn's firm shoulder and spoke to it in a strange tongue. The unicorn tossed its head again and pushed its nose into Bornias's palm.

"Ten bucks says he's telling the unicorn to never let us out," Ainsley told Megan.

"Probably. Why can't we go with you, Bornias?" asked Megan.

"Because it's too dangerous. You're much better off waiting here. I'll make sure someone comes in the morning to let you out. It doesn't have to be Lady Maudred, but I'll have someone watch you until I get back."

"But that could take weeks!" said Megan, throwing her hands in the air. "Our parents are going to freak out."

"I'll take care of it." Bornias assured her. "And it won't seem like two weeks. You'll get to explore the kingdom and you can go down to the valley. They have horseback riding, hunting, fishing—you'll feel like you're at a summer camp."

"We'll feel like we're in a prison," Ainsley corrected him.

Bornias sighed and patted the unicorn's head. "I'm sorry you feel this way, but I won't be changing my mind. I'll see you in a few weeks."

Ainsley glowered at Bornias from his seat, and Megan flopped across the bed, staring once more at the village below.

Bornias sighed again and disappeared through the solid wall.

Twilight Adventures

As soon as Bornias had left, Ainsley settled onto the bed beside Megan. "All right, what's the plan this time?" he asked in a hushed voice.

"What do you mean?" Megan didn't look away from the village.

"How are we going to get out of here?" he pressed.

She rolled onto her side and faced him. "We're not."

"What?" Ainsley sat up straight. "Why not?"

"Where are we going to go, Ainsley?" She gestured at the cliff's edge. "Just because you're wearing a cape doesn't mean you're Superman, you know."

Without waiting for an answer, he ran toward the river and cleared it easily in one leap.

"What are you doing?" Megan walked to the river's bank. "Bornias said not to go over there."

"Nooo. He said not to cross the bridge, and I didn't. Now let's get a closer look at what's in the wardrobe."

"Ainsley!" Megan stormed across the bridge. "Ainsley, stop."

"Help me with this, will you?" He slid the box of knacks from the shelf, but they were heavier than he had anticipated.

"Watch out!" He staggered under the weight and backed into Megan who bumped into Bornias's stone basin. The basin wasn't attached to the pedestal, so it tipped danger-ously. Megan spun around to secure it as the water in the basin sloshed over the sides.

But the water wasn't the clear liquid she was familiar with. It was an inky black, and Megan wondered if it was even water at all. Wiping her fingers through one of the puddles on the stone floor, she examined it, but to her surprise, the liquid was clear.

"Weird," she muttered.

"What's *that*?" asked Ainsley, peering over her shoulder.

"I don't know, but put that stuff back and get on the other side. You're going to get us into trouble."

Ainsley snorted derisively. "Please. Bornias isn't any-where near here. He probably—"

Ainsley stopped midsentence and stared past Megan, his mouth dropping open. "Look at that!"

The black water churned, creating small, rippling waves that began at the center and ebbed at the edges. When each wave reached the edge of the basin, it formed a gel-like ring. Different sections of each ring became lighter and altered in color until a picture appeared.

"That is cool," said Ainsley, staring in disbelief.

The image was of Bornias and Frieden, more than likely in Bornias's office, sitting on opposite sides of a table strewn with maps and books. The edges of the table were engulfed in a white flame that illuminated their faces, and they rested their elbows in it, heads bent low over one of the maps. Bornias appeared to be talking with Frieden, but Ainsley and Megan could hear no sound. It was as if they were watching a silent movie.

"What'd you do?" Megan demanded. "What is this thing?"

"I think it's some sort of . . . of location device!" said Ainsley. "After I mentioned Bornias, it showed us where he was."

"Let me try." Megan cleared her throat. "Where is Ainsley?" The liquid in the basin didn't so much as ripple.

"You must not have the magic touch like I do," boasted Ainsley.

Megan made a face at him, and they returned to the image. Bornias and Frieden were now walking down an unfamiliar slanted path. The men stopped in front of a heavy, wrought iron door, which Bornias touched with his fingertips. The metal glowed orange beneath his fingers, and the door swung inward.

Bornias and Frieden entered a wide corridor where a young boy in dirty coveralls guided them to a wooden gate on one side of the corridor.

Megan made a triumphant noise. "*That's* a stable. They must be in a barn of some sort."

"Are you sure?" asked Ainsley.

"Yes, see those harnesses tacked up between the stalls? And all the hay on the floors?"

She and Ainsley saw Bornias point to three different stalls, each with a different nameplate on it, and then Ainsley snapped his fingers.

"That's it! That's how we'll get out of here." He grinned at Megan with a fevered look in his eyes.

"What?" she asked nervously.

"Well, I figured that Bornias would probably magic himself to another city, but now we know he's going to travel like a normal person. We can *easily* follow him. All we have to do is sneak down to the barn and follow Bornias on horseback."

Megan couldn't join in his excitement. "And how are you planning on leaving this doorless room, *and* how do you plan to get through the stable doorway which Bornias had to magically open?"

"There has to be more than one way to get there," Ainsley figured aloud. "There must be some entrance from

Raklund Valley and an exit on the other side of the mountain."

"Okay, so how do we get out of *here*?" asked Megan.

Ainsley walked around the room and stopped at the wall with the trickling waterfall.

"You know, Bornias magicked the door but nothing else. I bet we could climb this rock."

"What, like you did the fence back home?" Megan asked with a smirk. "It's way too slippery."

"Well, we wouldn't climb up the *waterfall*, Megan. Besides, you wouldn't have any trouble. I've seen you on the ropes in gym. You're like a monkey."

Megan wasn't sure whether this was a compliment or an insult. "Forget it. I'm not scaling the mountain," she said flatly. "Even if we could get outside this room, we wouldn't have anywhere to go . . . except splat on the ground."

"There *has* to be a room on another floor that has a window," argued Ainsley. "All we have to do is climb through the window and leave through *that* door."

He stepped to the rim of the ledge and looked down. "And I know exactly where we can go. See down there?"

Megan joined him and saw a narrow row of ledges. "You want us to climb down to one of those tiny shelves?"

"We could totally make it down there," insisted Ainsley. Without waiting for a response, he opened the wardrobe and removed the sheets Bornias had placed there earlier, along with another set.

"Here, braid these together with the ones on the bed," he told Megan, tossing the bundle at her.

Megan sidestepped the throw and let the sheets fall to the floor. "I'm not one of your little lackeys that you can just boss around."

Ainsley threw his hands up in disgust. "Come on, Megan! Do you have to make everything so difficult? *This* is why you don't have any friends."

The tension in Megan's jaw increased, and she spoke through clenched teeth. "At least *my* friends are real. I bet not one of those losers that follows you around would be your friend if you weren't good-looking and popular."

Ainsley slammed the wardrobe door shut and snatched up the sheets from the floor. "What would you know about good looks?" he asked hotly. He stalked across the bridge with Megan following on his heels.

"I know that Bornias and Frieden aren't impressed by your 'good looks' and 'charm.'" As she said the words, Megan made air quotes with her fingers. "Not everybody thinks you're as great as *you* think you are."

Ainsley stopped walking and Megan almost bumped into him. He whirled around and got within inches of her face. "Get off my back. I'm not the bad guy you make me out to be, and you know it."

Ainsley held her gaze for a moment before turning away, his cloak swishing angrily around his ankles. He untucked the sheets from the freshly made bed and settled onto the cold stone floor.

"You don't have to come with me," grumbled Ainsley. "I'll just leave you here with Lady Maudred."

Megan raised her eyes to the starry night sky for support before sitting beside him. "Where are those sheets?"

———

They worked in silence for about thirty minutes, during which Ainsley couldn't resist correcting Megan's poor braiding skills.

"Can you explain to me why we're braiding these together?" she whined after Ainsley pointed out a flawed section for the tenth time.

"If we braid them into a rope, the rope will have more tensile strength than a single sheet would," he answered.

"You're pretty smart." Megan regarded him with something close to admiration, and Ainsley blushed.

"Don't act so surprised," he said, brushing off the compliment. "Beneath my charm and good looks, I'm a pretty intelligent guy."

Megan blushed, too, and returned to her work. A few minutes later, she held up her completed, though shabby-looking, rope.

"What do we do with this when it's done?"

"We push the bed to the edge and tie one end around one of the legs. Then we lower ourselves over the side of the cliff and down to the next level."

This turned out to be more difficult than it sounded. The bed was extremely heavy, and it felt as if it were made of lead instead of wood.

"At least we know we won't pull the bed off the edge when we go down the rope," said Megan with a grunt. She dug her heels into the ground and pushed with her back.

They managed to work the bed a foot from the ledge, and Ainsley secured the rope around one of the bedposts.

"I'll go first, I guess," he said. Now that the time had come, he was somewhat doubtful about his plan. He wound the end of the rope around his wrist and dropped to his hands and knees.

Megan wrung her hands as Ainsley backed toward the edge of the cliff. "Be careful."

He slid onto his belly and dangled his legs over the edge, pulling the rope taut, trying not to picture what would happen if the knot around the bed came undone.

"Ainsley, are you okay?" Megan kneeled on the ground beside him. "We don't have to do this if you don't want to."

"No, I'm fine," he lied.

He was more than a little relieved to find that the side of the mountain was riddled with crevices, making it easy for him to find a foothold. Inch by painstaking inch, he lowered himself down the rope, pausing every so often to locate a foothold. He was sure he imagined it, but it felt as if the bed was shifting, getting closer to the edge and closer to his head.

"By the time, you get down there, it'll be sunrise," Megan teased from above.

"Shut up." Ainsley had reached the end of the rope but the ledge below was still several feet away. He released the rope and let himself fall the remaining distance, landing squarely on his feet.

The ledge was a little wider than he had expected. Four people could sit comfortably, and he did so now to work out his nerves. As he had figured, the ledge connected to a palace window. The glass, or perhaps diamond, pane had been smashed out, and a few shards riddled the ledge. The remainder of the pane was jagged, and some of the sharpest points were encrusted with a golden dust.

Ainsley wiped at one of the points and rubbed the dust between his fingers. It was warm against his skin, and he wiped his hand vigorously against his pants to rid himself of the queer feeling.

Though the moon was shining, it offered little light into the room, so Ainsley cautiously poked his head through the window and listened.

"Ainsley? Is it okay to come down?" Megan hissed in a loud whisper.

"Yeah, there's nothing to it," he called up. "The rope's too short, though. You'll have to drop when you reach the end."

Megan was indeed a much better climber than Ainsley, and she was down the rope in a manner of minutes.

"Is someone in there?" she asked, gesturing to the broken window.

Ainsley shook his head. "I don't think so. It's too dark to be sure."

"This is a pretty big ledge," said Megan, glancing around. "What are all these?"

She pointed at the ground beneath Ainsley's feet. Deep grooves had been dug into the ledge, each about a foot long. The grooves ran in all directions, and in several, there was more of the gold dust.

"I don't know, but be careful around the gold dust," said Ainsley. "I think it might be some sort of magic."

Megan now eyed the ledge as if it were seething with scorpions. "Let's go inside."

She untied the cape from around her neck and laid it over the jagged glass on the bottom of the window.

"Wait," said Ainsley. He reached into his pocket and pulled out a sheathed knife as long as his hand.

"Where'd you get that?" asked Megan, snatching it from him and sliding the knife out of its casing.

"I stole it from Lady Maudred's house."

"Ainsley!"

"What? I wanted a souvenir. Look at the handle. The initials carved into it are the same as mine, so nobody will know I stole it." He tossed it through the broken window where it landed on the floor inside with a clatter.

"What did you do *that* for?" asked Megan.

"I wanted to see how far it was from the window to the floor so we don't end up jumping through a window near the ceiling or something," said Ainsley.

He swung one leg over the windowsill and his toes brushed the floor inside the darkened room. "This'll be easy," he said.

He climbed through the rest of the way and helped Megan inside. "Come on."

"Wait, don't forget the knife," said Megan.

Ainsley bent down and felt along the floor. His fingers swept across something and he grabbed at it. As he lifted the object, however, he realized it was much heavier than his knife.

"Did you find it?" asked Megan.

"No," said Ainsley, holding up the object he had come across. With what limited radiance the moon provided, they were able to see that it was a long, white bone.

Megan's eyes widened and she screeched like a boiling teakettle. "Drop it! Drop it!"

Ainsley let the bone fall from his hand. "Let's get into the palace," he said nervously. "Forget the knife."

They hurried away from the window, but darkness closed in around them until their panicked movement was reduced to a brisk walk to keep from bumping into anything.

"What do you think that bone came from?" asked Ainsley as they shuffled across the stone floor.

"I don't want to imagine," said Megan with a shudder. "Some sort of . . . creature must have used this room for a lair."

They shuffled forward several more yards.

"Geez, this room is big," said Ainsley. "How much further do you think we have to go before we reach the opposite wall?"

"Ow!" Megan's nose contacted with solid stone and she stumbled backward, falling onto her rear. "I think I just found it with my face," she said, feeling under her nostrils for blood.

"Next time, try using your hands," suggested Ainsley, running his fingers over the wall. "I think I found the door frame." He traced the edge of the door and found a seam where another door began. "They're double doors, but there's no handle."

"Try pushing," suggested Megan as she got to her feet.

Ainsley pressed against the doors. A thin ray of light shone through the seam followed by a clanking sound, but the doors didn't open.

"Help me," said Ainsley. "They must be stuck."

He and Megan laid their weight into a door. This time, the clanking was much louder and it was accompanied by strange screams.

"They're back!" a voice shrieked from the other side of the door.

Someone scurried across the stone floor, and the children heard a familiar echoing voice.

"Here now, Lord Taffington. Calm down. There's been nobody in that room for years. You can see that the doors are chained."

"That sounds like Healer Sterela," whispered Ainsley. "We must be in the infirmary."

The word "infirmary" echoed in Megan's mind, along with the image of two large black doors, chained together and bearing a sign.

Her stomach lurched and her arms broke out in goosebumps. "Ainsley," she said, her throat suddenly as dry as the discarded bone, "we're in the Illness Room."

An Attractive Accessory

"We're in the Illness Room!" Megan repeated, raising her voice a little more than she intended.

Ainsley felt as panicked as Megan sounded, but he knew better than to let it show. "Okay. We won't be able to get out this way," he said. "Let's just go back out the window and look around."

Walking back across the room was much easier; the moonlit sky acted as a beacon through the broken window. At one point, Ainsley stooped and straightened with Lord Maudred's knife in hand.

Boosting Megan out the window, he climbed up after her. When he reached the ledge, he began hopping around and rubbing his hands repeatedly against his clothes.

"Ah! Ah!" he cried.

"Are you okay?" asked Megan, watching Ainsley's strange dance.

"I must have gotten some of that gold powder on my hands. It burns like fire!"

"Her gold blood burned like fire . . ." murmured Megan. Then, "Ainsley, it's dragon's blood!" she exclaimed as the realization hit her.

Ainsley froze with his hands tucked under his armpits. "You're kidding. So, we've stumbled across a dragon's lair? I hope it's abandoned, or we're in trouble."

"The dragon must have been dying and came here for safety," said Megan.

"Yeah, but that doesn't explain the broken glass," Ainsley pointed out. "Why is it *out here* instead of *in there*?"

"You heard what Lady Maudred said about the Illness victims. I'm sure they went into a frenzy and broke the window. Let's get down before the dragon, if it's still alive, comes back."

Ainsley walked to the edge and looked beneath it. "How about there?" He pointed to another ledge five feet or so diagonally below theirs.

"I don't think I can make it," said Megan, eyeing the other ledge. "It looks too far."

Ainsley sighed. "Megan, when did you turn into such a chicken? Visiting another world is a once-in-a-lifetime opportunity. Take some chances!"

"Oh, no." Megan crossed her arms stubbornly. "I will *not* willingly jump thousands of feet to my death."

"That wouldn't happen unless you missed the ledge, and it's not thousands of feet . . . more like hundreds."

Megan rolled her eyes. "Oh, well in *that* case . . ."

Ainsley held up a hand to silence her. "Look, I'll go first again. If I make it, will you jump?"

"Fine."

Ainsley crouched on the ledge, pounced, and landed on the shelf below. "Nothing to it," he told Megan, though his legs felt as if they were made of gelatin. He held his arms out to catch her, but she waved him to the side.

"I need room to crash-land," she said.

"Suit yourself," said Ainsley. "Don't forget to keep your knees bent when you land."

Megan jumped, but her landing wasn't as graceful as Ainsley's, and her feet stung from the force of the landing, like thousands of needles pricking her.

"See? That wasn't so bad." Ainsley smiled at her and worked his knife into a latch on the window, which clicked free. He drew it open, and the smell of hay and manure greeted them, intermingling with the crisp night air.

"Jackpot!" said Ainsley softly. "We've reached the stables. He pocketed his knife and rested in the windowsill. "Am I good or what?"

Megan couldn't answer. She gasped and pointed at him but couldn't get any words out.

Ainsley saw the horrified look on her face and then someone jerked him backwards through the window and forced him against the stone wall. Whoever it was drew close to him, close enough for Ainsley to feel warm breath on his neck.

"Who sent you?" an angry voice hissed, tightening the grip on his shirtfront. "My father?"

"Leave him alone!" Megan cried, leaping through the window. She couldn't see very well in the dark, but she could make out two figures, so she kicked one of them hard in the leg.

"Ow! Megan, that was me, you dumbass!" Ainsley pushed the unknown figure away with all his strength and reached down to rub his leg. "Nobody sent us. We don't even know who you are."

"What are you doing here, then?" the figure challenged.

"We're running away," said Megan. "Our friends are leaving tomorrow and—"

"Megan, shut up," interrupted Ainsley. "Don't tell strangers our plans!"

"It's okay," the figure said in a calmer voice. "I won't say anything. I plan to escape this place myself."

They heard a muffled clatter, and then a flickering light materialized. It increased in size and brilliance until it illuminated a modest-sized room and brought the unknown speaker into focus.

A young man, no more than fifteen or sixteen was holding a rusty lantern in his dirty hands. His soft leather boots were an earthy brown, and his deep green pants clung to him like a second skin. Instead of a tunic, he wore a leather vest, beneath which he was bare-chested and bare-armed.

He passed the lantern to Ainsley and crossed the room to close a wooden door that had been left ajar. His walk was catlike, his footsteps whispering across the hay-strewn floor.

He settled opposite them on a rickety wooden chair, the light reflected in his eyes, an unusually deep green, like grass after a spring rain. His hair was a mop of brown curls that would have hung to his eyebrows if a worn leather headband hadn't held them back. Not a single freckle dotted his cheek, his skin clear and soft, except for a tiny scar on his upper lip. He held Megan spellbound and actually made Ainsley envious of his rugged good looks.

"So where are you headed?" asked the young man, looking from Ainsley to Megan.

Ainsley hesitated before he answered. "Pontsford. We're . . . going to live with our uncle."

"I'm headed there myself," the young man said with a nod. "They call me Garner."

He extended his hand to Ainsley, who shook it. "I'm Ainsley, and this is Megan."

Garner held his hand out to Megan who stared at it, as if she'd never seen one before. She looked from Garner to his hand and then at Ainsley for help.

"You'll have to forgive her," Ainsley spoke up. "This whole experience is coming as a shock."

"Ah, I understand," said Garner, withdrawing his hand, though his expression made it clear that he didn't.

Megan wished one of Sari's curtains would drop from the ceiling and hide her.

"If you don't mind my asking, how did the two of you end up on the ledge outside the stables?" asked Garner.

"We climbed down from King Bornias's living quarters," said Ainsley.

Garner raised his eyebrows. "Both of you?" He studied Megan with interest. "I'm impressed."

Megan cleared her throat and found she could speak as long as she didn't look directly at him. "It wasn't really that difficult. Anyone could have done it."

"Scale the side of a mountain? I doubt that so many maidens are as brave as you," said Garner. He leaned closer to Megan, and she swallowed audibly. "And where have you two been that has cobwebs?" He reached out and extracted a few of the cottony strands from her hair.

Megan felt herself growing lightheaded as his hand brushed against her cheek, plucking free more sticky threads. "We . . . we got lost in one of the rooms that hasn't been used for a while," she stammered. "I must have picked them up there."

Garner rolled the webs he had gathered between his thumb and forefinger, still watching Megan. "You're the first maiden I've known who wouldn't squeal about having cobwebs in her hair."

"There are bigger things out there to worry about . . . and I'm not your average maiden." Megan met his eyes and watched them crinkle as he smiled.

"No, you're not."

Ainsley had been silent this entire time, even when several inappropriate jokes about Megan came to mind. Now, however, she and Garner both looked a bit lovesick, which was making *him* sick.

"So . . . why did you attack us when we tried to climb in the window?" he asked Garner. "I take it your father has something to do with it."

"Yes," said Garner, pulling away from Megan. "He's been trying to force me to stay and do what *he* wants for the rest of my life, but farming isn't for me. Granted, I love working with the animals, but all the planting and harvesting doesn't speak to me."

As Garner spoke, he glanced at Megan, and though she didn't know why, she felt an overwhelming urge to wrap one of his loose curls around her finger and giggle like one of Ainsley's admirers.

"What do *you* want to do?" Ainsley asked him.

Garner leaned back in his chair so that it balanced on its rear legs. "I'm not really sure. I know I want to continue working with animals, so I'll probably try my hand at breeding zippers."

"Zippers?" asked Ainsley, picturing the zippers on clothing. "What are those?"

"A zipper is a crossbreed of horse and unicorn," said Garner. "They run incredibly fast, and they're easier to manage than unicorns."

"That's pretty cool," said Ainsley. "Are there any zippers or horses *here*? We need to get to the stables."

Garner lowered the front legs of his chair and stood.

"Well, there aren't any zippers, but we do have a few horses around here, though most citizens of Raklund typically ride scramblers. I can take you to the horses we *do* have, though."

"No," said Megan. "I think we should probably go look at the scramblers."

"All right, but we'll have to be careful," said Garner. "I'm friends with *some* of the stablehands, but the others won't like us being in here."

He turned down the lamp and opened the door, pressing a finger to his lips. "There's someone at the south end of this corridor," he whispered, head cocked to one side. "We'll have to wait for him to leave."

Megan and Ainsley stood quietly next to Garner, straining their ears, but they heard nothing. After a moment, Garner, opened the door the rest of the way and motioned for them to follow.

"The path is clear now."

The trio tiptoed down the hall past several doors identical to the one they had just left.

"Stableboy's quarters," whispered Garner.

They approached a gate, and Garner pushed it open quickly to keep it from creaking. The manure and animal smell intensified, and several of the stables' inhabitants grunted and bleated. Garner guided Ainsley and Megan past several scrambler stalls and down another corridor.

"This is my friend Farsid's section of the stableyard," he said. He whistled softly into the dark, and a moment later the boy in coveralls they had seen speaking with Bornias and Frieden appeared.

Garner spoke to the boy in a primitive-sounding dialect and the boy nodded silently. Garner patted him on the shoulder and turned to Megan and Ainsley.

"You'll be safe here. I've let him know what's going on. Don't venture past his area, though. The two other stable boys that watch the animals in this hall won't allow you to stay."

"Thank you," said Ainsley, shaking his hand.

Megan extended hers as well this time, and Garner took it, wrapping the rolled-up cobwebs around her little finger.

"For an unusual maiden, an unusual gift," he said with a grin. "I hope to see both of you around Pontsford." With that, he slunk into the shadows and disappeared.

Ainsley glanced at Megan, who was staring after Garner. "So you and Wilderness Boy, huh?"

Megan blushed, but luckily, Ainsley couldn't tell in the dim light. "Let's get some rest," she said. "We'll need to wake up early if we want to catch Bornias and Frieden."

"You just want to dream of Garner whisking you away," teased Ainsley, settling against a bale of hay and pulling the hood of his cloak over his head.

Megan didn't answer, though that was exactly what she intended to do.

———

"Well, well. Look who's waiting to see us off."

Megan opened her bleary eyes and squinted against the light of a lantern that Bornias held to his scowling face. Frieden and Rayne stood on either side of him wearing amused expressions.

"Did you not hear me last night when I told both of you to stay put?" asked Bornias.

"We're not staying behind," mumbled Megan, still groggy from sleep. She elbowed Ainsley to wake him and rubbed the sleep from her eyes. "You have to take us with you or we'll follow you anyway."

"You most certainly will *not*!" Bornias's mouth worked furiously. "You will stay here in Raklund out of harm's way."

"NO!" Megan jumped to her feet, all traces of sleep gone. "You can't push us around. We want to go home, and we'll follow you if we want!"

"We found our way down here," Ainsley added with a yawn. "We won't have any trouble following you."

"Oh, really?" asked Bornias with an angry smirk. "Suppose I were to bind you to the floor or turn your feet into rocks?"

Frieden placed a hand on his shoulder. "Er . . . Bornias, might I speak with you?"

"In a moment," Bornias practically barked over his shoulder.

Frieden squeezed Bornias's shoulder and bent low to his ear. "*Now*, if you wouldn't mind."

Bornias glared at Ainsley and Megan for a moment before turning away to follow Frieden. The two men spoke in low voices, their conversation punctuated by Bornias's wild gestures at Ainsley and Megan. At one point, Frieden mouthed something to Bornias who exclaimed, "Pocky Nates! Are you mad?"

"What's Pocky Nates?" Ainsley asked Rayne.

"Pocky Nates is a person," said Rayne, shaking his head. "He's a Ponzipoo and as crazy as they come . . . not that that's saying much. They're all a little bit crazy." He turned to face Ainsley and Megan. "I'm surprised you've never met him. He lives in Pontsford."

"Oh, Pocky *Nates*," said Ainsley with a feeble laugh. "I've always . . . heard it pronounced differently."

"Wow, Ainsley. Good save," whispered Megan sarcastically as Bornias and Frieden rejoined them; Bornias still looked upset.

"Well, children, Frieden has pleaded your case with me. You may come with us as far as Pontsford, where we'll be leaving you with a friend."

Megan was about to argue, but Ainsley elbowed her in the side.

"It's a deal," he said.

"Thank you for being so reasonable," said Bornias sarcastically. "Frieden, why don't you and Rayne come with me to get two more scramblers?"

The instant they were alone, Megan whirled on Ainsley. "Why did you give in so easily? Now we're just going to be trapped in another town."

"Relax," said Ainsley. "We'll wear them down on the road by proving how responsible we are, and they'll have to keep letting us come with them. Besides," he added with a sly grin, "don't you want to see Garner again?"

A Journey of a
Thousand Miles

"I am *not* riding one of those," Ainsley said with a pinched frown an hour later.

Several creatures that looked like cloven-hooved hippos were grazing among the trees outside the city.

Ainsley and Megan had helped Bornias and Frieden lead the animals up a ramp inside the stables and out through an exit guarded by more stone golems. The exit opened behind the lake where they had first arrived. When they stepped outside the palace, the gate closed behind them, blending seamlessly into the rock wall just like the entrance to the main hall.

"It's not too late for me to change my mind about allowing you to come, you know," Bornias threatened. "I can tell Rayne to return the extra scramblers to the stable."

"These scramblers are the best transportation money can buy outside of Pontsford," added Frieden, resting a hand on Bornias's shoulder to calm him. "Scramblers are much faster than donkeys, more durable than horses, and not as easily spooked."

"Why are they called scramblers?" asked Megan.

"Because of the way they run," said Frieden. "They live so high up in the mountains, very little vegetation grows and the water is still frozen snow. They have to run down the mountains every time they want to eat or drink, but because of their size, it's too dangerous for them to descend in a straight path, so they alter their running pattern."

Ainsley climbed onto his scrambler and glanced around in confusion. "Hey, where are the steering things?" he asked.

"Right here." Frieden pointed to a crease in the scrambler's skin above its shoulder blades.

"Holding onto a little wrinkle is supposed to keep me from flying off this thing?" Ainsley asked dubiously, wrapping his fingers around the ridge in the scrambler's neck.

"If you want your scrambler to turn a certain direction, lean your body that way," instructed Frieden, "and if you want to slow it, pull on the . . . erm, wrinkle, as you call it."

"Scramblers are very smooth runners," Bornias assured him, "and you'll be following a very flat trail. You'll be riding with Frieden along the Grimmett River. Rayne and I will be riding straight across the plain past Guevan."

"Why can't we all ride together?" asked Megan.

"We'll be taking the Quatrys with us, and it would be very unwise for one person to carry all the Quatrys," said Bornias. "We have to keep the Quatrys separated. Whoever stole the staff will surely come looking for them. Which reminds me—"

Bornias removed his belt and held it up for everyone to see. The silver buckle had a clasp on one side that Megan had never noticed before.

Bornias opened the face of the buckle, which had returned to its light blue tint, revealing four thimble-sized, colored jewels set into the silver.

"You've had the Quatrys the entire time? Even when we were back home?" Megan asked in amazement as Bornias removed a blue gemstone and a purple gemstone from the silver backing.

"Of course. I'm the king, aren't I? I have to make sure I am in control of at least some of the kingdom's interests." He handed the jewels to Frieden.

"Frieden Tybor, I make you an Honorary Guard for the Quatrys of Water and the Quatrys of Air. Under no circumstances are you to extract their power."

Frieden bowed and stuck the gemstones into a pouch tied around his neck. "You know I prefer the hum of a solid blade to that of a magic talisman any day, Bornias," he said. "Which reminds *me* . . ." He lifted a cloth-wrapped bundle from the back of his scrambler. "I have something for Ainsley and Megan."

"You do?" Megan nudged her scrambler closer.

Frieden unrolled the package and revealed two motley pelts that had been tanned and formed into belts. To each was fastened a scabbard, complete with a sword.

Ainsley, who had been hoping for magic staves like Bornias's, couldn't hide his disappointment. "Are these at least enchanted swords?" he asked as he unsheathed his and studied it with a critical eye.

"I'm afraid they are not," said Frieden, "so the magic must lie within the wielder."

"They're perfect," said Megan as she fastened the belt about her waist and drew the sword. She had assumed most of the weight was due to the belt, but her arm wavered as she held the sword aloft, its heavy blade bending her wrist towards the ground.

"Maybe you should take her sword back," said Ainsley as Megan struggled to hold the weapon upright but lost her grip, almost lopping her scrambler's ear off.

"I'll be fine," she said. "I just need a little practice. I'm just not used to something this heavy."

"Might I suggest riding with the sword in your dominant hand . . . so you can become accustomed to the weight." Frieden handed her the fallen weapon, and she accepted it without meeting his eye. With her earlier boasting, she knew he had expected her to at least be able to hold a sword.

"So, Bornias," said Ainsley, eyeing the remaining Quatrys that twinkled in his belt. "Who's carrying those?"

"I will be taking the green Quatrys of Land, and Rayne will be protecting the red Quatrys of Fire," said Bornias, snapping the face of the buckle shut.

"I could hold one for you, you know," offered Ainsley.

"As I have mentioned before," said Bornias, "the Staff of Lexiam is powerful enough to control a weak mind. The Quatrys can have the same effect, driving the wielder to insanity."

Ainsley nodded but felt a bit insulted that Bornias considered him weak-minded.

"We will meet up you in Pontsford to look for more clues," Bornias said to Frieden. "Your journey will take longer, so you best be on your way, and mind that you don't tarry on your trip. If something should go wrong, send me a signal and we will meet in Guevan."

Frieden nodded and gestured to the children before nudging his scrambler into a gallop alongside the lake. Megan and Ainsley waved goodbye to Bornias and followed after Frieden.

Megan didn't enjoy her first scrambler ride. She noticed that the scramblers did not seem to want to run in a straight line. Her scrambler would amble at an angle to the right, before changing its direction and running back towards the left. She started to feel nauseous as the scramblers continued to run in this zigzagging pattern and found it almost impossible to both handle her sword and remain upright on the scrambler's back.

Ainsley, however, enjoyed the unusual, albeit jerky, experience. They galloped along the west bank of the Grimmett River, and he could see deer-like animals with silvery eyes grazing in the tall grass on the opposite bank. Tiny green birds roosted on their backs, and as the deer grazed, the birds would swoop down and eat the little insects that leapt out of the way.

"Look at the deer, Megan!" he exclaimed, pointing.

"That's nice." Megan was too busy trying to keep her breakfast down to admire the scenery. "Frieden, will the scramblers ever start running straight?" she yelled.

Frieden glanced back at her and grinned. "Probably . . . after they get this mode of movement out of their system. It may be a little while, though."

Megan groaned and slumped on her scrambler's back, holding her stomach. It took the scramblers half an hour to finally develop a straight path, and it was then that she was able to enjoy the surrounding landscape.

Being in Arylon was like nothing either she or Ainsley had ever experienced. The air seemed sweeter and fresher than it did back home. The land was untouched by man, save for the villages and farms. There were no large smokestacks polluting the air, no sounds of blaring car horns or airplanes to break the peaceful stillness. The grass was lush and green, the countryside sprayed with flowers of all colors. The river beside them was like rippled crystal, clean enough to drink from.

By midday, Ainsley's appreciation of the landscape was overcome by a gnawing hunger in the pit of his stomach. He pointed this out to Frieden who agreed they should probably take a meal break. Megan was reluctant to dismount, however, feeling as though she could ride across the countryside forever.

"Trust me, we still have plenty of riding ahead of us," promised Frieden. "Besides, you'll get saddle sore."

They sat along the riverbank and let the scramblers graze close by. Frieden passed around a loaf of bread and some dried jerky he had pulled from his bag, and the threesome shared a water flask.

"Why can't we have some river water?" asked Ainsley. "It's not contaminated, is it?"

"Yes and no," said Frieden. "It's safe for the animals to drink, but it contains potion runoff from a witch's coven farther upstream. One can only imagine what brews swirl through the water. You might take a sip and grow two tails and a beak."

They laughed and gathered their things before continuing on their journey. When nightfall came, so did a chilling drop in temperature. While Ainsley and Megan dismounted and settled their scramblers for the evening, Frieden started a campfire with a fire pine pod he produced from his pack.

"How can it be so cold when it's about to be the hottest part of the year?" asked Megan, rubbing her aching sword arm.

"Well, for one thing, the hottest part of *our* year has just passed," said Frieden. "This is our harvest season. For another thing, we're by the Grimmett River where the escalariob live."

"Escalariob?" asked Ainsley.

"Look towards the sky," said Frieden. "What do you see?"

Ainsley and Megan tilted their heads back.

"I only see stars," said Megan. "Is that what you mean?"

Frieden smiled. "No. Ainsley, do you see anything?"

Ainsley, too, could see nothing but stars, though they seemed blurred to him, as if a haze were hanging in the sky. "I don't know. Everything looks kind of fuzzy."

"That would be the escalariob," said Frieden with a nod. "Tiny flying creatures that, for lack of a better word, swarm the skies from Raklund to Pontsford every harvest evening."

"I still don't understand," said Megan, now squinting skyward. "What do they have to do with why it's so cold?"

"To stay airborne, they have to flap their wings, and they do so at an accelerated rate. If you couple that with the millions of escalariob in the sky all making the same motion, the temperature in this region lowers fifteen degrees."

"So there are tiny bugs all around us?" asked Megan, swatting at the air in front of her face.

"Not *around* us," said Frieden. "To be more specific, above the treetops."

"So these tiny bugs are above us doing their day-to-day business?" amended Megan with a disgusted face. "I'm possibly covered in escalariob poop?"

"I don't think that's the kind of response Garner would want to hear from you," teased Ainsley. "You're supposed to be different than other girls, remember?"

Megan gave him a withering look. "Ainsley, there's a difference between having poop in your hair than cobwebs."

"Not really. They both come out of a creature's—"

"Perhaps we should retire for the evening," interrupted Frieden. "We have another full day of riding tomorrow."

They nestled into their blankets, but before he allowed himself to fall asleep, Ainsley rolled over to face Megan. "Don't fall asleep with your mouth open," he said with a grin.

———

They awoke early the next morning as the sun was rising. To Megan's relief, the escalariob had disappeared, but she raised her hood just the same while they ate.

Breakfast consisted of more bread and meat and a handful each of pink berries Frieden had found.

Ainsley sniffed at his cautiously, squeezing one between his fingers until a blood-red juice oozed out. "Are you sure these are safe to eat?"

"Positive." Frieden downed his own handful and winced. "They may not taste good, but jahwood berries ease muscle tension. I had a feeling you both might be sore from riding yesterday."

Megan held her nose and chewed her jahwood berries vigorously, eager for some form of relief from the muscle cramps in her sword arm. When she swallowed, it felt as if she had applied menthol to every inch of her body, and she found she could walk to her scrambler without hobbling.

They rode just as hard the second day, stopping only at lunchtime to eat and water their scramblers. A forest now ran along their left, which Frieden pointed out as the Pathis Wood, and it was filled with the trilling of thousands of birds, the trees covered in thick, green foliage.

While they rested, Frieden explained what some of the animals they had seen were. The deer-like creatures were the motleys, and their silver eyes had a hypnotic effect that protected them from frontal attacks by predators.

"What about attacks from the rear?" asked Ainsley.

"Every motley carries a bird on its back," said Frieden, pointing to a motley who was having its ears pecked by one of the sparrow-sized birds. "In exchange for food and shelter, these backhoppers, as they are called, trill warnings of potential danger to their hosts and eat the fleas that dig into their fur. Theirs is a symbiotic relationship, so it benefits both parties."

They watched the backhopper work for a moment while its motley sampled rotted fruit beneath a tree.

"Fascinating creatures," murmured Frieden.

"How do you know so much about animals and plants?" asked Megan. "Are you a . . . a biologist or something?"

Frieden frowned. "I don't know what a biologist is, but before I became governor I was a nascifriend, if that's what you mean."

"Nascifriend. What's that?" asked Megan.

"A nascifriend is someone who studies and appreciates all nature, from the tiniest plant to the largest animal," said Frieden. "We also care for those who cannot care for themselves."

"We?" repeated Ainsley. "There are a lot of nascifriends then?"

Frieden nodded. "Most fey and elfkin are nascifriends, as well as a few select beings from other races."

"So why did *you* stop once you became governor?" asked Megan. "I mean, it's not like you couldn't do that on the side, is it?"

Frieden never got the opportunity to explain, for at that moment, a deafening series of cracks resounded from the forest, as if something were crashing through the underbrush and uprooting trees.

Megan, Ainsley, and Frieden jumped to their feet as one.

"What was that?" asked Megan. Her left elbow banged against the hilt of her sword, and she reached across her waist to grasp it, more for comfort than defense.

"I'm not certain, but it's coming from somewhere in the Pathis Wood," said Frieden. He unsheathed his sword, and Megan did the same with hers, mimicking Frieden's stance with the weapon. Ainsley knew nothing of swordplay and had a feeling his martial arts would be ineffective on whatever hurtled through the woods, so he grabbed the reins of the scramblers and pulled them away from the river, feeling rather inept.

Then the screams began. One, at first, so blood-curdling that it made even Frieden turn pale. The scream wasn't one of pain or fear but of anguish and hatred and was joined by two more screeching voices. At this, the supposedly brave scramblers jerked at their reins and broke free of Ainsley's grasp, tossing him to the ground and almost trampling him in their haste to flee.

"It's good to know we have their support," muttered Ainsley as he got to his feet.

"What's making that noise, Frieden?" Megan asked, her voice barely above a whisper.

"If that sound comes from what I think it does," said Frieden, pushing her and Ainsley toward the river, "we face a 'them,' not an 'it'—grimalkins, and we have no chance of outrunning these hellcats."

Reaching beneath his cloak, he extracted the pouch containing the Quatrys and tossed it to Ainsley. "Protect these."

"Can't we use the Quatrys to drive away the grimalkins?" asked Ainsley.

Frieden gripped his shoulder so hard Ainsley winced. "You heard Bornias. Besides," he glanced over his shoul-

der, "I'd rather face these creatures the nascifriend way —
on their terms, without magic."

"But—"

"Leave this place," he urged, looking from Ainsley to
Megan. "Cross to the other bank, get your scramblers and
ride hard towards the north."

Ainsley took the pouch and tucked it into his breast
pocket.

"But you said we couldn't outrun these . . . things," argued Megan.

"*We* can't. *You* can. I'll hold them off so you can escape." Frieden pivoted so that he faced the forest. The
conversation appeared to be closed in his mind.

"But what if they . . . what if you . . ." Megan couldn't
bring herself to say the words, afraid of sealing Frieden's
fate.

He lowered his sword for a moment and turned to look
at Megan with a smile. "I am not afraid of death, but it
will take more than a few grimalkins to tear me from this
world."

Another crash sounded in the forest, this one much
closer. The birds within were squawking in cacophonous
unison, like a tone-deaf orchestra tuning its instruments.
They flew from the treetops, as if trying to distance themselves from the monsters below. Several motleys dashed
out of the forest toward the river, but bolted farther upstream when they saw Frieden, Ainsley, and Megan.

"You're running out of time," said Frieden, prodding them with his free hand. "Go now, and don't look back."

Ainsley nodded and grabbed a protesting Megan by the arm. The two of them jumped into the river and waded across, clambering up the bank. When they reached dry ground, Megan clutched Ainsley by the front of his tunic. The panic in her eyes augmented what he already felt.

"We are not leaving Frieden to die." Her voice quavered, threatening to dissolve her words into sobs, but she set her jaw.

Ainsley squeezed her shoulder and leaned close. "Don't worry. We're not going."

"What?" Megan released him, having expected an argument.

Ainsley pulled her behind a large thorn bush out of Frieden's line of sight. "I've got the Quatrys, don't I? We'll stay and help Frieden."

Megan sniffled and frowned. "But, you heard Bornias. The magic in the Quatrys is too powerful. I don't think you could use them even if you knew how."

Ainsley held his finger to his lips, and for a moment, it seemed as if the whole forest had followed his bidding. The birds stopped squawking, the insects stopped buzzing, and even the wind appeared to have ceased blowing.

"That's not a good sign," Megan whispered to Ainsley, looking over the top of the shrub with him.

Then, with another ear-piercing scream, three gigantic catlike creatures burst into view. At the sight of them,

Megan gasped and fell backward, but Ainsley caught her before she hit the ground and pulled her back to her feet.

The grimalkins, as mammoth in size as horses, were hideously grotesque, nightmarish demons brought to life. They brandished six-inch claws on their front and back feet, and their bodies appeared to be all muscle, covered with a thin layer of grayish skin. They cracked long whip-like tails in the air as they ran, but their heads were the most horrific.

Large pointy ears, twitching and turning in every direction, were set atop feline heads with eyes as black as night and snapping jaws filled with two rows of sharp teeth.

Megan turned to Ainsley. "I think Frieden's going to need that help."

Running the Risk

Frieden slid a round metal shield from his pack and grasped it firmly in his right hand. He regripped his scimitar with his left, swishing the sword through the air a few times as if testing the weight.

The grimalkins slowed their advance as they drew closer to him. Stalking forward on padded paws, they wailed softly in an eerie song.

Side to side, Frieden stepped, one foot over the other in an intricate dance, waiting for the first creature to approach him. The grimalkins, in turn, stretched their muscular forelegs, unsheathing their knifelike talons to the fullest length. One of them flattened its ears against its bony skull and hissed at Frieden.

The battle was about to begin.

Almost as one, the grimalkins launched themselves at Frieden, teeth bared and paws raised to strike. The closest grimalkin swiped at Frieden who deflected the blow with his shield while ducking another's thrashing tail. He rolled to the side just as the third grimalkin pounced on the spot where he had been kneeling.

Frieden leapt deftly to his feet and smashed the closest cat in the face with his shield. A sickening crunch resounded as metal met bone, accompanied by the anguished yowl of the injured beast. It tried to snag Frieden with its claws, but he eluded its grasp and brought the butt of his sword down hard on the cat's skull. Dazed, the grimalkin staggered drunkenly in circles while the other two moved in for the kill.

When one of them lifted a paw to strike, Frieden slashed it across the chest, smearing his scimitar with blood. He whirled and raised his shield seconds before the other grimalkin snapped its yellowed teeth at his head.

"He's doing great, isn't he?" Ainsley whispered to Megan, but she had now lifted her hands to her eyes and could see nothing.

Ainsley turned back to watch Frieden who appeared to almost have a second creature beat down, but then the first grimalkin rejoined its kin. It was back to three against one, and Frieden appeared to be straining a little to avoid the swipes and bites directed at him.

"He can't beat them, can he?" asked Megan, peeking through her fingers.

"Not alone." Ainsley reached into his pocket and fingered the pouch containing the Quatrys. Loosening the drawstrings, he shook out the purple gem. "How do these things work?"

As if it had heard him, the Quatrys vibrated, tickling his palm, and a voice whispered in his mind. *"What would you wish of me?"*

Ainsley almost dropped the Quatrys in surprise. He looked at Megan. "Did you say something?"

She shook her head, wincing as Frieden narrowly avoided being whipped by one of the grimalkin's tails.

"It was not her, but I, the Quatrys," spoke the voice. *"How may I serve you?"*

"I . . . uh . . . want to help my friend," he whispered to the Quatrys. He felt rather foolish talking to a colored rock. "Can you . . . can you help me do that?"

"Of course, my master," came the whispered reply. *"I am at your command. Allow me a moment to draw my strength."*

"Megan," he tapped her on the shoulder. "I need you to do me a favor."

She looked at him, and her gaze settled on the purple Quatrys glinting in his palm.

"Ainsley—"

"Just . . . trust me," he said. "I know you're a fast runner. Can you draw the grimalkins away from Frieden without getting hurt?"

Megan looked around and spotted a tall tree nearby with several sturdy-looking lower branches. She nodded, getting to her feet.

"Go!" said Ainsley.

She bolted out from behind the bush, heart jackhammering in her chest. At a closer distance, the grimalkins were even more terrifying, and for one horrific moment, her legs felt stuck to the ground.

"Run, Megan!" Ainsley hissed at her as Frieden sliced at the front paw of a grimalkin, clipping its talons to the quick.

Megan took a deep breath and held her sword above her head, waving it from side to side. "Here! Over here!" she screamed. To her satisfaction, and dismay, all three grimalkins snapped their heads in her direction.

She would never forget the look on Frieden's face at that moment. It was as if someone had plunged a blade into his heart and pushed him from a cliff's edge.

"Megan!" was all he said before the grimalkins screamed in unison and closed the gap on their new quarry.

Megan flung the sword down and turned on her heel, sprinting upstream towards the tree. She launched herself into the lowest branches and pulled herself higher and higher, vaguely aware of the scratches she was amassing on her arms and face from the sticks and leaves that jutted off the branches.

Below her, Frieden fought with the grimalkins to keep them from the tree, but he was only able to engage two of them. The third one leaned back on its haunches and leapt towards Megan, claws outstretched. She screamed and pressed herself against the trunk.

The grimalkin missed her torso by inches, and Megan gasped in relief until she realized her cloak still dangled about her neck. She unclasped it just as the grimalkin made a second lunge for her. It snagged the cloak with its talons, but now unfettered, the cloak slipped from Megan's shoulders and fluttered to the ground where the grimalkin worried it to shreds.

Megan knew the cloak wouldn't hold its interest for long and had started to climb again when her ears began to ring with a strange vibration.

Ainsley had emerged from behind the bush, holding the Quatrys before him. He furrowed his brow and the wind level around them rose, creating a blast of air that knocked the grimalkins off balance.

Frieden stumbled as well, but he seemed to be aware that something unusual was going on. He threw himself flat against the ground. The ringing became louder, and the grimalkins were lifted off their paws and swept back towards the forest.

Frieden rolled onto his back and sat up to face Ainsley, his face white and his expression one of shock. Ainsley closed his palm, but as Frieden jumped up and leapt nimbly across the river, Ainsley knew he had seen.

"How did you do that?" demanded Frieden, practically nose-to-nose with Ainsley.

"I-I'm not really sure," stammered Ainsley. "I just sort of willed it to act, and it did."

Frieden regarded Ainsley with a look that was a cross between admiration and anger. "Bornias will need to know what has happened," he said sternly. He glanced from Megan in the tree to the grimalkins, as if weighing the consequences. "But I could use your assistance in getting rid of these monstrosities."

The grimalkins had shaken their enormous heads dazedly and were now getting to their feet, growling at Frieden and Ainsley.

Ainsley reached into his pocket and handed the Quatrys of Water to Frieden; together, they approached the river.

"I'm going to need a very frosty wind from you," Frieden told Ainsley. "If you can make it cold enough, we'll be pelting the grimalkins with chunks of ice. Will you be able to control your aim?"

"I think so. I'll try," said Ainsley as the yowling grimalkins sauntered closer.

Frieden smiled at him in encouragement. "Let's get started," he said.

The familiar ringing of the Quatrys filled the air again, but this time, it sounded in two different pitches. The water in the river began to churn and form into orbs the size of grapefruits, as if they were balls of dough being shaped by some giant hand. Frieden lifted them out of the stream, and Ainsley hit them with a blast of icy wind so that they smashed into the face of the grimalkin leader with a slush-like consistency.

"You need to think colder," Frieden told Ainsley, looking a bit worried.

The attack had done no more than anger the grimalkins, which had almost reached the opposite bank of the river. Frieden created more spheres of liquid, and this time, Ainsley was able to successfully turn the water into ice, which crackled as it hardened.

He pelted the grimalkin leader between its dark, haunting eyes and the cat creature let out a yowl, jerking its head from side to side. The other grimalkins studied their companion with mystified expressions, but they too were soon howling with pain as a barrage of ice pelted them.

"You handle the Quatrys very well," Frieden said to Ainsley as they launched a fourth volley of ice bombs. "Care to try for something bigger?"

Ainsley nodded at Frieden who began increasing the size of the water balls. Ainsley had a bit more difficulty freezing and controlling them as they grew larger, but they had their desired effect.

Ainsley struck the chief grimalkin squarely in the face with a bowling-ball-sized chunk of ice. The ice block shattered when it made contact, spraying the shards everywhere, including into the cat's eyes. The grimalkin rubbed its eyes with the backs of its paws. The other grimalkins, which were wizening up, backed away from Frieden and Ainsley, hissing and spitting. Frieden and Ainsley bombarded them with one more shower of ice before all three grimalkins finally turned away and stalked back towards the forest, their whiplike tails snapping in anguish.

As soon as the grimalkins were out of sight, Frieden and Ainsley collapsed onto the grass, breathing as if they'd just completed a minute mile.

"Well done, Ainsley," Frieden gasped. "It's too bad you don't live in Arylon. You would make a fine Protector."

Ainsley smiled and wiped the sweat from his brow.

"As for you, Megan," Frieden glanced at the tree, "please climb down before you fall."

Megan hurried to the ground but took her time reaching Ainsley and Frieden. She had never seen Frieden angry before and wasn't sure what he might do. Once she reached him, however, he threw his arms around her and hugged her close.

"You must *never* do anything so foolish again. Do you understand me?"

She nodded and considered telling him it was Ainsley's idea, but Ainsley already looked as if he had suffered enough.

When Megan had jumped down from the tree, he had seen the cuts that criss-crossed her bare skin, as well as her shredded cloak on the ground. Now that he had a moment to reflect, he realized that he had asked her to do something that would have gotten most people killed.

"I'm . . . uh . . . glad you're okay," Ainsley told her. "Sorry that . . . sorry."

To Frieden's credit, he said nothing further on the issue but released Megan and studied her arms and face. "I hate to do this to you, Megan, but," he turned to Ainsley, "do you still have that jar of mossfur?"

"Sure." Ainsley fished the jar from the pocket of his breeches and handed it over.

"Please, no," said Megan, wrinkling her nose.

"Megan, if you don't use mossfur, some of these cuts could get infected and take longer to heal," warned Frieden.

"Fine. I'll smell like raw sewage," she said, rubbing the salve on her arms and face.

Ainsley sniffed at the air. "Actually, it's a nice change for you. I think Garner would really like it."

"At least he's mature . . . unlike some people," said Megan, thrusting the jar at Ainsley's chest. She left to join Frieden who was now kneeling on the ground with his back to them.

"Hey, Frieden, what—" Megan stopped short as she drew nearer to him. His eyes were shut and he held the flat of his sword against his palms, the hilt submerged in a pewter bowl of cloudy, white liquid.

"Frieden?" she whispered, leaning close and waving her hand in front of his face. His eyelids snapped open to reveal pupils as jet-black and haunting as a grimalkin's. Megan gasped and stepped backwards into Ainsley who had followed her.

"What's wrong with him?" asked Ainsley as the black in Frieden's pupils retracted until his warm, green irises were visible once more. Frieden snapped back to a state of wakefulness, wiping the handle of his sword before returning it to its sheath.

"We can continue our journey, now," he said. "But we will be stopping at Guevan instead of riding straight into Pontsford."

Megan and Ainsley watched Frieden for a moment, hoping he would volunteer an explanation for what he had just done, but Frieden merely dumped the liquid into the grass and whistled to the scramblers.

"Uh, Frieden," said Megan, as their mounts trundled forward from their hiding places, "what were you doing just now?"

"That belt buckle Bornias wears, aside from housing the Quatrys, is actually a communication piece between him and I. He and Rayne will know we encountered difficulty and will meet us in Guevan."

"He's going to get all that from your eyes turning black?" asked Ainsley.

"It won't appear that way to him," Frieden assured him.

"How can you be sure?"

"How else do you think I summoned him back to our world?"

———

When they arrived at the Guevan outpost, Rayne and Bornias were already waiting for them, and Bornias was dancing from one foot to the other, wringing his hands.

"What happened?" he called as soon as they were in earshot. "Is everyone all right?"

"We're fine," Frieden assured him. "We were attacked by a few grimalkins, but we chased them away. I've never seen a grimalkin below the falls, though. I have a feeling they weren't there by accident."

"How were you able to scare off grimalkins?" asked Rayne, sounding impressed.

Frieden and Ainsley looked at each other, and Frieden cleared his throat. "We . . . used the Quatrys to drive them away."

"What do you mean 'we'?" interjected Bornias, his eyes narrowing suspiciously.

"Well, you see . . ." began Frieden, but Ainsley spoke up in his defense.

"It was all my idea. I used the Quatrys of Air and Frieden used the Quatrys of Water."

"You what?" Bornias's hands lifted towards his beard and everyone winced.

"Megan was in danger, so we had to!"

"Did you not consider the danger you were placing *yourself* in?" barked Bornias. He reached for Ainsley who stepped outside his grasp. "Quit moving!"

Ainsley froze as Bornias held him at arm's length and opened one of Ainsley's eyes widely, inspecting it for so long that it began to water from the dry air. Then he did the same thing with Ainsley's other eye before stepping back in bewilderment.

"It's amazing." Bornias shook his head. "You seem perfectly fine."

"Duh," said Ainsley, blinking until his eyes felt moist again. "We told you we could take care of ourselves."

"Oh you still think so, do you?" Bornias reached toward his beard again.

"Uh . . . Frieden," spoke up Rayne. "You say those grimalkins shouldn't have been below the falls. Kaelin lives in that area. Do you suppose he might have been involved?"

"It could be possible," replied Frieden. "We can inquire around the outpost and see if anyone has seen anything unusual. It's getting close to sunset anyway, and it will be too dark to travel soon."

"Let's start at Parksy's Den, then," said Bornias. "He's one of my most loyal informants."

"This wouldn't have anything to do with the fact that Parksy's Den serves the spiciest firepots in Arylon, would it?" Rayne asked with a grin.

"Oh, no. It has *everything* to do with that," said Bornias. "After what I've just gone through, I'm going to need at least three."

Seeing Red

The Guevan outpost was an unexceptional, crude town shaped by restaurants and inns, with a few shops scattered here and there. It was not the place to settle down and raise a family. Even in the middle of the day, people were stumbling out of buildings, drunk from too much ale and mulled wine. Scruffy beggars dressed in rags sat outside some of the establishments, hands outstretched.

Ainsley entertained everyone with a dramatic recount of his battle with the grimalkins as they walked toward Parsky's Den. He was kind enough to mention that Frieden had offered him a little bit of assistance, and Frieden was kind enough not to contradict Ainsley's story.

They passed buildings constructed out of wood that were rotting with age and termites. There was no lettering on the doors of the buildings to denote what sorts of goods or services were offered inside; instead, each had a picture painted on it of what the merchant had to offer. Ainsley paused in his recount long enough to point this out to Bornias.

"The outpost is mainly a waypoint for travelers, and since many do not speak the same tongue . . . well, a picture really is worth a thousand words," explained Bornias.

They reached an intersection and turned right down a much busier side street, at the end of which stood a two-story building. The building was covered in stucco with the exception of its wooden doors, upon which pictures of a loaf of bread, a mug, and a bed were carved. The building appeared to be the only non-wooden structure in the town.

"This is Parksy's Den," Bornias told Megan and Ainsley. "Parksy doesn't spend much time around anyone but adults, so he's not particularly fond of the younger crowd. As long as you act mature and stay out from underfoot, however, he'll let you sleep inside."

With that admonition, Bornias pulled open one of the heavy doors. As they entered the tavern, they were greeted by a great deal of noise and a flurry of feathers. A large circular pen had been erected in the middle of the dining hall, and it was occupied by a flock of gray birds the size of turkeys.

"Doo-dahs," Frieden said to Ainsley and Megan, pointing at the enclosure.

A man in a freshly starched apron entered the pen to the cheers of a noisy crowd. Upon his appearance, the doo-dahs began squawking madly and darting about the pen, trying to avoid his grasp. The diners laughed and jeered as the man slipped several times in bird droppings before seizing one of the doo-dahs by the leg.

Everyone in the tavern applauded and whistled, and when the man in the apron carried the protesting doo-dah through the kitchen doors, they resumed their personal conversations and merriment.

"What was *that* all about?" asked Megan.

"Parksy prides himself on fresh fried doo-dah, and he lets his customers choose their own dinner," said Bornias.

"You mean they're going to kill that bird?" Megan clutched her stomach. "And I thought the scrambler ride was going to make me sick."

Just then, a waitress stepped away from a customer's table and rang a large brass bell by the kitchen door. The cheering recommenced as a gigantic bear of a man with ash blond hair barreled through the kitchen entrance into the dining hall.

"That's Parksy," Bornias told Ainsley and Megan. "He's the fastest doo-dah catcher in the restaurant."

Parksy didn't bother to tie on an apron. He simply rolled up his sleeves, cracked his back, and sauntered into the pen.

If the doo-dahs had been panicked by their last pursuer, they were ten times worse with Parksy, scampering about the pen as fast as their little legs could carry them. Parksy was quick and nimble on his feet, however, and he caught a doo-dah in a matter of seconds without slipping once. He held the bird up to the customer, who nodded, and the patrons all cheered.

"I believe that's a new record, Parksy!" hollered Bornias.

Parksy bowed and turned from his audience to glance at the doorway. He grinned at Bornias and handed the squawking doo-dah to a passing waiter, who hurriedly put his tray down to take the bird.

"Silverboss!" roared Parksy. "Where have you been hiding? I've missed your money! Come and sit!"

Parksy guided Bornias towards a solitary booth in the rear, not seeming to have noticed the other party members, or perhaps not caring. He whisked some crumbs off the tabletop with a rag from his pocket and gestured for Bornias to sit down.

"Have a seat," he bellowed. Ainsley and Megan hastily slid into one side of the booth, not wanting to test the enormous man. Bornias removed his cloak, talking to Parksy all the while.

"Have you seen Evren recently?" he asked in a low voice. "We think he might be brewing trouble."

Parksy raised one of his blond eyebrows and glanced around before bending to whisper in Bornias's ear. He whispered so loudly, however, that even Megan and Ainsley could hear him.

"He was here last week. Gittings, the young man who works our late shift, was cleaning the floorboards around closing time when he overheard Evren talking to some dark-haired fellow. He mentioned something about the Staff of Lexiam."

"Did Gittings happen to mention who the man with Evren was?" asked Rayne.

"No," Parksy said with a shake of his massive head. "He never mentioned the other fellow. I don't think Gittings knew him."

"Parksy, would it be possible to speak to Gittings?" asked Bornias.

Parksy slapped his dishrag against his hand. "I suppose so. He's sleeping right now, but I could rouse him for you."

"I would appreciate it, old friend," said Bornias. "While you're up, I could also use a purple firepot."

"Make that two," spoke up Frieden.

"I'll have a black," said Rayne. Frieden and Bornias gaped at him in surprise.

"Black? Really?" asked Bornias.

"Please, Grandfather, I've been drinking black firepots for years," said Rayne with a grin.

"And for the young 'uns?" asked Parksy.

"Milk, I think," said Bornias.

Parksy nodded and headed back to the kitchen. Along the way, he paused to speak with one of the servers who nodded and started up a staircase at the side of the dining room.

"Well, it looks like we have our mastermind," said Frieden, turning to everyone at the table. "Evren must have been the one who sent the grimalkins. Now it's just a matter of catching him."

"The question is, though, does Evren have the staff or does our thief still have it?" asked Rayne.

"I think it's safe to assume that the staff has not yet come under Evren's control," said Bornias. "We haven't born witness to any sort of mass destruction, and I have a feeling Evren would be most eager to try out the staff once he had control of it."

Parksy returned a few moments later, carrying a tray loaded down with drinks. "Gittings will be right down," he said as he passed out the beverages. He handed Rayne his black firepot last, along with a large towel.

Everyone at the table waited for Rayne to take a drink, and he obliged them all by chugging half the stein in one gulp. He expelled a tremendous belch and smiled around the table. Whatever effect the firepot was supposed to have didn't seem to bother him.

After about three seconds, however, Rayne developed a facial twitch and his eyes watered as if he had been presented with a freshly cut onion. His forehead beaded with sweat and his nostrils flared.

Bornias and Frieden watched the transformation, grinning. "A little warm, is it?" Bornias asked his grandson.

Rayne smiled at him through pursed lips.

"Can I try some of that?" Ainsley asked Rayne, who was now banging his fist on the table and clearing his throat repeatedly.

"You'd better try a purple first," said Frieden, pushing his firepot towards Ainsley.

Flecks of black pepper floated on the surface of the drink. Ainsley raised the stein and sipped at the firepot tentatively. It tasted a bit like jalapeno juice, but didn't seem like anything he couldn't handle. He took a bigger swallow. This time, the firepot had its desired effect. As the liquid in the mug slid past Ainsley's lips and down his throat, it left a fiery trail, heating the inside of his mouth like a furnace.

"What does it taste like, Ainsley?" asked Megan, who sniffed at the stein cautiously and sneezed. "Is it really hot?"

"Not at all," said Ainsley, but the sides of his nose were beginning to shine with sweat, and he could almost feel steam coming out of his ears.

"The black one is ten times hotter than this," said Frieden, pushing Ainsley's glass of milk closer to him.

Ainsley took a sip of the milk to cool his tongue, but instantly spat it across the table.

"Ugh! This isn't milk! It's awful!"

Megan, who had been about to take a drink from her own mug, pushed it away.

Bornias took Ainsley's cup and sniffed at it. "There's nothing wrong with this. You've just never had beetle's milk before."

"What?! Gross!" exclaimed Ainsley, making a face as though he'd just drunk vomit.

"How do you milk a beetle?" asked Megan, fascinated.

"You don't milk the beetle. It produces the milk as a defense mechanism to make it inedible to backhoppers," said Frieden.

"If a bird can't stand the taste of this stuff, what makes you think a human would?" asked Ainsley, regarding his mug in disgust.

Bornias shrugged his shoulders. "It's an acquired taste, I guess—like firepots."

Across the table, Rayne mopped his sweat-drenched forehead with the towel Parksy had given him.

"Maybe you'd rather have a milk, young Rayne," jibed Parksy.

Rayne held his hand up in protest and wiped at his face once more with the towel. Raising his stein with a flourish, he chugged the remainder of the fiery drink. When the last drop had passed his lips, he slammed his mug down on the table, and everyone in the booth applauded. Parksy slapped Rayne heartily on the back, causing him to let out a loud belch.

"Water, please," said Rayne hoarsely as the second draw of firepot took effect.

Parksy hurried to get a pitcher of water and returned with a sleepy-eyed young man in tow.

"This is Gittings," said Parksy by way of introduction. He handed the pitcher of water to Rayne who guzzled from the jug, not bothering to pour the water into his glass.

"Good afternoon, Gittings," said Bornias. "Parksy tells me you work the late shift here."

"Yeah, that's right," said Gittings, brushing greasy, sand-colored hair from his dull eyes.

"Did you happen to overhear a conversation last week at closing time?"

"I overhear lots of conversations, mister," said Gittings with a grin. He was missing a few teeth and those that remained were in need of a good scrubbing.

"This particular conversation," said Bornias, lowering his voice, "had to do with a magical staff."

Gittings screwed his face up for a moment.

"There may have also been mention of some magical stones," prompted Frieden.

Gittings's face relaxed a little. "Oh, yeah. I remember those two guys. The red-headed one was flirting with my girl," he scowled.

Bornias and Frieden looked at one another.

"That's our Evren," said Frieden.

"What did the other man look like?" asked Rayne, his voice still raspy from the firepot.

Gittings shrugged his broad shoulders. "I dunno. Couldn't see his face. I didn't want them to know I was eavesdropping, so I stayed down low. I knew it was the red-headed fellow because I'd been keeping my eye on him all night, and he didn't leave that booth once."

"What were they saying about the staff and the stones?" asked Bornias.

"Well, it was the redheaded one who was doing all the talking. The other fellow just sat there, nodding his head. The redhead was telling the other that he was going to need him to steal the staff and bring it to him in . . . Pontsford I think it was? He wanted the other fellow to meet him at some bar there. I don't remember the name of it, though," said Gittings with a frown.

"That's all right," Bornias assured him. "The information you've provided has been valuable enough."

"Can I go back to sleep now?" Gittings asked Parksy with a sleepy yawn.

"Of course. I'll wake you when your shift starts." Parksy clapped a hand on Gittings's shoulder, and Gittings lumbered sleepily across the dining room.

"Anything else I can do for you right now, Silver-boss?" asked Parksy, surveying the dining room. The tables were beginning to fill up, and several people were waiting by the door.

"Just one more thing, Parksy. We will need lodging for the evening. Do you have any spare rooms?"

"For you, Silverboss, of course," said Parksy with a grin. "I'll return with a key as soon as I help these folks at the door. We're understaffed tonight."

Ainsley turned to Bornias as Parksy left the table. "Do you suppose Evren knew Rayne was going to have the staff unprotected?"

"He couldn't have," said Rayne. "I didn't decide to do it until the last minute."

"Maybe his plan was to take the Staff of Lexiam during the actual ceremony," said Frieden.

"The thief was probably watching Rayne for days before the staff was taken," said Bornias, chewing his lip thoughtfully. "He saw an early opportunity and he seized it."

Parksy returned to the table a moment later, carrying a flat slab of wood from which a copper key dangled.

"Heya, Silverboss," he said, as he handed the key to Bornias. "One of the people who just came in said there's a man outside waiting to speak with you . . . says it's important."

Bornias raised his eyebrows. "Someone wishes to speak with *me*?"

"Maybe it's Evren," said Ainsley. "Maybe he wants to make a deal."

"Allow me to go in your stead, Grandfather," said Rayne. He rose from his seat abruptly and bumped the table, almost upsetting the drinks. "It's my fault the staff was stolen, and it is my responsibility to get it back."

"But Rayne, this is a highly sensitive issue," said Frieden. "If it isn't handled correctly, we may lose our one chance."

"If I am to be king, then I should be allowed to demonstrate my diplomatic abilities," said Rayne with a disdainful sniff.

"But——" Frieden was cut short by Bornias.

"It's all right, Frieden. I trust Rayne can handle this."

Frieden pursed his lips and crossed his arms; Rayne nodded at his grandfather and hastened for the exit. As soon as he had disappeared from sight, Frieden leaned towards Bornias.

"Don't say anything," warned Bornias. "Rayne has a point. It's about time he learned to be accountable for his actions."

"But sire," objected Frieden, using Bornias's title for the first time that either Ainsley or Megan could remember, "surely Rayne's abilities could be tested with a simpler task than this."

"On the contrary, I think this is the perfect test," said Bornias, dabbing at some drops of firepot that had fallen into his beard. "True character is reflected in the worst of circumstances."

Frieden looked at Bornias dubiously and took a swig from his glass.

"If you and Rayne are both looking for the staff, who's ruling the kingdom?" asked Megan, swirling the milk in her mug.

"The Silvan Council is handling internal affairs," said Bornias. "Anything more serious, for example if someone should recover the staff, is being reported directly to me."

"There's a Silvan Council?" asked Ainsley. "Who's on it?"

"Protectors and Silvan Sentry mainly," said Frieden. "Most of them were in the meeting you sat through, but the Council Leader wasn't able to attend."

"Who's the Council Leader?" asked Megan.

"Lord Maudred," said Bornias. "He was chosen after Lady Maudred's first husband passed on, but—" Bornias's face took on a pained expression and he raised a shaking hand to his forehead. "Something's happened to Rayne," he said, paling. "I must go to him."

Parksy sauntered back to their table, frowning. "I wouldn't suggest going out in this weather. In fact, I think you all might be staying for more than one night. It's quite a blizzard out there."

"Really?" asked Megan eagerly. "Snow?"

"Parksy, winter's not for another season yet. It can't possibly be snowing," said Frieden.

"Oh no? Take a look for yourselves." Parksy pointed at the entrance of his building.

A crowd of people was pushing into the tavern through the heavy wooden doors, a flurry of snow sweeping into the room behind them. They shut the doors with a great effort against a driving wind that caused their cloaks to flap madly. The customers already seated looked around with interest, and some even got up from their chairs to witness the aberrant weather for themselves.

"Frieden, take Ainsley and Megan upstairs," said Bornias, his voice tight. He pulled out his staff and waved it at the room key lying on the table. The key glimmered, then turned green with tarnish. "Lock them in the room and then join me outside."

Frieden nodded grimly as the crowd within the tavern continued to grow. "Come on, Ainsley, Megan." He hurried to his feet, giving them a hand out of the booth.

"Frieden, what's going on?" asked Megan as Bornias ran across the room towards the doorway. "Is it Evren?"

"It certainly looks like it," said Frieden, steering them up the flight of steps at the side of the dining room. They passed a stampede of people descending in a panic, and Ainsley was nearly knocked to the ground by a rather sharp elbow in his shoulder.

Frieden stopped before a room with a picture of a flower on it. He unlocked the door and rushed the children inside. A candle stood on a tall dresser by the door, and Frieden cut a notch in it with a knife from his pocket.

"I'm going to join Bornias now. If I don't return by the time the candle gets down to this notch, climb out the window and down the ladder on the side of the building. Get to the stables and ride back to Raklund."

With a swish of his cape, he turned and left the room. The bedroom door locked with a click and Frieden's footsteps faded away.

Ainsley settled on the bed and watched the snowfall outside while Megan paced the room. Soon, however, Megan's nervous energy had moved her in front of the window, and Ainsley could see nothing but her shaking figure.

"Megan, relax . . . and get out of the way."

"I can't!" Megan faced him with her hands on her hips. "Don't you see how bad this is? What if Rayne, Bornias, *and* Frieden get captured or something?"

"Then we head back to Raklund like Frieden said."

"And leave them to die?"

Ainsley rolled his eyes. "Don't be so dramatic, Megan. I'm sure they—" He paused. "Do you hear that?" He slunk across the room and held his ear against the door.

Megan joined him. Footsteps, swift and solid, were beating a path down the hallway.

"Maybe it's Frieden," she whispered.

The footsteps on the balcony intensified as someone drew closer to the room where Ainsley and Megan were hiding.

"It sounds like someone heavier than Frieden," said Ainsley, his heart beating a little faster. "Keep quiet."

The footsteps stopped in front of the bedroom door, and Ainsley and Megan crouched behind the bed, drawing shaky breaths. A man's voice they didn't recognize muttered something, and Megan dug her fingernails into Ainsley's arm as the doorknob jiggled.

"Move!" Ainsley pushed Megan towards the window just as the bedroom door exploded into a thousand pieces, slivers of wood hurtling across the room. Megan screamed as a man in a scarlet cloak appeared in the doorway, his face hidden beneath a cowled hood.

"You are friends of King Bornias, are you not?" The man's voice was like velvet.

"Who wants to know?" asked Ainsley, his hand going into the pocket that held the Quatrys.

"An old associate from his past." He glanced into the hallway. "Take me to him quickly, or others will suffer the same fate as the crown prince."

In one fluid motion, Megan unsheathed her sword and pointed it at his heart. "We're not taking you anywhere. Get on your knees."

The cowl shook from side to side. "I must see King Bornias. *Nexia silgorosh!*" The sword in Megan's hand glowed orange, and she screamed, dropping the searing-hot metal. She recoiled and backed against the window, holding her blistering fingers against her stomach. Fumbling with the window latch, she attempted to throw the window open, but the sudden snowfall had frozen it in place.

Ainsley stood between her and the man in red, the Quatrys now clutched in his clammy right hand. "You heard her. On your knees!" The now familiar ringing sound filled the room as Ainsley used all his strength to generate a violent wind.

Somehow the man in red knew what was coming. He raised his hand in front of him and muttered another incantation.

"Ilja mosda sefrem!"

The wind passed directly through him, like water through a sieve, but it pushed everything else, the rickety four-poster bed, the banged-up dresser, the splinters of wood, against the opposite wall with a tremendous racket. Ainsley's current of air was so powerful, in fact, that it curled back around the room and knocked him into Megan, forcing both of them against the window.

The glass pane couldn't withstand their combined weight. With a sickening, crackling crunch, it shattered behind them, and they plummeted through the wintry air towards the ground below.

Strangers in a Strange Land

Megan let out a bloodcurdling scream as everything flashed by in a blur. Ainsley snatched at a handful of her clothing and gritted his teeth, silently entreating the Quatrys for help.

The air around them rang, and their descent slowed until they were hovering inches above the ground, the swirling snow beneath their feet evidence of a rolling wind that seemed to have cushioned their fall.

They landed on their backs with a soft thump, and Megan glanced towards the second-floor window where the man in red looked down on them before quickly disappearing from view.

"Come on. We've got to get to the scramblers," she said, pulling a pale, sweat-drenched Ainsley to his feet.

"But what about Bornias and—"

Megan shook her head. "We can't wait for them. Don't you know who that was?"

"I'm not—"

"It was Evren! And now, thanks to you and your magic obsession, he knows we have one of the Quatrys, so he'll be coming after us."

Ainsley would have argued with her about his magic "obsession," if not for the uneasy feeling in his stomach. The power had come much quicker this time when he had called upon it, almost as eager for him to use it as he was.

Megan noticed his hesitation. "Ainsley, you need to be careful with magic. You don't know enough about it."

"Look, forget about that for now," was all he could say. "We *do* need to keep moving, but we should try and find the others."

They stumbled through the snowdrifts, barely aware that the flurry had stopped, until they reached the front of Parksy's Den. A raging fire had engulfed the entire block, with the exception of the stucco tavern. People scurried about in a frenzy, some of them running away from the blazing buildings, others running toward them trying to put out the fire using whatever water the snowstorm hadn't frozen.

Frieden stood among the crowd gathered at the base of the fire, valiantly trying to extinguish it using the magic from the Quatrys.

"I see Frieden," said Megan, "but where are Bornias and Rayne?"

"I don't know. Evren made it sound like something bad, though." Ainsley stood on tiptoe and scanned the crowd until he felt a hand on his right shoulder. He followed the hairy hand to the sleeve of a red cloak.

"Evren." The name caught in his throat, so that the second syllable was only a whisper on his lips.

"What?" murmured Megan, hypnotized by the vicious fire roaring and crackling in front of them.

The man pulled back his hood and regarded Ainsley with an anxious expression. "I'm not Evren," he said. "But I will need that Quatrys you're carrying. I'll offer you a trade . . ." He drew Megan's sword from the folds of his cloak, but doubled over as Megan kicked him hard in the shin.

"Run, Ainsley!" she cried, for she hadn't heard the man's words, she had only seen him brandishing a sword.

Megan elbowed her way through the crowd, dragging a protesting Ainsley behind her. "Come on," she said, heading for the stable. She pulled her bewildered scrambler from its stall where it had been nibbling at a bale of hay. "We have to ride."

Ainsley made no motion to follow. "Megan, wait a second."

Megan shook her head and pulled herself up onto the scrambler's coarse back. "It's not safe here any more. Evren attacked Rayne and started those fires," she said. "He'll be after us next."

Before Ainsley could stop her, she dug her ankles into her mount's side and dashed out of the stables. Ainsley yelled a stream of curse words after her before climbing onto his own scrambler and giving chase.

She had gotten a good head start on him and it was almost ten minutes before Ainsley managed to catch up. When he did, he yelled, "Where are you going? Raklund is that way." He pointed to his left.

"We can't go back to Raklund. Evren will be expecting us there," she said before coaxing her scrambler into a faster pace.

Ainsley matched her stride for stride. "That wasn't Evren," he said in exasperation. "Evren has red hair and, probably, lighter skin. The man in the red cloak had brown hair and dark skin. Plus, he said he *wasn't Evren*!"

Megan finally reined in her scrambler and wheeled it to face Ainsley, who had done the same. "Let's just say that it wasn't Evren. How do we know that this man isn't working for Evren, hmm? Bornias said Evren would have used a henchman to steal the staff. Maybe he sent his henchman to finish the job."

Ainsley didn't answer right away.

"Well?" pressed Megan.

"You could be right, but—"

"We need to keep moving before Evren, or whoever he is, catches up with us."

"Well, where do you suggest we go?" asked Ainsley sourly. "I mean, since you seem to be the expert on this country."

Megan removed a rolled-up piece of parchment from her bag and unfurled a detailed map of the area.

"And you call *me* a thief?" asked Ainsley. "Who'd you swipe that from?"

"Barsley told me I could have it. I didn't steal it," she said righteously. "Now, we'll camp out in the forest tonight here, where the Silver Falls form the Grimmett River," she pointed at a spot on the map, "and then tomorrow, we'll go looking for everybody."

She made it sound simple, but Ainsley knew better. "Camp in the forest? Are you crazy? Did you even see the grimalkins that came out of that place?"

"Yes, I did," said Megan, rolling up her map. "And I also happened to be listening to Frieden when he told us about them. Grimalkins don't move around after dark because they have very poor night vision. We can't stay out here in the open and risk being spotted, and we can't ride all night because we won't be able to see where we're going. It's really the only logical alternative." She tapped him on the head with her map and slid it into her pack.

"Yeah, all right," Ainsley said with a frown. "But just out of curiosity, how are you expecting to find everyone tomorrow?"

"Kaelin Warnik will help us."

———

Despite Megan's qualms about riding at night, it was well after dark before they reached the forest. The scramblers seemed grateful for the rest and waded into the river as soon as their riders dismounted.

As Ainsley and Megan stretched their legs, they listened to the water churning softly at the base of the falls. Had they not been in a strange world in an uncomfortable darkness, the rhythmic drumming of the water as it splashed onto the rocks below would have been soothing. Instead, it just seemed a distraction, masking the sounds of any enemies that might be waiting to ambush them from behind a nearby tree.

"Let's get to the top of the falls," said Ainsley. "We'll be able to spot anyone coming from the south."

They stumbled a little as they climbed, and a crop of thorny bushes slowed their progress, Ainsley being the unfortunate discoverer of this obstacle. The thorns were needle-thin, and Ainsley didn't realize what he had come across until he had several imbedded in his arms and legs.

"At least the thorns will slow anyone else trying to climb up here," said Megan consolingly as she maneuvered through the bushes.

"Easy for you to say," he grumbled, wincing as he pulled out each sliver and tossed it on the ground. "You're not a human pincushion."

Once they reached the top, Megan helped Ainsley extract the thorns he had missed. While Ainsley bathed his arms and legs in the cool river water, Megan dug in her pack for food. They ate a cold meal of bread and cheese, which wasn't very filling, and tried to make themselves comfortable on the hard ground.

"What makes you so sure that Kaelin will help us?" asked Ainsley, tearing a large chunk of bread off the loaf sitting between them. The bread was already getting stale; by tomorrow, it could probably be used to drive stakes into the ground.

"He's friends with Bornias and Frieden, isn't he? I'll bet if he knew they were in danger, he'd do anything for us."

Ainsley snorted and stuffed his bread into his mouth. "I doubt that," he said, spraying breadcrumbs everywhere. "He wasn't even willing to look for his own nephew,"

"Well, he was at first," countered Megan. "I'm sure he had a good reason for giving up. And you know what else? I'll bet he's got one of those birdbaths like Bornias, and we can use that to find them."

"You really think he's got one of those?" asked Ainsley.

A silky voice responded before Megan could. "Of course he does. All *great* wizards do, you know."

Ainsley and Megan jumped to their feet and looked around for their mysterious visitor. Ainsley glanced upward and elbowed Megan, who followed his gaze. A large tawny cougar was resting lazily in a tree above them.

"You should never expect your enemies to approach from the logical direction," the cougar purred. "It's always best to watch your back."

The cougar leapt from its tree branch to the ground below with a soft thump. "You must be friends of Bornias. I'm Sasha," the mountain lion bent her forelegs in a slight bow. "I know someone who's been looking for you."

"E-Evren?" Ainsley craned his neck to follow the large cat. She circled him slowly, as if sizing him up for a meal.

"Oh my, no," she said, swishing her black-tipped tail. "I would never associate with such a loathsome creature. The man of whom I speak is Kaelin Warnik. Have you heard of him?"

Megan, who had instinctively reached for her now-absent sword, relaxed a little. "Yes, we have, and we . . . uh . . . actually need to talk with him."

"Excellent," purred Sasha. "Then this works out best for all, doesn't it? If you'll follow me, I can lead you to Kaelin."

"How do we know we can trust you?" asked Ainsley.

Sasha stared at him with unblinking cat's eyes. "You don't, but I think you'll be safer with me than with the grimalkins that prowl these woods at night. I spotted one not far from here."

Ainsley turned to Megan. "I thought you said grimalkins don't move at night."

"I lied," she said with a shrug.

Sasha hissed in laughter at the loathsome look Ainsley gave Megan. "You're a crafty girl. I admire that. What's your name?"

"Megan, and this is Ainsley," she said pointing at her scowling companion.

A familiar, hair-raising scream sounded from upstream.

"Grimalkins." Ainsley reached into his pocket.

"We don't have much time," said Sasha, tilting her head to one side. "She's no more than twenty yards from here."

"What do we do?" asked Megan, starting to regret her woodland hideout. "We can't outrun it! It'll track us down and kill us!"

Sasha pawed at the ground with her front claws. "There's a root that grows up here. It's used in neutralizing powders and—Aha!"

Sasha managed to dig up a long brown tuber, which she promptly bit in two and spat back onto the ground.

"Ugh. It's rather bitter, but it can help us mask your scent. Chew on the root, then spit it out."

They did as she told them, the acidic juices causing their mouths to water and pucker.

"Now what?" asked Megan.

"Now we leave the forest quickly and quietly," said Sasha.

"What about our scramblers?" asked Ainsley.

"They'll be all right. They've got tough hides, so the grimalkin won't bother with them. Now, get moving!"

Sasha padded upstream, and Megan and Ainsley followed as quietly as they could. After riding the scramblers, it wasn't as easy traveling on foot. They journeyed through the night, Sasha pushing them at a relentless pace. She allowed them to rest when the sun came up, scavenging for food as they slept, and by nightfall, they were moving again.

As the full moon reached its highest point on the second day, she announced that they were at last approaching Amdor. Ainsley and Megan almost collapsed from exhaustion and relief. Megan's feet and back were aching as they climbed a steep hill at the edge of the community, and Ainsley dragged, more than lifted, his feet across the dewy grass.

Amdor was little more than a row of brownstone cottages nestled on the edge of a lake, which fed the Upper Grimmett River. It looked like a summer camp, complete with stables and a riding pen and surrounded by a tall wooden fence. At the entrance hung a sign that read, "*Amdor,*" with a smaller sign beneath it reading, "*We're not tired, just retired.*"

"Here is where I take my leave," said Sasha, resting on her haunches. "I have some business to attend to, but you will be safe in Amdor. Kaelin lives in cottage five. He'll be waiting for you."

They watched her saunter away before stepping through the opening in the fence. As they did so, they each felt a tingling sensation that started at the scalp and washed downward to the soles of their feet.

"Weird," said Ainsley, shaking himself. "My skin just felt like it does when my foot falls asleep—except this was my entire body!"

"I know. Mine too," said Megan, rubbing at the goose bumps on her arms. "This is a wizard community, isn't it? It's probably some kind of magic."

They climbed the steps to a cottage with a red number five painted on its door, and Megan hesitated a moment before stepping forward and knocking. She and Ainsley waited nervously, shifting from one foot to the other until the door clicked and a dark-skinned man stepped onto the torchlit porch, smiling at them.

It was the man in red.

Reunion

"I see Sasha succeeded in bringing you to me," he said. He smiled again, and his left cheek dimpled. The air of evil he had projected in Guevan had vanished, as if the snow there had washed him clean.

Ainsley and Megan exchanged a confused look. "We're . . . we're actually looking for Kaelin Warnik," said Ainsley.

"And you've found him," said the man.

"Um, okay," said Megan. She looked him up and down but could see nary a wrinkle or gray hair. "Aren't you a little young to be retired?"

Kaelin laughed affably, the torch flame reflected in his warm brown eyes. "You'd be surprised how often I get asked that question." He gestured towards the open doorway. "Please, come inside. I've been worried about you."

Neither Ainsley nor Megan moved.

"Why were you chasing us?" asked Megan.

"Yeah, and what was all that talk about needing to speak to Bornias?" added Ainsley.

Kaelin's sunny visage faded, and he stepped onto the porch, closing the door behind him. "I wasn't chasing you with the intent of hurting you. In fact, I'm rather sorry you burned your hand and that the two of you fell out of the window. I can tend to your wounds when we get inside. As for Bornias," he paused as if unsure whether to continue, "let's just say I know something about the Silverskin legacy that he doesn't."

"What does *that* mean?" asked Megan.

Kaelin seemed hesitant to answer and when Ainsley's stomach grumbled like an agitated garbage disposal, Kaelin looked almost relieved to have a change in subject. "I'd say it's been a while since you ate a good meal, yes? Would the two of you like to come inside and get some food now?"

Ainsley nodded and moved towards the door, but Megan held him back. "I'm sorry," she said to Kaelin, "but I don't think we feel safe entering your home. Not when we know you're so skilled at magic."

"Well, if that's your concern, you needn't worry. When you walked through the entrance of Amdor, did anything strange happen to you?"

Ainsley spoke up. "Yeah, it felt like ants were crawling all over me."

"That's because you've entered a no-magic zone," explained Kaelin. "Any magic in your body was . . . neutralized, if you will. Which means I have no magical powers here either. Listen," he said, placing a hand on the doorknob, "if you don't want to come inside, how about if I bring some food out to you?" He turned to go back into the cottage, and Ainsley cast a look at Megan.

"No, we'll come inside," she said hurriedly.

They entered the front room of Kaelin's home to the smell of roasting meat, and Ainsley's stomach roared again. The roast turned on a spit in the living room fireplace, and the polished wood floor in front of the hearth was strewn with several soft pallets and plump pillows.

This living area occupied half of the front room; the other half was Kaelin's kitchen, crowded by a squat potbelly stove, butter churn, and breakfast nook.

Kaelin gestured for them to sit down at the benches in the breakfast nook. "Now, you are Pagan and Antsy, correct?" he asked, pointing from Megan to Ainsley.

They looked at each other and laughed. "Close," said Megan. "I'm Megan and he's Ainsley."

"How did you . . . almost know our names?" asked Ainsley.

"I've heard Bornias mention you when I've been watching him in my summoning pool. Which reminds me," Kaelin continued as he removed two plates from a shelf, "there's something I've been meaning to ask you two. Where were you born?"

Ainsley and Megan looked at one another, stumped by this unexpected question.

"Why do you want to know where we were born?" asked Ainsley.

Kaelin set the plates on the kitchen counter. "Well, it's really just the strangest thing. When I looked in my summoning pool the other day, I saw Bornias and Frieden, I even saw your scramblers, but I didn't see you two. I could see and hear Frieden and Bornias talking to you, but it was as if they were talking into empty space."

Kaelin opened a narrow door on the wall beside the stove, and a chill wind slid through the nook. The door led to a smaller room that appeared to be some sort of refrigeration unit, judging by the abundance of hanging meats and fowl. Kaelin had to step in sideways to fit through the narrow doorway.

"I did some research on it over at my friend Poloi's . . . he's the community's historian . . . and the only thing I could find on the subject had to deal with foreign visitors." Kaelin pushed the "refrigerator" door shut with his foot, his arms laden with tomatoes, cheese, and a wooden tub of what appeared to be butter.

"Poloi said it meant foreign to this world, but that would be absurd, wouldn't it?" Kaelin chuckled as he began cutting tomatoes.

"Heh, that is a pretty crazy idea," said Ainsley, his eyes darting about the kitchen for a decent change of subject. "So, how . . . um . . . do you keep that little room so cold?"

Kaelin paused midslice and gave Ainsley a baffled look. "With fire pine pods, of course. Once you've used up the heat, you freeze them."

"Oh, well, we . . . we travel with the Carnival, so we don't see things like that too often," said Megan, kicking Ainsley under the table.

Kaelin cocked his head at them as if deciphering their lies, but if he knew the truth, he made no mention of it. He finished building the sandwiches, and as he set them before Ainsley and Megan, he glanced out the window at a sundial in his front yard.

"After you eat, you two should get some rest. Your friends will arrive soon."

"You saw them in your summoning pool?" asked Megan.

"I did," he said, walking to the fireplace to turn the handle on the spit. "I have a rather advanced model that gives me greater coverage, *and* I can pick up sounds." He said this with a hint of pride.

Ainsley bit into his sandwich and gulped down a few mouthfuls before speaking. "If this is a no-magic zone, how can you use your summoning pool? Isn't that magic?" he asked.

"You're very swift of mind, Ainsley," said Kaelin with a grin. "But my summoning pool is down by the lake, outside the borders of Amdor. We can see Bornias and Frieden there if you'd like."

Wolfing down the remainder of their food, Ainsley and Megan followed Kaelin through a back doorway onto another porch, which was littered with piles of wood and bags of fire pine pods.

"Why do you need the wood if you have the fire pine pods?" asked Ainsley.

"Call me old-fashioned, but I still enjoy the sounds and smells of a crackling fire," said Kaelin. "Plus, the wood adds a smoky flavor to my cooking that I can't get from fire pine pods."

The trio descended the porch steps and traversed a stretch of grass to the gravelly lakeshore where the summoning pool stood. The pedestal of Kaelin's pool appeared to be made of a silvery metal, and the basin was clear, like glass.

"How come your summoning pool looks so much different than Bornias's?" asked Ainsley. "His is made of stone."

"I find that lipothis—that's the metal, and enchanted diamond make much better conductors than stone," replied Kaelin. "Of course, it's an incredible amount of trouble to enchant the diamond, which is probably why Bornias hasn't done it."

"Can I try and summon Bornias's image?" Ainsley asked eagerly.

"I'm sorry, Ainsley, but I have my pool set up so it will respond to me alone," said Kaelin. He hummed a single note, and the liquid in the summoning pool began to ripple. "*Admis creeba focál*," he said.

Bornias's image shimmered onto the surface of the pool. He and Frieden had exchanged their scramblers for horses and were galloping across an open field, their faces grim and anxious.

"*Nofra dinsi*," said Kaelin.

Bornias and Frieden grew smaller as the summoning pool broadened its view. Kaelin studied the landscape for a moment.

"They're past the falls," he said. "That's good. They should be here in a few hours."

"Where's Rayne?" asked Megan. "I don't see him."

"He went a separate way from Bornias and Frieden," said Kaelin. "*Admis creeba prowid*."

The image of Bornias and Frieden was replaced by one of Rayne walking along a crowded street.

"He's gone on to Pontsford," said Kaelin. "For which I am very grateful."

"You know if you're not going to tell us your big secret, you shouldn't keep saying weird things like that," said Ainsley sourly.

"I am sorry, Ainsley," said Kaelin with a smile. "You're right, of course, but don't let it frustrate you. The secret will be revealed soon enough."

The Revelation

A few hours after noon, Megan awoke to the sound of voices from outside. She heard footsteps on the porch and the rustle of cloak against boots as Kaelin hurried to meet his visitors.

As soon as Kaelin had stepped outside and closed the door, Megan sat up in her makeshift bed on the living room floor and crawled to a window overlooking the porch. Squinting in the bright sunlight, she saw Bornias and Frieden tethering their horses to the porch railing and had to suppress a squeal of glee.

"You must have seen me coming," Bornias told Kaelin, wrapping the younger man in an affectionate bear hug.

"It has been too long, old friend," replied Kaelin in a husky voice.

"Unfortunately, troubled times prevent social calls," said Bornias, as Kaelin clasped hands warmly with Frieden. "We could use your help with several evils that have befallen us."

"I think I may be able to alleviate some of your troubles, my friend," Kaelin told Bornias. "Your young associates Ainsley and Megan are here with me."

Bornias's face, which had been wrought with worry lines, slackened, and he looked as if he might cry. "Where are they?"

"They're inside, asleep," said Kaelin, putting his arms around his two friends. "Come now. You must both be tired after your journey. Let us go indoors and get you off your feet. I have something important to tell you."

Megan did a frantic crawl back to her pallet and dove under the blankets just as the front door opened and the men stepped inside. She peeked through her eyelids and saw Bornias heave a sigh of relief as he gazed down at her and Ainsley. Megan shrunk beneath her blanket, for Bornias looked as if he wanted to smother them both in hugs and kisses. To her momentary relief, he did nothing more than sit on the floor beside them.

When Bornias removed his damp boots, however, a nauseating odor of old cheese and manure nearly made Megan gag under her blanket. Even Frieden and Kaelin wrinkled their noses at the staggering smell emanating from Bornias's feet.

"Why don't I get the two of you something to eat? Roast motley sandwiches, perhaps?" Kaelin dashed from the room without waiting for an answer.

"Good gracious, Bornias, don't poison Ainsley and Megan in their sleep," said Frieden, waving his hand in front of his face. "When was the last time you changed your stockings?"

"Just last week," said Bornias, sounding surprised. "I only have three pairs."

Frieden made a face. "Bornias, that is foul! Go and wash your feet," he said in a scolding voice. "And throw those stockings away. I'm sure Kaelin has a pair he'll let you borrow."

Bornias shrugged but got up, carrying his dirty stockings in one hand. When he vacated the room, Frieden gathered his boots and put them outside.

"Is it safe in there?" asked Kaelin, peeking his head around the corner of the kitchen.

Frieden settled onto the pillows beside Megan, who quickly shut her eyes and let out a very fake snore. "Yes, he's washing up. I told him he could borrow a pair of your stockings."

"Ugh. He can keep them." Kaelin carried a tray of sandwich trimmings back into the living room. "It's amazing that the king of Raklund has but three pairs of socks.

You'd think he could afford one pair for every hour of the day."

Frieden laughed and helped himself to two pieces of bread and some slices of roast motley. "Since you're awake, Megan, you might as well have something to eat, too," he said, without looking away from his food.

Megan blushed but sat up and fixed herself a sandwich.

"I've never met a worse fake-sleeper," added Kaelin with a smile before turning to Frieden. "Ainsley and Megan won't tell me where they're from, by the way, so I'll ask you. They look like First Gaters."

"They are," said Frieden.

"First Gaters?" repeated Megan. "Why do you call us that?"

"The Staff of Lexiam has allowed us to discover gates into other dimensions, as I'm sure Bornias has already told you," said Kaelin while Frieden crunched upon a piece of fruit. "So far, we've found twelve. Your world was the first one we discovered."

"I thought nobody was supposed to know that other worlds existed," said Megan, picking at her sandwich.

Frieden swallowed. "Well, the governor of the Protectors always knows, and of course, so does the king."

"Does Rayne know?" asked Ainsley's voice from beneath a pile of cushions, startling Megan so that she dropped her sandwich. Ainsley unearthed himself and rubbed his bleary eyes, then retrieved the fallen sandwich, dusted it off and took a bite.

"Rayne doesn't know yet," said Frieden. "He was supposed to find out after his coronation, but since that didn't happen . . ." Frieden trailed off as Bornias entered the room, a fresh pair of stockings dangling from his arm.

"This whole incident of the missing staff is actually what I wanted to speak with you about," said Kaelin. He disappeared and returned with two chairs, setting them so that they faced one another.

"Please, sit, Bornias." Kaelin indicated one of the chairs as he perched on the edge of the other. Looking slightly nonplussed, Bornias did as he was instructed.

"You see," began Kaelin, "Evren has been acting a little suspicious lately. He's been visiting Amdor far more often than he ever has in the past—"

"Ha! We were right. It *was* Evren!" interjected Ainsley.

"Let Kaelin finish," Bornias told him, pulling on a clean stocking.

"Well, I started watching Evren in my summoning pool to see what he was up to. He made numerous trips to Pontsford, and on one occasion, I tracked him into Guevan."

Kaelin paused for a moment and rubbed his hands across the front of his robes, his legs bouncing up and down. Bornias stopped pulling on his second stocking, leaving it in a roll around his ankle.

"What is it, Kaelin?" he asked in concern.

"I have to tell you something that will seem unbelievable and probably more than a little alarming."

"Kaelin, I think after what we've been going through, nothing could alarm us," said Frieden with a smile.

Kaelin laughed, a short, mirthless laugh and wiped his hands down his robes again. "No, this . . . this will definitely come as a shock. It came as a shock to me."

"What did you see?" asked Ainsley. His half-eaten sandwich dangled limply from one hand.

Kaelin took a deep breath. "When Evren was in Guevan, I saw him talking to someone about the Staff of Lexiam and . . . the face was familiar to me."

Frieden, Bornias, Megan, and Ainsley leaned forward expectantly, but Kaelin didn't elaborate.

"Well?" prompted Bornias after a minute or two had gone by.

Kaelin stood and began pacing the room. "It's a funny thing really. I ran through this scenario a dozen times before you arrived, practicing what I would say, and how you would respond. Now, that the time has come I-I'm not sure I want to tell you."

Bornias stood and grabbed Kaelin by the shoulders. He guided Kaelin back to his chair and sat down clasping the young wizard's hands in his old ones.

"Can it really be that bad, Kaelin? Whatever it is, old friend, you can tell us. Was it your sister? One of the Protectors?"

Kaelin sighed and bowed his head. He looked up at Bornias with a somber expression, and for the first time, lines of age and worry wrought his face.

"Bornias, it was Rayne."

Bornias pulled his hands away from Kaelin's with a quick, jerky movement, and a collage of emotions washed over him. His eyebrows rose in disbelief, but the look in his eyes conveyed anger; his cheeks turned even ruddier than usual, as if Kaelin had just shamed him, and his bottom lip quivered slightly.

Kaelin withdrew his own now-empty hands awkwardly and folded them in his lap, pressing his lips together in a tight line. Frieden had his head buried in his hands and was shaking it from side to side.

Ainsley and Megan watched in silence, expecting Bornias to throw himself into a rage and attack Kaelin. For several minutes, however, the only sound was the crackle of the fire and the shuffling of Megan's feet from side to side.

Finally, Kaelin cleared his throat and spoke up. "Maybe, I should get everyone something to drink," he said.

He started to get to his feet but Bornias banged his staff on the floor in front of Kaelin, barring his path.

"You're not going anywhere until you explain this . . . slander you're proposing to me," said Bornias. The myriad of emotions on his face had been replaced with pure ire.

Kaelin lowered himself back into his seat and glanced at Frieden, as if silently begging for help.

"I'm afraid I have to agree with Bornias on this one, Kaelin," said Frieden. "Rayne is a Silverskin, and a protector of the staff. He would not want to see any harm come to it."

Kaelin sighed and ran shaky fingers through his hair. "I know it doesn't sound true, but I saw Rayne talking with Evren. They were drinking firepots at Parksy's, and Evren asked Rayne to bring the Staff of Lexiam to Pontsford."

Frieden turned to Bornias with an uncomfortable look on his face. "This fits with Gittings's story."

"Maybe it was someone disguised as Rayne . . . a shape shifter," said Bornias stubbornly. "Or maybe it was someone who looked like Rayne."

"Bornias, what reason would someone have to disguise himself as Rayne?" asked Kaelin. His voice remained calm, but his hands were clenched.

"Maybe someone *wanted* to be seen and overheard. Maybe they hoped word would get back to Raklund that the future heir was going to deceive his people—to stir up political unrest."

Kaelin bit his lip and stared up at the ceiling, as if looking for guidance. Before he could speak again, however, Frieden interceded.

"Bornias, I have to say that Kaelin may have something. Your theory seems a trifle . . . implausible."

"Damn it, Frieden," snapped Bornias. "Whose side are you on?"

Kaelin cleared his throat again. "In your favor, Bornias, someone did try to get word back to the palace," Bornias looked smug at this minor victory, "but the guards wouldn't listen to me. They discounted me as a traitor for abandoning the king."

"You came to Raklund? Why didn't you speak with a Protector?" asked Frieden.

"The Silvan Sentry wouldn't let me past the entrance," said Kaelin. "They're still bitter towards me about the . . . incident with Losen."

"Well, you still haven't offered any other reason for believing that Rayne would take the staff," said Bornias.

"I saw him with my own two eyes," said Kaelin, the exasperation finally working into his voice. "What more do you want?"

"How about a reason why Rayne would be willing to help Evren? Did you see Evren hand him some money or offer him some sort of magical powers?"

"No," said Kaelin with a frown, "but . . ."

"Well, there you have it," interrupted Bornias. "It was just a case of mistaken identity."

He settled back in his chair, looking satisfied with himself, and finished pulling on his stocking. Kaelin threw his hands in the air and grunted in disgust.

"Actually, Bornias," said Frieden, "now that I've been thinking about it, Rayne *has* been showing signs of strange behavior."

"What do you mean?" asked Bornias, giving Frieden a look that almost dared him to speak against his grandson.

"Well, about a week before the staff was taken, I found him sitting in the Hall of Staves every morning, just staring at the Staff of Lexiam, entranced. And another thing," Frieden said quickly before Bornias could interject, "Do you remember when we questioned the Silvan Sentry that were with Rayne? They said they tried to stop him from leaving Raklund with the staff, but he threatened to have them dismissed; Rayne told us it was *their* idea."

"What are you saying, Frieden?" asked Bornias.

Frieden regarded him with something close to pity. "I'm saying that Kaelin may be right," he said.

Bornias shook his head slowly, pulling at his beard. "No," he muttered. "No, no, *NO!*" He kicked the tray of food across the floor, and half its contents splattered against the living room wall. "How dare you accuse my grandson of such treachery?" stormed Bornias, getting nose to nose with Kaelin.

Kaelin closed his eyes and swallowed hard. "I'm sorry, Bornias. I saw what I saw."

"Liar!" shrieked Bornias. He clenched his fists as if he might take a swing at Kaelin. "You are a liar! This is all your doing, and now you've turned Frieden against me as well!"

Kaelin opened his eyes, an unmistakable anger flashing in them. "Don't point the finger at me, Bornias. I'm sorry about this, but it is the truth."

He reached within his cloak, but Frieden slid his sword from its scabbard and held the blade against Kaelin's throat. As the blade grazed his jugular vein, Kaelin held his hands up submissively. In one of them, he now clutched something.

"What's that?" asked Bornias, snatching the object from Kaelin's hand. "Some little trinket? Are you trying to *buy* your way back into my good favors?"

"Of course not, Bornias," said Kaelin, pushing Frieden's sword away with his fingertips. "It's a key."

"Ah yes, this will definitely make up for all that you've just done," said Bornias sarcastically.

"Come with me, and you'll see what it goes to," said Kaelin. "Then perhaps you'll cool down a bit."

He led the way through a door on the left side of the hall that opened into a sunlit room. On the wall closest to the living room, a crowded bookshelf held such titles as *Minimal Curses* and *Knack Attacks*. On the opposite wall, cloaks and conical hats hung from hooks, and a mounted wooden rack was stacked with around twenty staves.

Slender and about six feet in length each, they were made of varying materials, most of them wood. Some had objects affixed to one end for channeling powers or drawing power from the surroundings. Others were rather plain and looked like simple walking staves. Ainsley wondered if Kaelin would notice if one was missing.

"Don't even think about it," Megan whispered in his ear.

"All right, Kaelin," growled Bornias. "Where is this wonderment you dragged me in here for?"

Kaelin walked to the bookshelf and pulled at the books on the middle row. They came off the ledge as a cohesive unit, and he dropped them on the floor where they made a hollow thumping sound—fakes, meant to distract trespassers from something far more valuable.

When Kaelin had removed the row of books, he revealed a long iron box. With a grunt, he lifted it off the shelf and set it on a table cluttered with bottles and sheets of parchment. The box had a hinged lid, in the center of which was a keyhole.

Bornias started towards the box with the key ready, but Kaelin covered the keyhole with his hand.

"What is it *now*?" asked Bornias irritably.

"What you're about to see," said Kaelin, "will prove, once and for all, that I am not lying to you about Rayne. You'll understand that I did what I had to."

Bornias studied Kaelin for a moment. "If it's possible, you've made me more anxious than I was before."

Kaelin pulled his hand away, and Bornias fitted the key into the keyhole and turned it. The lid clicked open and

Bornias lifted it cautiously, as though expecting a viper to spring out at him. He peeked under the lid and, after deciding that nothing dangerous resided in the box, threw it back the rest of the way, revealing a cloth-covered object.

He lifted the edge of the cloth but dropped it quickly and turned to Kaelin, face drained of color. "What . . . how did you . . . when did you . . ." he sputtered. "It can't be."

"What is it, Bornias?" asked Frieden, lifting the edge of the cloth. "Oh my." He goggled at the object. "Kaelin, this . . . this is amazing."

Ainsley and Megan peered around him. Nestled among the velvet was a transparent crystal baton with a golden orb on one end.

"I don't get it," said Ainsley with a frown. "It looks like one of those stirring rods we use in chemistry . . . except, you know, bigger."

He reached out to touch it, but Frieden knocked his hand away. "You may be strong enough to control a Quatrys, Ainsley, but you can't handle the Staff of Lexiam."

"*This* is the Staff of Lexiam?" Ainsley snorted. "I'm not impressed."

"What were you expecting? Blinking lights and switches? It doesn't need to be extravagant to be useful," said Bornias, as he lifted the staff out of the box.

"Take it outside of Amdor," said Kaelin. "Test it if you don't believe me."

"I think I shall have to." Bornias headed out the back door with the rest of the party on his heels.

Once beyond the no-magic border, he turned the staff over and fire streaked through the inside of the staff, scorching the glassy interior to an ashen black. Without Bornias even moving it, a wave of water washed across the length of the staff, removing the black ash, and making the staff appear clear once more. The water inside evaporated, leaving only the ashy residue settled in the bottom. Bornias shook the staff vigorously, and the ash was gone.

"Did *you* do all that?" asked Megan in awe.

"I removed just the ashes," said Bornias. "The staff was cleansing itself from its last use. That is," he glanced at Kaelin, "if it *is* the real staff of Lexiam. Frieden, grab one of those logs for me."

Frieden selected a log and dropped it on the ground by the lake. Bornias lifted the staff in front of him, and it flared to life. A finger each of red, blue, green, and purple lightning traveled up and down the staff, crackling excitedly. Each strand of colored lightning was attempting to dominate the others, glowing brighter and stronger than its fellows, before being suppressed by another strand.

The staff hummed resonantly and, to his surprise, Ainsley felt the Quatrys in his pocket vibrate to the humming.

Bornias waved the staff at the log and it burst into flames. He waved the staff again, and the log began to spin through the air, as if trapped in a miniature twister. Bornias waved the wand a third time, and the air grew cooler as the sky around them darkened. A storm cloud rolled in above the burning log; lightning flashed, and a thunderclap shook the ground where they stood. Moments later, the cloud unleashed a barrel of rain, drenching the log and extinguishing the fire.

"Cool," said Ainsley.

"Indeed," said Bornias, waving the staff again so that the cloud dissipated. He turned to Kaelin with an astonished look on his face. "It *is* the Staff of Lexiam. I felt it tingle in my soul."

"I knew it would,"Kaelin said with a smile. "I speak the truth, Bornias."

Bornias handed the staff to Frieden and shuffled to the back porch, looking dazed as he sat upon one of the steps.

"How did you get the staff, Kaelin?" asked Frieden.

Kaelin picked up the sodden log and tossed it into the lake. After wiping his hands on his robes, he turned to face his friends.

"Well, after I saw . . . Rayne speaking with Evren, I knew it wouldn't be long before he took the staff to Evren, so I watched and waited. The day before his coronation, I saw Rayne leave Raklund with a band of guards. I wasn't sure what he was doing, but I had the feeling he was going to leave the guards behind and return to Pontsford. I reacted without thinking, rode in, and stole the staff."

"They didn't recognize you?" asked Frieden.

"I had my hood pulled up. I rode in a straight line for Pontsford so they would think that was where I was headed, abandoned my horse halfway, then turned into an eagle and flew back to Amdor."

Megan leaned towards Ainsley and whispered out of the corner of her mouth. "Did he just say he turned into a bird?"

"Out of all of this, *that's* the part you find hard to believe?" Ainsley whispered back.

Bornias shushed them. "Kaelin, why didn't you tell me what was going on?"

"I *tried* to return it to you in Guevan," said Kaelin, spreading his arms in exasperation, "but Rayne came outside instead of you, and he attacked me and tried to take back the staff." Kaelin hung his head. "We fought over it, like children over a toy."

"Would I be correct in guessing that you two were responsible for the fire and the blizzard, then?" asked Bornias.

Kaelin nodded. "I think he set off the staff a few times in an attempt to distract me. When we started drawing a crowd, I finally had to knock him unconscious to make him let go."

"*You* were the one who attacked my grandson?" asked Bornias with a tinge of anger. "He looked as if an entire gang assaulted him."

"I did what I had to do," said Kaelin stoutly, "and I'd do it again. Even though I'm no longer with the Protectors, I still feel an obligation to uphold the creed, Bornias."

"What's the creed?" Ainsley asked Frieden in a low voice.

"It's written in a language that's been dead for thousands of years, but the rough meaning is that the protection of the Staff of Lexiam comes above all else, even friends and family. It cannot be allowed to fall into the wrong hands."

"Which, unfortunately, it almost did," said Bornias glumly.

"Come now, Bornias," said Kaelin, sitting on the porch beside his friend. "You have the staff back. That should bring you great relief."

"How can I be happy, Kaelin?" asked Bornias, waving his hands emphatically. "If all this is true, then what you say about Rayne must also be true. He is a traitor to his family and to his people, and I am an embarrassment to the Silverskin name."

"At least you have the Staff of Lexiam and the Quatrys together again," said Frieden consolingly.

"Yes, all except for Rayne's Quatrys," said Bornias with a sigh. "I suppose we should place the ones we have back in the staff. Frieden, Ainsley, hand your Quatrys to me."

Ainsley reached into his trousers and closed his fingers around the purple gemstone but couldn't bring himself to remove his hand from his pocket. He didn't *want* to give up his Quatrys. He reveled in the surge of power he felt when he used it.

"Don't let him separate us," a familiar voice spoke in his mind. Ainsley found himself inexorably charmed by its tone. *"You are a much better master than he ever was."*

Ainsley relaxed his grip and waited for Frieden to offer his first. Maybe after Bornias had Frieden's Quatrys, he wouldn't need Ainsley's.

Frieden opened the pouch hanging from his neck, held his hand beneath it, and shook it upside down.

But nothing came out.

Frieden frowned, felt around inside his cloak and patted his breeches. "I . . . can't seem to find it," he said, sounding almost embarrassed.

"Maybe I have both of ours," said Bornias, reaching into the breast pocket of his tunic. "That's strange," he muttered. "I can't seem to find mine either."

Ainsley reached into his pocket and shoved the Quatrys deeper inside. "Mine's gone too!" He mustered as much surprise as he thought sounded genuine.

"Bornias," said Frieden slowly, as Bornias removed his cloak and shook it out. "Do you remember when we were carrying Rayne to Parksy's Den?"

"How can I forget?" asked Bornias. "He kept stumbling into us. I thought he was going to rip the shirt right off—" Bornias stopped mid-sentence and swore under his breath. "Rayne must have swiped it out of my pocket," he said.

"Mine too," said Frieden.

"He must have taken mine while we were at the table." Ainsley felt Megan's eyes drilling holes into the side of his head.

"So, we're pretty much back where we started," said Bornias, tugging on his beard again.

"The one thing I don't understand," said Kaelin, "is why Rayne didn't stay with the two of you if he knew someone else had the Staff of Lexiam."

"I don't know," said Bornias with a shake of his head. "He seemed quite driven to go to Pontsford. Maybe he assumed you would go there. Or maybe he had agreed to meet Evren at a pre-arranged time."

Frieden turned to Kaelin. "Can we use your summoning pool to track down Evren and Rayne?"

"Of course," said Kaelin with a nod. "I can get one more view in before I need to use a new summoning tablet."

Frieden and Bornias started across the grass with Kaelin. They seemed to have forgotten about Ainsley's Quatrys, and a feeling of relief flooded him. Now he and the Quatrys could stay together, and nobody could take his strength from him.

Something clamped around his arm and Ainsley jumped.

"Ainsley and I will wait inside," Megan called to the men, her hand still clenching his arm like a vise. "He can watch the cottage, and I need to take a bath anyway. I haven't been clean in three days."

"There's a large tub in my bathroom," called Kaelin. "And the soap is in a bag by the towel stand. All you need is a pinch, mind. That soap powder is ultra-concentrated."

As soon as all three men were out of earshot, Megan turned to Ainsley with eyes full of worry.

"We need to talk."

Fire and Ice

It took Megan several minutes to fill Kaelin's bathtub from the hot spring under the floor, but when she submerged her body in the warm, soothing water, she knew her efforts had been worthwhile.

She had found the bag of soap resting on a stack of purple towels and pulled out a pinch, looking doubtfully at the miniscule amount before sprinkling it into the water. Aside from a few bubbles that erupted at the surface, nothing else happened.

Megan reached back into the bag and took out another dash of soap. Then another. Then a handful. By the time she was satisfied with the amount of foam in the water, she had used over half the bag. She flung the half-empty bag aside and settled back into the water, closing her eyes and letting her arms dangle outside the tub.

She could hear the men moving about outside and pondered over the day's events, as well as all that had happened since they arrived in Arylon. Most of her thoughts disturbed her, the ones about Ainsley in particular.

Ever since he had used the Quatrys to help Frieden stave off the grimalkins, Ainsley seemed . . . different. Any time someone mentioned anything to do with magic, he got an almost *hungry* gleam in his eye. And just now, when Bornias had asked Frieden and Ainsley to hand over their Quatrys, Ainsley had looked pained by the request, as if Bornias had asked him to tear out his soul and give *it* up.

Megan had, of course, confronted him when everyone else had walked to the summoning pool, but Ainsley had laughed and given her a playful shove. She decided not to press the issue for now, but she would definitely be keeping a closer eye on him.

Something tickled the front of her neck, and Megan reached up distractedly to scratch it. She paused, however, when her fingers encountered bubbles before they even reached her throat. When she opened her eyes, she saw that the level of foam in the tub had risen considerably.

She gasped as the film of bubbles continued to increase, until it threatened to spill over the edge of the tub and onto the floor. Megan scooped up an armful of froth and flung it out the open bathroom window, but it was like trying to empty a sinking ship with a teaspoon.

The more she stirred up the water by removing bubbles, the quicker new bubbles would form. It wasn't long before they had covered the entire bathroom.

Someone knocked on the door.

"Megan? Are you okay?" Ainsley called from the other side. "There's some white stuff oozing out from under the door."

"I'm fine. Don't come in here," she warned, grabbing a robe from the bathroom cupboard. "I had a little trouble with the bath water." The soapy mess was up to her ankles now.

"Put something on. I'm coming in!" Ainsley opened the door with his eyes jammed shut. "Are you decent?"

Megan finished tying her robe shut. "Yeah."

Ainsley opened his eyes and his jaw dropped. "Holy shit!" he said with a laugh closing the door behind him. He pointed at the mess around her and the tub that still belched forth a fluffy lather. "You used more than a pinch of soap."

"Is that all you came in here to say?" snapped Megan. Glancing around for something to mop up the mess with, her eyes fell on the stack of purple towels on the shelf. She grabbed them all and dropped them on the floor, but to her horror, they began to dissolve in the soapy water, their purple coloring spreading across the wood.

"No!" she shrieked at the towels. She tried to save the ones she could but to no avail. They disintegrated in her hands, staining her skin a rich purple. "Help me!" she entreated Ainsley who was doubled over with laughter. Before he could do anything, there was a knock on the door.

"Ainsley? What are you doing in there with Megan?" asked Bornias. "You better both be fully dressed."

Megan took a deep breath and threw open the bathroom door to find a crowd gathered on the other side. She quickly tucked her hands under her armpits to hide them.

"I . . . had a little trouble with the soap," she told Kaelin who stood at the front of the crowd.

Kaelin said nothing; instead, he gaped at his bathroom and moved his lips mutely, as if lost for words. He looked to Ainsley who backed away, hands raised.

"Don't look at me. I just got here, too."

"I guess you can't use magic to clean this place, can you?" asked Megan, looking pitifully at the now lavender heaps of foam behind her. Kaelin continued to stare at the disaster, his lips pursed.

"I tried to clean it up," she rushed on, "but when I went to mop the floor with your towels, they dissolved in the bubbles and stained the floor purple."

"Purple?" asked Bornias. He and Frieden chuckled knowingly.

Megan untucked her hands from her sides and held them out. "I didn't know," Megan said to Bornias. "What does he need dye tablets for anyway?"

When Kaelin finally spoke, his words were harsh and halting. "They . . . weren't . . . dye . . . tablets. They . . . were summoning tablets."

"I'm really sorry," said Megan, biting her lip. "I'll clean it up, I promise."

But Kaelin shook his head and breathed deeply before he responded. "The mess isn't what upsets me. Yes, you stained my floor, but you used my last tablets, and I'm not sure Nick has any more in stock."

Megan didn't have an answer for that, except to moan and hold her arms out to Bornias. "What am I going to do about my arms?" she wailed. "I can't stay like this forever."

"Cheer up, Megan," said Ainsley. "Now, you have a new and uniquely bizarre feature to add to your repertoire."

Megan turned to choke Ainsley with her grape-colored hands, but Bornias grabbed her by the back of the robe.

"White-washing tonic will get your skin back to normal," he said calmly. "Get dressed, and you and Ainsley can go to Nick's to buy some. While you're there, you can see about getting a few summoning tablets for Kaelin."

"But I don't have any money and I don't know where to go!" complained Megan, on the verge of whining.

"Two doors down—cottage seven," spoke up Kaelin, "and you can tell Nick to bill me for the items."

Megan dressed, and she and Ainsley walked across the lawns to cottage seven. While they walked, Megan asked Ainsley about what they had seen in the summoning pool.

"Only what we already knew," he said, picking up a stick and running it along the brick wall of a nearby cottage. "Rayne was waiting in Pontsford and Evren was riding to meet him."

"So, when are we leaving?" she asked.

"Soon. Bornias says we'll need to gather some supplies and get some horses ready first, though."

A minute later, they stood on the porch of cottage seven. Megan banged the knocker against the wooden door, and it creaked open, the smell of cloves wafting towards them. A stooped man in white robes and a black half-apron appeared at the doorway.

"Hello," he said softly, his almond-shaped eyes regarding them each curiously. "Welcome to Nick's Knacks. My name is Nick Oh. Please come in."

He gestured them into his cottage, which had no living room proper. Instead, it had been arranged like a shop with shelves lining the walls and three large display racks erected in the middle of the floor.

Three large stoves crowded one of the kitchen walls, and one of the stoves had all of its burners occupied by steaming pots. A long counter took up the opposite wall with a sign hanging above it that read, "Mix Your Own Knacks." Two people, a man and a woman, were sitting at the counter on wobbly wooden stools. The woman was busy grinding something with a pestle, while the man, an older wizard with failing eyesight, was squinting at a book chained to the wall.

"Nick, what's this word?" he asked loudly.

Nick smiled at Megan and Ainsley. "Excuse me. I'll be right back," he said, walking to the kitchen.

Nick peered over the man's shoulder at the contents of a recipe. "It says needlerose. Where are your glasses, Brin?"

The old wizard pulled some leaves from a jar. "I lost 'em. Haven't gone for a new pair because Amikri hasn't been home. He's been visiting family in Raklund."

While the two men talked, Nick stopping often to read the name of an ingredient to Brin, Ainsley and Megan wandered around the storeroom, goggling at all the bizarre merchandise.

One of the racks in the middle of the room contained bags of different soil samples, leaves, and crushed flowers. A sign perched on top of the rack read "Earth."

Another one of the racks, labeled "Water," contained hundreds of flasks and vials. Megan selected one of the flasks labeled "Crystal Falls" and turned to Ainsley, waving the clear container.

"I don't get it. It just looks like water."

Ainsley responded by holding up an empty jar.

Megan squinted at it but couldn't see any contents. "What's that?" she asked, returning her own container to the rack.

"It says 'Mangy Forest Breeze,' but there's nothing in here." He glanced at the signs atop the racks. "Earth, air, water . . . it's like the Quatrys, isn't it? I wonder where he keeps his fire items?"

"I keep them outside," said Nick from behind them. "If you don't see what you need here, let me know. I can always make a special order."

"Did you gather all these things?" Megan gestured at the room.

Nick nodded. "It takes me months at a time to get everything. In fact, I'll be leaving for Icyll tonight to pick up some more ingredients. I'm out of soulfire and a few other popular items."

"Icyll? Isn't that far away?" asked Megan.

"Yes, but it's all right. Our historian, Poloi, agreed to watch my shop if I pick up an Icyllian atlas for him while I'm there, and I have a friend accompanying me. Did you find any knacks that interest you?"

"We actually needed a whitewashing tonic and some summoning tablets," said Megan.

Nick tapped his wispy-haired chin. "Hmm. Whitewashing tonic I have, but summoning tablets are on back order. I'm passing through Pontsford on my trip to put in requests to my sister Natty. She runs a knack store there, and she can track down a load of summoning tablets for me from the Port of Scribnitch. Would you like to order them in advance?"

"They're actually for Kaelin Warnik," said Megan.

"Oh, for Kaelin." Nick fished a slip of parchment and quill from his apron pocket. "Well, I'll make sure to write that down, so Poloi knows to set some aside for him. How many will he be needing?"

"Do you have any specials?" asked Ainsley. He had meant it as a joke, but Nick didn't bat an eye.

"Well, I normally don't do . . . specials, but if you buy five summoning tablets, I'll throw in a free bottle of Instant Ice."

"*One* bottle?" asked Ainsley shrewdly.

Megan stepped in front of him. "We'll take it," she said before Ainsley managed to haggle them out of the cottage. "And we . . . uh wanted to put this on Kaelin's bill."

"He told us to," added Ainsley.

Nick finished scrawling on his parchment and folded it. "Very well. I trust you, and even if I can't, I never forget a face."

He tossed the square of parchment onto an end table by the door and walked to one of the shelves, removing a pint-sized jar. From a box on the same shelf, he removed a pinky-sized tube, which was covered by a cap with a built-in dropper.

"This is the whitewash tonic," said Nick, handing the jar to Megan, "and this is your complementary bottle of Instant Ice." He handed Ainsley the tube. "Would you like to test it? I've got a trial area outside the zone."

"Sure!" Ainsley followed Nick down a hallway and out the back door.

"Ainsley, we don't have time to play around!" Megan hissed in his ear, but Ainsley ignored her as Nick led the way to a patch of scarecrows behind his cottage.

The trial area looked like a mock battlefield. The scarecrows dangled from their posts, some missing arms or legs, while others had been completely destroyed, littering the ground with heaps of straw and tatters of clothing.

"I never clean it up," said Nick. "It's become somewhat of an attraction with visitors."

The woman that had been inside Nick's shop was now testing her brew on a nearby scarecrow. She poured a vial of liquid atop the scarecrow's head, and it slowly began to rise off the ground. It stopped its ascent after a few feet and hovered there. The woman shook her head and walked back towards Nick's cottage.

"Needs more dragonfly essence," she told Nick in passing.

"That was amazing," said Megan, gaping at the floating scarecrow.

"Matilda's one of the best knackmakers," said Nick. "It's extremely difficult to make a good levitation formula, but she seems to have almost mastered it." He turned to Ainsley. "Well, go on. Try out your product."

Ainsley chose a particularly overstuffed scarecrow and was about to open the tube of Instant Ice when Nick put a hand on his shoulder.

"Wait a moment. Let's make this more exciting, shall we?"

Nick tossed a handful of red powder at the pole holding the scarecrow, and it instantly caught fire. The flames began to lick their way upwards, tickling the feet of the scarecrow.

"There you are," Nick said to Ainsley, who looked back and forth from the fiery straw man to his tiny container of Instant Ice. "All you need for a blaze this minimal is two drops. You don't want to waste it, you know. Put a little on the arm there," he said, indicating a not-as-yet burning limb.

Ainsley stepped cautiously toward the flames and squeezed two drops of potion onto the scarecrow's arm.

The result was unbelievable.

As the droplets settled into the hay, the arm developed a frosty texture. Soon, it had frozen solid, encased in a thick layer of ice. The ice began to spread past the arm and down the torso. When it encountered the fire, it was not melted, nor was it deterred. It appeared to be *consuming* the fire.

Hisses and pops filled the air as the two elements battled for control over the scarecrow. In the end, the frozen water was the conqueror. It iced over the flames in a crackling frenzy, until the scarecrow looked like a giant Popsicle. The ice stopped when it reached the blackened pole, where the flames had already died out.

"That was awesome!" cried Ainsley, as the frozen arm, too heavy to remain elevated without support, ripped free from the torso and fell to the ground with a thump.

"Wasn't it?" asked Nick with a grin. "Now, the Instant Ice will stop working once it encounters something of a lower temperature, but it will affect human flesh in a similar way, so be very careful not to spill it on yourself or others."

Someone giggled on the back porch, and Megan and Ainsley turned to see Matilda resting her hand on the chest of a handsome, red-headed man, her head tossed back in laughter.

"Oh, Evren, you are too much!"

Magic Rules

Ainsley shot Megan a *Don't-say-anything* look, and she pursed her lips.

After Matilda had gone back inside, Evren sauntered down the porch steps but paused upon seeing Ainsley and Megan. "Oh! I apologize if I'm interrupting anything, Nick." His voice alone, soothing as an ocean wave lapping at the shore, could have amended the intrusion; the words he chose were a mere formality. "I didn't realize you had company."

He winked at the Ainsley and Megan and flashed a brilliant smile. They returned it politely and stepped back a few feet.

Nick ambled forward and patted Evren on the arm. "It's all right, Evren. We're just having a little fun. What do you need?"

"Nothing that can't wait," said Evren, nodding at Ainsley and Megan. "I'll finish packing for our trip. Would you please send me a message when you're ready?"

"Of course," said Nick, and Evren disappeared into the cottage.

"He's going with you on your trip?" Ainsley asked Nick as soon as Evren was out of sight.

"Yes, he's very eager to learn the trade," said Nick. "Not to mention that it always helps to have another wizard along when you're traveling—in case you run into trouble."

"That makes sense," said Ainsley, dropping the tube into his pocket and pulling at Megan's arm. "Well, thank you for the Instant Ice."

"Yes, and thanks for the whitewashing tonic," said Megan, waving her bottle.

"Just soak your arms in that for five minutes," said Nick, smiling as they walked away. "I'll see you later."

———

"Evren's here!" Ainsley blurted as he and Megan threw open Kaelin's front door. Bornias glanced up in surprise from the bags he was packing, but Frieden cast Ainsley a dubious look.

"That's not possible. We saw Evren riding to Pontsford."

Bornias held up a hand. "Maybe not, Frieden. We saw Evren riding across Devil's Plain, but we only *assumed* he was going to Pontsford."

"We're *sure* it was him," added Megan. "Nick called him Evren, and he had the red hair and everything."

"How did he know where to find us?" Frieden asked Bornias. "We're in the no-magic zone. He shouldn't have been able to track us."

"Forget about that," said Ainsley with a wave of his hand. "We have to get out of here, Bornias! If he finds out that we have the staff—"

"Do you think he'd kill us? We're safe in the no-magic zone, aren't we?" Megan blurted out.

Bornias whistled loudly and three voices quieted at once. "Let's not panic," he began. "Evren may not even be looking for us. Did he mention what he had come for?"

"He's going with Nick on some trip for more knack ingredients," said Ainsley. "Or at least, that's what Nick thinks."

Bornias looked confused at this and scratched his beard. "Why would he be going on this trip with Nick if he's after the staff? Is he buttering up to Nick?"

"What do you mean 'buttering up'?" asked Megan.

"Nick is Master Mage of the Community of Amdor," said Frieden as Bornias paced the floor in thought. "They address any magical concerns in Arylon and report back to Hylark," he added at the looks of confusion on Ainsley and Megan's faces.

"I thought everyone in the community was retired," said Ainsley.

"Retired from active service, yes, but they don't consider what they do work. More like . . . a hobby."

Megan screwed up her face in thought. "So, Evren wants to stay on Nick's good side because . . ."

"The Amdorians are the wisest, most learned wizards on the continent. They have access to tomes of knowledge that most wizards would give their eyeteeth for. If Evren ever wants to get his conniving hands on those volumes, he needs to be accepted into the community."

Bornias stopped pacing. "Which makes his interest in Nick's trip understandable, but why would he be going when he's so busy looking for the Staff of Lexiam? He should be going to Pontsford, not Icyll."

Ainsley turned to Megan. "Nick said they were going through Pontsford on the trip, didn't he?"

Megan nodded. "To turn in an order to Nick's sister."

"Ha!" bellowed Bornias. "So, that's Evren's game. He's going to meet Rayne to get the staff and Quatrys."

"But Rayne doesn't have the staff," Megan pointed out. "What do you think Evren will do to Rayne when he finds out?"

Footsteps thumped on the front porch, and everyone froze. Frieden put a finger to his lips and crept behind the door, his sword ringing softly as he unsheathed it.

The door creaked open, and Kaelin walked into the cottage, taking in the crowd that was poised to ambush him.

"What's going on?" he asked curiously, as four sets of shoulders relaxed. "Am I being regarded as the enemy again?" He jumped as Frieden stepped out from behind the door.

"We thought you might be Evren," said Frieden.

"Evren's here?" asked Kaelin, shutting the door behind him. "I thought he was almost to Pontsford."

"So did we," said Bornias. "Kaelin, we need you to buy us some time so we can reach Pontsford before Nick and Evren."

Kaelin looked baffled but nodded. "I can do that. I'll go over to Nick's and start a conversation about knacks. Nick loves to talk about them, and Evren wouldn't dare go anywhere with two Amdorians in front of him."

"Excellent. Are the horses ready?" asked Bornias, cinching his pack.

Kaelin nodded again. "But two of you will have to share. We only had three available."

Kaelin hugged Bornias and Frieden tightly and shook hands with Ainsley. Instead of a handshake, he presented Megan with her sword.

"I hope I will see you both again soon," he nodded at her and Ainsley, "under better circumstances."

———

The group journeyed for two grueling days and had but a few short hours left until they reached Pontsford. The sun was setting, however, and Bornias announced that they would not attempt to ride into Pontsford until morning, so they settled around a campfire for yet another meal of dried meat and bread.

Ainsley had eaten so much jerky and stale bread, he doubted he would ever eat a sandwich again. He enjoyed sleeping outside under the stars, however, and found himself growing comfortable with his surroundings, almost as if Arylon were a second home.

Megan, on the other hand, was not adjusting as well to the new world. At night, she chose to curl up in a fetal ball and pull her blanket over her head so that she could see the outside world but be invisible to it. She had confided to Ainsley several times on the ride that she wished they were back on Earth.

Ainsley often shared her feelings, but he had been away from home so many times, it didn't really bother him. Instead, he spent each night talking about this strange, new world and learning about its inhabitants.

"Do a lot of retired wizards run shops out of their homes?" Ainsley asked on the last evening.

"Actually, almost every wizard in the Community of Amdor runs a legitimate business apart from their research duties," said Bornias. "They're well enough off that they don't need to, but they enjoy staying active and keeping up with the events."

"Retirement can get pretty boring, I hear," said Frieden.

"How does a wizard retire?" asked Megan, her voice muffled through the blankets.

"Most witches or wizards earn a living working for a private party—usually royalty or guilds," said Frieden.

"Doing what?" asked Ainsley.

"Offering protection, advice, or whatever their customer wants that they can provide. Some wizards choose to specialize their talents in specific areas, while others try and learn absolutely everything about . . . absolutely everything."

"Like Kaelin," said Bornias. "He's incredibly talented, and that's why he was able to retire so early. He could work more if he wished, but he doesn't need the money."

Megan poked her head out and tilted her face toward the fire. After the sun had set, it had grown very chilly on the plain. "Why would a wizard need to work anyway?"

"Yeah, can't they just conjure up some money or food or whatever they need?" asked Ainsley.

Bornias shook his head.

"No wizard can create something from nothing. The closest thing they could do is transfigure a rock into gold or a loaf of bread, but it would be a temporary enchantment, and the wizard would be very broke with a stomach full of rocks."

Ainsley and Megan laughed at this.

"You think it's funny," Frieden spoke up, "but you'd be surprised how many young wizards and witches have tried to trick a merchant with fake coins and ended up on Arylon's Most Wanted List. My cousin, Quinto, is on the run for purchasing a horse with gold he transfigured from rabbit droppings. The merchant says he'll turn Quinto into a skunk if he sees him."

"Kaelin mentioned that whole shape-shifting thing before," said Ainsley as he gnawed on a piece of jerky. "He said he turned into an eagle, but I don't get it. Can anyone do it?"

"Yes," said Bornias, poking at the fire with a stick. "But the rules are difficult. For example, you can't change into someone else without prior contact with them."

"And in most cases, the contact has to be in the form of a willing handshake," added Frieden.

"So, you can imagine that people are wary of strangers who want to shake their hand," continued Bornias.

"You said 'in most cases' it has to be a handshake," said Megan. "What are the exceptions?"

"Creatures that don't have hands," said Frieden with a smile.

"There's also a consequence of shape-shifting," said Bornias. "It causes the shifter to age five years for every change."

Ainsley whistled under his breath. "That definitely wouldn't be worth it."

"What if you want to change someone else?" asked Megan. "Like that merchant who's after Frieden's cousin?"

"That's known as the Curse of Sargon, and it's only reversible by the person who casts it," said Bornias. He added a few sticks to the fire, and they crackled enthusiastically in the flame. "The problem with casting it on another being is that the caster must give part of their soul in the process."

"Who would want to do that?" asked Megan.

"You'd be surprised how much some are willing to sacrifice for revenge," said Frieden.

"What about other curses?" asked Ainsley. "Like cursing someone to death?"

"It's not possible," said Bornias, shaking his head. "You can curse someone to make them *ill*, but magic will *not* kill a creature for another. It will always refuse to cooperate, and then it will turn on you and kill you."

Ainsley mulled this over. "Okay then. What about cursing someone to make them sick? What does that entail?"

Bornias didn't speak for a moment; he merely gazed into the fire. "It worries me that you ask these questions, Ainsley," he said.

Ainsley blushed and settled back against his rucksack. "I'm just curious," he said, nudging a half-blazing log with his foot to push it farther into the flames.

"Don't worry about him, Bornias," added Megan. "He's always been this disturbed. He did his science fair project last year on animals that can regenerate lost body parts."

"I *hope* that this is no more than a phase," said Bornias. He paused for a moment and then continued with his explanation. "Most cursing requires an item of the individuals—something personal, like a letter from a loved one or a cherished gift."

"And . . . what are the consequences there?" asked Ainsley, eyes lowered to the flames.

"The same thing—loss of soul. The unfortunate thing is that you never know how much you'll lose with each curse."

"That's too dangerous for me," said Megan.

"Well, that's the point," said Frieden. "Otherwise, people would be turning into rabbits and breaking into hives left and right."

"Let's talk about something else," said Bornias, stretching out on his blanket. "Something less macabre that doesn't suit Ainsley so well."

"Let's talk about Kaelin," suggested Megan. "I noticed he lives by himself. Does he have any family?"

"We already know the answer to that," Ainsley scoffed. "They died in the swamp."

"Only his nephew," corrected Bornias. "His sister Sasha stops by to stay with him every now and then, but she spends most of her time alone."

Megan's eyebrows raised. "Sasha? We met a mountain lion named Sasha."

"That's her," said Bornias with a nod.

"It's because she tried to trick a merchant, isn't it?" asked Ainsley.

Neither Frieden nor Bornias chose to answer, and there was an awkward silence around the campfire.

"We could talk about curses again," he warned.

"Actually, to explain Sasha's plight, we have to," said Bornias. "She wasn't turned into an animal by another wizard. She inflicted the Curse of Sargon upon herself."

"Why would she do that?" asked Megan with a yawn.

"I don't know for certain. Kaelin's never discussed it with me, and I've never found the right time to ask about it. I can only assume that she felt guilty about what happened to her son."

"Well, how come she doesn't turn back into a human when she enters the no-magic zone?" asked Ainsley in confusion.

"A curse cannot be reversed by any magic other than that of the wizard who exacted it," said Bornias. "Sasha must choose to forget her past and release herself from the curse."

———

"It's stupid, really," Megan told Ainsley as they doused their campfire the next morning. "She made a mistake, and she was young."

"Maybe after we help Bornias, we can help her," he replied. "I bet her son's still alive somewhere."

Megan snorted. "Don't be dumb. You heard how vicious the people were that attacked the Silvan Sentry. Why would they spare a young boy?"

"Ainsley, Megan," Bornias sidled his horse up to them. "Let's go. You can talk on the way to Pontsford."

They departed their campsite, eager to complete the journey. With the exception of a few rolling hills, the grassland was as flat as parchment. Only a few trees and shrubs dotted the landscape, as though tastefully arranged by an artistic giant. The evenness of the plain allowed them to see quite a distance ahead, and Bornias pointed out the city of Pontsford when they were still several miles away.

But there really was no need to point out a city such as this.

Ainsley turned in his saddle to Megan. "Do you see . . . ?" Megan nodded, in awe of the architectural anomaly before them. Ainsley could see the city reflected in her wide eyes and his face split into a yard-long grin.

He could never compare Pontsford to a city on Earth, even if all its inhabitants were human and all its buildings made of steel and concrete, for no other city in the world *he* knew floated among the clouds.

Pontsford Aloft

As they neared Pontsford, they saw it was at least fifty vertical feet from the ground to the front gates. The entire city cast an immense shadow, and people were actually traversing the ground beneath it without the slightest expression of care. No ladders or ropes led up to the city, but several wooden poles had been staked into the ground coinciding with the walls of the city above.

Megan tilted her head back until she almost lost her balance. "How do we get up there?"

In answer, Bornias pointed at a man on horseback underneath what appeared to be the front gates to Pontsford.

Man and horse were standing on a broad metal square that rested on the ground. The man leaned over and placed his hand atop one of the wooden poles.

A moment later, there was a hissing, like the brakes on a bus, and the metal square was propelled up to the city gates by an enormous jet of air. The square, apparently some sort of lift, remained airborne as the man nudged his horse onto a platform outside the city gates. The lift dropped back down a moment later carrying a white-haired dwarf.

"That's so cool!" said Ainsley. "It's like an elevator, isn't it?"

Frieden looked confused at the word 'elevator,' but Bornias smiled. "The airpads are more than an elevator. They, and the warding posts, are guardians of the city. Watch." He directed their attention back to the airpad.

The dwarf had stepped onto the grass, and a hideous-looking troll had rushed forward to take his place. The troll placed a crusty, wart-covered hand on the wooden warding post, but nothing happened.

Furious, the slow-witted creature resorted to punching and biting the wood until a streak of lightning shot from the warding post and zapped him in the shoulder. He howled with pain and anger and stepped back, kicking the warding post, which sent another lightning bolt hurtling at his stomach. The troll shrieked in rage and abandoned the warding post, making a beeline for the next one, where he was promptly stung with another electric current.

"Of course, most creatures are smart enough to give up after just one try," said Bornias, chuckling. "The warding posts determine who gets access to the city and who doesn't. Trolls and orcs, for example, will always be denied entrance, unless a friendly creature accompanies them. At that point, they are still investigated before being allowed within the city walls."

They rode to the warding post by the front gates as the troll finally skulked away in defeat, his singed hair smoking. Bornias gathered everyone onto the airpad and laid his hand atop the warding post, which hissed like a boiling teakettle.

A moment later, they were shooting upwards, drawing closer to the city in the sky. At the top, they passed through security, two giants and a wizard, fairly quickly and were soon within the city walls.

"So, where do we go first?" asked Ainsley.

Dozens of streets branched off from Eastride, the main avenue, each lined with colorful buildings of odd shapes and shades. The people walking the streets were almost as different as the buildings that surrounded them.

Elves gracefully sidestepped the throngs in the crowded streets, dwarves trudged around in surly packs, and fairies flitted over the heads of the crowd. There were also several ethnicities neither Ainsley nor Megan had ever seen before.

Men and women with wings growing from their backs soared above the city, and a group of young children, who were playing a stick-and-ball game on one of the street corners, all had vibrant orange skin and flaming red hair that was literally alight.

"I suppose we should start at Pocky's," said Bornias, dismounting. He handed the reins to one of the stableboys at the city entrance. While Frieden did the same, Bornias explained that the streets of Pontsford just weren't big enough to accommodate thousands of people and their horses.

"Besides that, imagine the smell and the filth on your boots," he added.

"But the city's so big," said Ainsley. "It'll take us forever on foot."

"Not if we know where we're going," said Bornias. "Once you see enough of the buildings, you'll understand."

As they walked, Ainsley began to realize what Bornias meant. All the buildings seemed to follow a particular pattern. They were colored and shaped based upon what they sold. The clothing stores, for example were blue, but the men's stores were shaped like squares, and the women's like ovals.

Outside of one store that was shaped like a colossal birdcage, a merchant was telling a confused young man, "It's the orange triangle." The wrinkles in the man's forehead disappeared, and he thanked the merchant and headed off down the street. The merchant turned and walked back into his shop beneath a sign that read "Unfamiliar Familiars."

Displayed in the window was a crate of cats that had eyeballs dotting their bodies, and a placard in front of them that said "Siall Cats—Homely but Helpful."

"What are familiars?" asked Megan, looking up at the sign.

"A familiar is a mage's companion," said Frieden. "It can help the mage channel power or perform other functions that its species excels at. Those siall cats, for example, would make excellent warders or spies."

"Spies?" Ainsley laughed. "With eyes all over their bodies? I think people might notice."

"Not if they appear to be ordinary cats. Have a look at the one that's asleep." Frieden pointed to a corner of the crate at a dozing siall. Its myriad of eyes were closed, and with the fluffy fur that covered the eyelids now visible, it appeared an innocent housecat.

"The siall can choose to keep all of its eyes closed, except for the two on its face, when it is needed to sneak into an enemy building. Once it has found a secure location, say in the rafters, it can open all its eyes and communicate to its master what every eye sees."

Ainsley's own eyes darted from one magical creature to the next. He turned to Bornias. "Can we go in?"

Bornias looked ready to give a firm no, but Frieden intervened. "I'll take them. You go on to Pocky's. It might actually be for the best if they don't meet him just yet."

Ainsley nodded and smiled at Bornias who sighed. "Very well. Don't be long, though. It should only take me a few minutes at Pocky's."

He disappeared down the street, and Ainsley, still grinning, pulled open the door. A man in mage's robes greeted them.

"The right familiar can maximize your magical ability. May I help you choose the right one for you?"

"We're just looking around, thank you," said Frieden.

"Very well. Our aquatic specimens are to the right, and our flying specimens are in the back." The man bowed and stepped away to help a woman tapping a glass case that held nothing but a miniature stone castle.

Ainsley led the way to a row of tanks against the right wall.

"Why would anyone want an aquatic familiar?" asked Megan.

"Well, many kingdoms are surrounded by moats," said Frieden. "And some mages prefer a life at sea."

"That makes sense, I guess." Megan paused before two of the largest tanks, each about five feet square. The top one held a violet jellyfish that was pushing through the water with its many tentacles.

"A jellyfish?" Ainsley stepped up to the glass. "How can *that* be a familiar?"

"That's not just a jellyfish, my dear boy." The salesmage appeared behind them. "You've no doubt heard of the man-of-war? This is a man-of-peace."

Ainsley and Megan both burst out laughing.

"Of course, we just shorten the name to 'mop' because we seem to get the same reaction from everyone," the salesmage said with a frown. "Nobody takes the poor creature seriously."

"What does a . . . mop do for its wizard?" asked Ainsley, still grinning.

"They have a marvelous ability to communicate with other aquatic creatures, which can come in quite handy for the mage who seeks a favor from the sea."

"That would be very useful," agreed Frieden, "but I imagine they gather a hefty price."

"In Kingdom Coalition currency, they start at ten thousand gold," said the salesmage. He pointed to a pricing chart where the coalition currency was listed, as well as several other forms of payment.

"I want one!" blurted Ainsley, looking to Frieden with pleading eyes. "I want a familiar."

The salesmage broke into a broad smile and clapped his hands together. "A wise decision, my young mage friend."

"Excuse us a moment," Frieden told the salesmage before steering Ainsley to an empty corner of the store.

"Ainsley, *what* would you do with a familiar? If all goes well, you should be home soon."

"Then why is it a problem for me to have one now?" asked Ainsley. "You guys can sell it when I leave. I just want to experience everything while I'm here."

Frieden smoothed his mustache. "I don't know . . ."

Acting as if Frieden had already given his approval, Ainsley sauntered down one of the aisles stocked with various containers of food pellets. "Which familiar do you think I'd do best with?"

"Well," said Frieden, "I think—?"

"None." Megan appeared in front of Ainsley, blocking his path. "I don't think you should get one at all."

"Huh? Well, nobody asked what you think," said Ainsley, "so why don't you mind your own business?"

Frieden placed a hand on Ainsley's shoulder. "What do you mean, Megan?"

"You should *see* how obsessed he is with magic, Frieden." Megan shouldered past Ainsley. "It's all he likes to talk about, and whenever someone else mentions it, he gets this *crazy* look in his eyes." She leaned back with arms crossed. "Getting him a magical pet would be a bad idea."

Ainsley grabbed a jar of pellets and thrust it at Megan. "Have some. I know your kind prefers dog food, but they don't seem to carry that here, so this will have to do."

Frieden snatched the jar from Megan before she could maim Ainsley with it. "Both of you calm down. Ainsley, Megan is *not* a dog or," he scanned the jar label, "a hairy-rumped baboon. Megan, I have never seen Ainsley looking the slightest bit maniacal, but you may have a point about being overexposed to magic."

The salesmage walked toward them with a wide, superficial smile. "Have we made a decision?"

"Yes, I don't think we will be making a purchase today," Frieden told him. "Thank you for your time."

The mage's smile slipped a little. "Not a problem. If you change your mind, you know where we are." He bowed and turned away.

"Why do you feel the need to ruin my life?" Ainsley snapped at Megan as they stepped out into the busy street. "Does it *kill* you to see me happy?"

"Oh, please." Megan rolled her eyes. "I'm doing you a favor. You're so obsessed with magic that you can't see how it's affecting you."

As she waited for a group of amphibious merpeople to walk past, Ainsley grabbed her arm and turned her to face him. "Are you kidding me? I'm getting the chance to do something that," he glanced up and down the street before leaning in close, "that people from *our* world only dream about doing. What's wrong with *that*?"

"There's nothing wrong with magic," said Megan, wrenching her arm free. "But you seem to want more of it than you can handle." She hurried after Frieden, who waited on a street corner where a wooden post designated the crossroads as Weeberwall and Cluckety.

Ainsley stormed after them, imagining various ways to push Megan from the city's edge but still make it look like an accident.

"Why do they have such weird street names in this city?" Megan asked Frieden as Ainsley joined them. "They're really hard to pronounce."

"They're names of the famous Ponzipoo who founded this city, though there's not many of them left anymore."

"So *they* were the ones who came up with this city in the sky? Did they have a lot of enemies or something?" asked Megan.

Her nonchalance at destroying Ainsley's chance to get a familiar infuriated him, and he decided that she deserved to feel as miserable as he.

"Why, Megan?" he asked innocently. "Thinking of ways to avoid *your* enemies? Oh, wait a minute." He snapped his fingers. "I forgot. You don't have any because everyone loves you, right? You have *loads* of friends."

"Oh, please, Ainsley." Megan laughed, but her cheeks were beginning to burn.

"Let's see, how many friends *do* you have?" Ainsley continued. "The numbers must be mind-boggling!" He held up his thumb, then his index finger as he said, "There's Frieden and Bornias and . . . well, there *was* me, but you ruined that, and then you *wish* Garner was your friend, but, let's face it, he was only nice to you because it was dark and he couldn't see what you *really* looked like . . ."

"Shut up!" Megan drew her fist back and swung at Ainsley's face, but Frieden intercepted the blow with the palm of his hand.

In the first angry gesture either Ainsley or Megan had ever seen him display, Frieden pushed on their shoulders, forcing them into a crouched position. He followed suit, staring them both down until they lowered their heads sheepishly.

"The two of you are going to get us banned from the city if you cannot be more careful," he said. "I understand that you are still young, but I also know you are both more mature than this. In our current predicament, we need unity, not division, among us. Understand?"

Ainsley and Megan nodded.

"Sorry, Frieden," said Megan.

"Me, too," said Ainsley.

"Good." Frieden smiled, pulling them to their feet. "Now, while you were arguing, you overlooked something interesting." He pointed to a shop on the opposite street corner.

Shaped like a square wooden shield, it had been inverted so that its normal bottom point became a spire. The doors had bronze handles that looked like miniature pikes, and above them, a hammered metal sign bordered with colorful gemstones announced the shop as "Blades and Baubles."

In the left-hand window, several teenage girls in satin and chiffon ballgowns stood chatting and laughing happily, flashing jeweled bracelets and gesturing at necklaces that encircled their slender décolletage. A woman inside the shop approached the girls and walked around one with a tiara nestled in her blond locks. She touched the blonde on the arm, and the girl froze in place, motionless as a mannequin as the woman unhooked a gold-link bracelet from the girl's wrist and draped it over her own.

"That is pretty cool," agreed Megan. "Life-like dummies."

"Actually, I was talking about *this* window." Frieden pointed at the store's other display to the right of the door.

Four men in various stages of military regalia were engaged in a mock battle, and before them on a wooden display rack rested several swords with copper hilts that had different insignias etched into them. The ends of each handle curved outward and then up to meet the blade, which appeared to be hewn from lipothis and looked sharp enough to slice a diamond in half.

"They're beautiful!" exclaimed Megan. She turned to Frieden with pleading eyes. "Can I have a quick look?"

"I don't see why not," said Frieden, glancing down the street Bornias had taken. "Though we probably shouldn't stay too long."

Megan pulled open one of the doors, and a medley of chamber music, girlish laughter, and clashing metal greeted them. A trio of pocket-sized fairies flitted toward them and settled, one each, upon their shoulders. Ainsley and Frieden headed towards the swords, and Megan felt herself being pulled towards the girls in the gaudy jewelry.

"Um, I'm not really interested in that," Megan told her fairy. "I wanted to see the weapons."

A brief look of surprise registered on her tiny face, but the fairy nodded and guided Megan back across the room where Frieden waited by himself on a wooden bench.

Ainsley had discovered a back room blocked off with a veritable curtain of spider webs that had ensnared a sheepish-looking man. The words, "Shoplifters will be caught" were woven in the threads above his head.

"What's back there?" Ainsley asked the thief who was struggling to free himself.

"Enchanted articles," the thief answered as a length of crystalline chain slithered onto the floor from inside his pantleg. He smiled ruefully at Ainsley. "I'm normally a decent fellow, but when it comes to magic, I just can't help myself." The man fought his bindings and managed to bend forward, but as he gathered the chain, a golden chalice rolled out of his tunic and bounced off his boot.

"It's like looking into a mirror, isn't it?" Megan whispered over Ainsley's shoulder.

"You're crazy," Ainsley growled at her. "*I'm* not stealing magical items." As he said this, however, the Quatrys tucked into his pocket vibrated against his leg. He clamped a hand over it and tried to act natural, avoiding Megan's shrewd gaze.

"Didn't you come in here to look at these swords?" he asked, stepping down to the window display. Doing what he had seen the woman in the other window do, he touched the battling mannequins on their arms. They all stiffened in poses of violence, and Ainsley slipped through to the weapon rack, careful not to touch any of the fighters.

"Here." He grabbed one of the swords and turned, not knowing Megan was directly behind him.

"Watch it!" The point of the sword grazed her midriff, and she jumped backward, knocking into one of the mannequins who sprang to life and promptly beheaded his sparring companion.

"Oh, dear," said the fighter, his expression freezing in concern as Megan tapped one of his boots. She started to reach for the other mannequin's head but decided against it, unsure of what might happen should just the head be rejuvenated.

"Sorry," said Ainsley, helping her to her feet. "I didn't know you'd be right there."

Pride dented and shop patrons staring at her, Megan had a scathing remark for Ainsley waiting on the tip of her tongue. When she looked up at him, however, something outside caught her eye. The anger that had been boiling inside her evaporated, replaced with glee.

Standing in the middle of the crowded street, an unabashed grin on his face, was Garner.

Reflection

"Why do you have that crazed look in your eye?" Ainsley asked Megan, nervously scanning her clothes for possible concealed weapons.

"It's Garner!" She waved, and to her delight, he started towards the shop doors. She whirled to face Ainsley and grabbed him by the shoulders.

"He's coming in!" she squeaked in an unusually girly manner.

Afraid she might head-butt him out of excitement or start squealing like the girls at his school, Ainsley leaned back, her grip too tight for him to break free.

"I thought you didn't care about guys or whether or not they liked you."

"I don't. I didn't. But I do now!" She released Ainsley, and he escaped to a corner of the window display. "With Garner it's different," she said. "I feel special when he smiles at me . . . like *he* thinks I'm special, you know?"

"Yeah, you're 'special,' all right," said Ainsley, making a crazy motion by his head.

Megan ignored him and continued gushing. "I mean, you said guys only go after pretty, popular girls, but here's one that's not wrapped up in all that shallow stuff. He's perfect! What's taking him so long, anyway?"

She stepped towards the window and looked out at the street, Ainsley peering over her shoulder.

He winced, knowing how Megan would react to what she saw.

Garner now stood before the entrance of Blades and Baubles with two beautiful girls his own age draped on each shoulder. They were giggling and flirting with him, and he was drinking it in with a smile.

Megan made an indiscernible sound in her throat and lowered herself onto the divider between the window and shop. "Well, I guess you were right all along, Ainsley," she murmured. "Looks *are* everything." She looked up at him with a wavery smile. "So much for having a good personality, huh?"

Ainsley sat down beside her. "Megan, you're not really—"

"Are we ready to go?" interrupted Frieden. "I expect Bornias is waiting for us to meet him." He stepped down to their level and glanced out the window at Garner. "Well, look at that." He chuckled to himself. "He certainly is a lucky fellow, isn't he?"

"Oh, yeah," snapped Megan as angry tears sizzled against her burning cheeks. "A beautiful girl on each arm. That's what all guys want, isn't it? Instead of a hag like me, they'd rather be with one of those girls." She turned to point out the window, but it had disappeared, replaced by a wall of mirrors. "What—" She looked to Frieden and Ainsley, but they were gone as well, and in their stead were more mirrors.

Megan spun around, beset on all sides by her own reflection . . . and that of an open wooden crate, on the lip of which her salesfairy now perched.

"What's going on?" Megan kneeled beside the crate, wiping at her face. "Where are my friends?"

The fairy smiled but said nothing. Instead, she dove into the crate and emerged clutching a square bottle no bigger than a thimble. Holding the bottle behind her back, she shook her wings and filled it with fairy dust, then doused the contents with a stray tear caught from Megan's cheek.

Disappearing once more into the crate, she returned with a needle that looked like a sword in her wee hands. She pricked her arm with it, allowing two droplets of blue-gray blood to splash into the bottle, and then corked the container. After swirling the bottle's contents together, she triumphantly held up the result of the mixture.

Megan peered closely at the contents and saw what looked like a tiny pearl resting at the bottom.

"It . . . it's beautiful," she said, though she couldn't figure out why the fairy was so pleased. The fairy held up a finger and felt inside her skirts, extracting a spool of golden thread. Tying a length of it around the neck of the bottle, she wrapped the makeshift necklace around Megan's neck.

Planting a kiss on Megan's forehead, the fairy smiled. "Seek the truth and hold it fast," she intoned. "It will not betray you." Then, she and the crate disappeared, leaving Megan alone with her reflections.

Megan wondered if the necklace had possibly changed her appearance, but the myriad of Megans blinking back at her hadn't changed.

"At least I'm not all red and puffy from crying," she said with a sigh.

Lifting her hair away from the necklace, she noticed how the dainty gold thread offset her strong chin and augmented the golden flecks in her eyes. She tried to straighten the bottle so that it hung level but found that it tilted to one side because of the weight of the pearl. She smiled one of her lopsided smiles and then laughed because it matched the bottle so.

"You seem to be in better spirits."

Megan turned in surprise. Frieden and Ainsley had reappeared, as had the rest of the city.

"I am," she said, still smiling.

"Well, Garner's gone, so you don't have to worry about running into him," Ainsley told her. He watched her tuck something under her tunic but couldn't tell what it was.

At the mention of Garner, Megan remembered what had upset her in the first place, but the more she thought about it, the less sense it made to be upset.

"Is he? That's too bad. I wished we could have said hello."

"Huh?" Ainsley's eyebrows furrowed in confusion. "I thought that when you saw him with those girls—"

"Well, it's not like we're dating or anything. He can hang out with whomever he wants. I'm not going to be in this world much longer anyway, so it's good that he has other interests."

"I think that is a very mature way of viewing this," said Frieden with a nod of approval.

Ainsley gaped at Megan. "Okay, something must have happened to you when you disappeared because you didn't act this way five minutes ago. Where were you?"

"Just having a moment of reflection," she said with a lopsided grin. Then she linked her arms through his and Frieden's and led the way outside.

———

Megan felt much more lighthearted as they stepped into the street, though she didn't quite know why. Ainsley noticed it, too, and took advantage of this opportunity to pull Megan back a few paces and offer an apology.

"Frieden and I were talking while we waited for you," he said as they followed Frieden through the crowd. "And I just wanted to say sorry for trying to make things difficult."

Megan didn't question him, but she did almost trip over her own feet in surprise. His sincerity puzzled her — not because it was so unlikely but because she felt so confident that he meant what he had said.

"Thank you," she responded. "And I'm sorry for always getting on your case about . . . caring how you look."

Ainsley had been hoping she would also mention her accusations about magic, but he still accepted her apology because she gave them about as often as he did.

They stopped on a street corner, and Frieden pointed to an oblong, cloud-shaped building painted purple. "*That* is where Pocky lives. I expect Bornias is still inside."

"Well, let's go join him," said Ainsley.

As they neared the building, however, he and Frieden halted in their tracks.

"Oh my." Frieden stared at the façade of Pocky's home. "This could be difficult."

Dozens of door openers, brass and silver, knob and handle, jutted from the purple wall like a bizarre home improvement store display.

"How do we get into the building?" asked Ainsley.

"I'm not sure," said Frieden, scratching his goatee. "I was expecting Bornias to meet us out here. I guess we try all of them, starting with the most logical ones first."

Megan stared at Ainsley and Frieden, mystified by their inability to enter a building. "Try all of what?"

Frieden and Ainsley raised an eyebrow at one another before returning Megan's stare. "The . . . uh . . . door-knobs, Megan," said Ainsley, gesturing at the building. "There's, like, over a hundred."

Megan looked from Ainsley to the building and back again. She spotted a single cast-iron handle at about waist level. "Why don't you guys try this one?" she asked, pressing down the lever. It clicked, and a camouflaged door pulled away from the rest of the wall, revealing a dim hallway.

"Well done, Megan," cheered Frieden. "You got it on your first try."

"How did you know which knob to pick?" added Ainsley as he watched the remaining door handles disappear.

"I don't understand what you're talking about," said Megan with a frown. "There was only one to choose from." She looked up at Frieden. "Wasn't there?"

Frieden stroked his goatee. "I'm not sure, but we should re-explore this subject later. For now, we need to get inside before *none* of us can find a way in."

Megan studied the outer wall while Ainsley followed Frieden, then pulled the necklace from under her tunic, wondering if it had powers to restrict vision. The bottled pearl winked in the sunlight but didn't look as if it held anything sinister.

"Are you coming, Megan? We don't want to lose Frieden." Ainsley looked back at her from the base of a tall staircase, and she tucked the necklace away, hurrying after him.

They needn't have worried about Frieden continuing without them. He was standing at the top of the staircase, looking down a hallway of doors to his right. He turned his head and looked dazedly at the other hallway, which was also lined with doors.

"You see all these doors, right?" Ainsley whispered to Megan.

She nodded, thunderstruck.

"Obviously, only one of these will lead us to Bornias," said Frieden. "The only trouble is, I don't know which one."

Frieden ventured down the left wing and opened the first door on his right. Something from behind it roared, followed by a burst of flame. Frieden slammed the door and turned to Ainsley and Megan.

"That's obviously not the right door," he said. His eyebrows looked a bit singed, and they could smell burning hair.

Frieden turned back around and tried the door to his left, opening it slowly this time. Green smoke curled out from the sides of the door and floated into the hallway. Frieden sputtered and clutched at his throat, pushing the door shut with his arm. He stepped out of the hallway into the fresh air, gasping and gagging.

"Maybe you should let us try," said Megan.

"Or maybe we could try knocking on the doors to see if anyone answers," suggested Ainsley.

"*That* sounds like a better idea," said Frieden, knocking on the door he was about to open.

"Come in!" said a voice from the other side.

Frieden smiled triumphantly, but at the same time, Ainsley had tried knocking on a door beside Frieden's.

"Come in!" said the same voice from behind Ainsley's door.

Frieden sighed and turned around, knocking on the door that had just emitted the green gas.

"Come in!" said the familiar voice.

"Well, so much for that idea," said Frieden, rubbing his temples.

While he and Ainsley discussed their next plan of attack, Megan strolled down the opposite hall. From the other side of a door midway down the right wing, voices drifted to her—Bornias's and another she couldn't recognize.

"This is a tough one," said Bornias.

"Not too tough for a king so wise," said the other voice.

Megan turned and beckoned to Ainsley and Frieden who were in the process of braving another door. Ainsley was holding an iron hat rack like a spear, while Frieden, his back against the wall, flung the door open wide.

A piercing screech filled both halls and Megan stuffed her fingers in her ears. Frieden and Ainsley didn't seem bothered by it, however. Their jaws slackened and their tense expressions relaxed into dreamy ones.

Ainsley dropped the hat rack on the ground with a clang as the most beautiful song carried to him from the cherry red lips of an alluring copper-haired girl. Sprawled across a divan, she beckoned him to her with a hand as delicate and white as porcelain.

Ainsley tried to push past Frieden into the room, but Frieden seemed just as eager to reach the girl.

"Frieden, get out of here. That girl's too young for you." Ainsley elbowed Frieden in the stomach and slid past.

"Not so fast." Frieden grabbed Ainsley by the hood of his cloak and dragged him backwards. "She may look young with her hair cropped so short, but this is definitely a woman. Try and find someone your own age."

"She *is* my age," said Ainsley, yanking his cloak from Frieden's grasp. "And what do you mean? Her hair almost reaches her waist. It's not short."

Frieden, who had been breathing into his hand and sniffing it, paused. "Wait a moment. You *are* seeing a dark-haired woman in a silver scholar's robe, are you not?"

Ainsley looked around but couldn't see the person Frieden was describing. "I only see the red-haired girl in the blue dress."

Without cause, the door closed behind them, and Frieden winced. "Oh dear."

Out in the hallway, the screeching ended abruptly, and Megan pulled her fingers from her ears, crossing the floor to join Ainsley and Frieden. Before she even reached the middle of the hallway, however, Ainsley flung the door open, his face stark white and bloody scratches on his arms.

Behind him, Frieden struggled with a hideous bird-woman that was clawing and snapping her way forward. Ainsley retrieved the hat rack he had discarded and charged back into the room, and after several well-placed jabs, he managed to detach the creature from Frieden. She hissed at him, and he and Frieden backed away, holding the hat rack in front of them as a buffer.

"*What* were you doing?" demanded Megan, as Ainsley and Frieden slipped into the hallway, shoving their weight against the door to seal it.

"We were lured inside by the siren's song," gasped Frieden, wiping the blood from his torn lip.

Megan gaped at him. "You were attracted by all the noise that grotesque . . . thing was making?"

"Siren's song isn't meant to appeal to women," said Frieden. "It's meant to lure men to their death."

"Ah," she said, nodding, "Lucky for me. Listen, while you two were flirting with the she-beast, I found Bornias!"

"Are you sure?" asked Ainsley. He held out his injured arms. "I don't think I can stand another wrong door."

"Yes, I'm sure. I could hear him talking."

"Did he say 'come in'?" Ainsley asked sardonically.

"Trust me," she said as Ainsley and Frieden fell into step beside her. She opened the door before either of them could stop her, and they both flinched.

Nothing happened, however, as Megan stepped inside, where Bornias sat at a table with a white-haired man.

"Hello!" the man said with a gleeful smile. "I was wondering when we might see you."

"Some of us got distracted," said Megan.

"Ran into a bit of trouble, eh?" asked the man cheerfully, getting to his feet. He was tall and lean, his hair cropped short against his head, revealing pointed ears.

"Pocky," Frieden addressed the old man, "Some of your tricks are a little . . . dangerous. You might consider replacing them."

"Never," said Pocky, his mist-gray eyes hinting at laughter. "Everyone needs a little excitement in their lives."

"I'll take the excitement without the unnecessary bruising, thank you," said Frieden.

Pocky patted Frieden's head and let his lower lip protrude in a mock pout. "Awww, poor fellow. Too much adventure for you?" He took hold of Frieden's face with one hand and touched Frieden's lip with the other. A glow emitted from beneath Pocky's fingers, and when he pulled his hand away, Frieden's swollen lip was fully healed.

"Many thanks," said Frieden dryly. "Though I shouldn't have needed that at all."

Pocky just grinned in response. He instructed Ainsley to hold out his scratched arms, and after Ainsley complied, Pocky blew on the scratches. The cuts disappeared as easily as if he had been blowing eraser dust off a piece of paper.

"Thanks," said Ainsley, rubbing his arms in awe.

"Pocky has informed me that he knows where Rayne is," said Bornias.

"Fantastic," said Frieden. "So why are we wasting our time here?"

"He refuses to give me a straight answer," grumbled Bornias. "He's making me guess."

"I provided you with clues," said Pocky in his defense, returning to the table.

"Your clues don't even make any sense."

"What are they?" asked Frieden. "Surely the four of us can figure it out."

"Actually, the *three* of you. She," Pocky pointed at Megan, "may not assist."

"Why?" asked Megan in astonishment.

Pocky waggled a finger at her. "Because you know too much, my dear, and that takes all the fun out of the game."

"But—"

Bornias held up a hand. "Please, Megan, if we keep arguing like this, Rayne will be gone by the time we figure out his location."

"Oh, Rayne won't be going anywhere," said Pocky enigmatically.

"Well, then. What are the clues, Pocky?" asked Frieden.

"They're actually in a song I wrote," Pocky said with a grin. He pulled a tuning fork out of his pocket, but before he could strike it, Bornias thrust a piece of parchment at Frieden.

"Here, I've written it all down."

Pocky frowned in disappointment as Frieden read aloud:

Your good friend Rayne

Heir to the throne
Is in a place that's so well-known.
It's name is three words long, you see
The first one being simple 'The.'
The second is essential to deciphering this rhyme.
    The answer's in the clue, you'll find, so don't waste
too much time.
The third word is the base of life.
It makes the world go 'round.
    Once these clues three you've figured out, the young
prince will be found.

"You never make it easy, do you, Pocky?" said Frieden with a sigh. He scanned the paper, his lips moving as he silently reread the lyrics with Ainsley looking over his shoulder.

"Well, at least we know the first word is 'the,'" offered Ainsley.

"That doesn't do us much good," said Bornias. "Do you realize how may restaurants and shops in Pontsford start with the word 'the'?"

"It says the second word is in the clue," said Frieden, tapping the parchment. "Does that mean the actual word is in the line of the clue, or that the clue reveals the word?"

Megan, who had been obediently mute during this entire process, could hold her silence no longer. She had seen the answer when Pocky had given them the clues. She didn't know how, but it was almost as if the three words had jumped out at her.

"The word is in the line," she said, glancing quickly at Pocky.

"Girl!" said Pocky in exasperation. "One more word out of you and I'll turn your lips into butterflies!"

Megan smiled but Pocky shook a bony finger at her. "It won't be as amusing when they fly off your face, and you have to chase them across the city."

Megan sat at the table, pursed her lips and covered them with her hand. Pocky nodded in satisfaction and turned back to Ainsley, Bornias, and Frieden.

"You three, forget she said anything."

"It says that the second word is essential, but that doesn't tell us anything," said Frieden.

"Let's come back to that one," said Bornias. "The third word is the base of life. What does all life need to survive?"

"Air," said Ainsley.

"Water," said Frieden.

"Both," sighed Bornias. "You can't survive without either element."

"Wait a moment," said Frieden, his eyes lighting up. "Air and water are both elements. *Elements* are the base of life!"

"So, this place is called The 'something' Element?" asked Bornias with a frown. "I don't know any place with a name like that."

"I do," said Frieden, looking excited. "The second word *is* essential."

"Yes, we've established that, Frieden," said Bornias.

"No, I mean 'essential' is the second word! Rayne is at The Essential Element."

"I've never heard of it," said Bornias.

"It's a rather seedy tavern where most of the city lowlifes hang out, but it serves an outstanding ale."

Bornias raised an eyebrow at Frieden. "You've frequented this 'seedy tavern'?"

Frieden waved his hand dismissively. "I haven't been there in some time."

"I see," said Bornias, not sounding as though he believed this. "Well, then. I suppose we'd best get moving. Frieden, even though you haven't been to this tavern in some time, I expect you can still find your way?"

———

"What exactly is Pocky anyway? He looks kind of like an elf," said Megan as the group walked down the street in search of The Essential Element.

"Well, Ponzipoos *are* members of the Elven family," said Frieden. "Second cousins once removed or something like that. They possess all the Elven powers of healing, but none of their immortality. They also happen to be tricksters and nascifriend, if Pocky's menagerie of monsters didn't make that apparent."

"So, what does Pocky do for a living?" asked Ainsley, sidestepping an overturned cart of vegetables. A man with two heads was gathering up the fallen vegetables, though the work was going slow, as the two heads kept arguing with one another. "Is he a vet—er, animal doctor?"

"He sells snowflakes and icicles," said Bornias, taking a right on Richpoor Street. "There's not much of a demand for them this time of year, so he busies himself tending to his creatures."

"You know, if I were in any other world, that sentence would not have made sense," said Ainsley, shaking his head. "But since I'm here, I have to believe it's true."

After a few more streets, Frieden pointed to a barrel-shaped building situated next to an enormous five-story library. "There's The Essential Element," he said.

Bornias glanced at the street sign. "Hmm. I've been in this part of town to use the library," he remarked. "I wonder why I never noticed that place before."

As he spoke, a group of men wearing velvety purple cloaks and highly polished boots emerged from the pub, talking animatedly, waving their polished gold canes in the air for emphasis.

"Ah, this explains it," said Bornias, indicating the affluent men. "I don't enjoy mingling with *their* type."

"Bornias, your entire kingdom is filled with people like this," said Frieden, leading the way into the tavern.

"Exactly, and you see how much time I spend there. I'd rather be on Earth."

With its many fineries, The Essential Element was more a parlor than a bar. A string quartet played chamber music on a round marble slab that hung from the stained-glass ceiling. The many tables occupying the floor space were not wood, but wrought iron structures with glass tops, their curvy, iron legs imprinted with leaf patterns that matched the legs of their cushiony chairs.

The clientele of the saloon dressed the same as the men they had seen outside, with the exception of the ladies, who wore gowns like those at Blades and Baubles, their hair coiffed into sophisticated upsweeps similar to Lady Maudred's.

"Are you sure we're in the right place?" Bornias asked Frieden as the group was met with haughty, disapproving looks. "I thought you said this was a seedy tavern."

"Positive," said Frieden, ignoring the stares and strolling towards the polished ebony bar. "Some of the shadiest people are also the wealthiest."

The floor plan had not been designed to allow four people to walk side by side, and as they approached the bar, they found themselves passing exceptionally close to a table where a woman in silken robes was speaking in loud whispers to a bespectacled man with a handlebar mustache.

"You're sure my husband is the primary benefactor?" the woman was asking.

"I'm certain." The man fingered his mustache delicately. "If your grandfather were to . . . pass away, you and your husband would be swimming in riches."

The woman's eyes shone with greed. "And it's completely untraceable?"

"They'll think he died of natural causes," the man assured her.

Frieden cast Bornias an I-told-you-so look before smiling at a greasy-haired man who looked misplaced in the establishment.

"Good evening, sir," said Frieden.

"Hello yourself, Frieden. What's with the 'sir' bit? Will you take your usual?"

Frieden didn't dare look at Bornias.

"Haven't been here in some time, eh?" asked Bornias.

"On occasion, I go to the library and stop in here for a bite to eat," said Frieden, but he was blushing as he turned back to the bartender. "No thank you, Roderick. We're actually looking for someone."

The bartender looked mildly surprised. "I wouldn't consider you to be engaging in such . . . shady dealin', Master Frieden. You don't look the type."

"On, no, Roderick," Frieden was quick to correct him. "I'm not here on business. A friend of mine asked me to pick him up. I think he may have been waiting for some time."

Roderick seemed to know who Frieden was talking about, and he frowned, pointing to a table in the far corner. "That fellow's been here all day, talking to himself and wailing like a baby. Actually managed to scare away some of my regulars. Is he yours?"

The party of four followed the length of Roderick's pointing finger to a crazy-looking man in tattered clothes that was seated at an isolated table, murmuring to the air and occasionally weeping into his mug of ale.

Bornias seemed to recognize the man at once, and his face drained of color.

"Rayne!"

The Naked Truth

Bornias hastened to the corner table, followed closely by Frieden, Ainsley, and Megan.

Rayne had fallen into such disrepair, it was amazing that Bornias had recognized him at all. He was covered with dirt and blood, except for two clean streaks on his face where tears had been running down his cheeks. His hair was sticking out in odd directions, and some of it was missing on both sides of his head. In both his hands he clutched tufts of hair, which he had obviously wrenched from his scalp.

"Rayne?" Bornias ripped off a piece of Rayne's already shredded cloak and poured some of the ale onto it. He swiped at Rayne's face to clear off the dirt and blood, but Rayne did little more than wince as the alcohol made contact with his wounds.

"He was acting much crazier when he first got here," said Roderick, who had come up behind them. "Bawling about some rocks or something."

"Could you please get us a towel and a warm glass of water, Roderick?" Frieden asked him.

Bornias sat down by his grandson and this seemed to relax Rayne. At any rate, he wasn't gripping his bunches of hair so tightly.

"What happened, Rayne?" Bornias asked softly. "Did something happen to the Quatrys?"

Rayne's calm exterior broke and he shrieked, raising his arms to pull more hair free of his head. Frieden and Bornias wrestled his arms to the table, but that didn't stop the screaming.

"Gone! All gone!" wailed Rayne.

"Where did the Quatrys go, Rayne?" Bornias asked.

Rayne was becoming more agitated, and it was all Frieden and Bornias could do to keep him in his seat.

"My master took them, but he is angry with me. I have failed my master!"

Rayne screeched and started talking to himself again.

Frieden turned to Bornias. "Do you think he's talking about Evren?"

"He couldn't be," said Bornias. "There's no way Evren and Nick could have beat us here. We would have seen them."

"It wasn't Evren," murmured Megan. "A woman took the Quatrys from him."

"What? Megan, you just heard him say his master was a guy," said Ainsley.

Megan shook her head and clutched at her chest. "No, she's not. His master is a woman."

"How do you know?" Ainsley challenged her.

"I can see the woman in his words," she said. It really wasn't a good explanation, but it was all she could come up with to explain the picture that had popped into her mind while Rayne had talked.

Ainsley slapped the table with his palm, and everyone, including Rayne, jumped. "I knew it!" He pointed at Megan. "Something happened when you disappeared, didn't it?"

"What are you talking about, Ainsley?" asked Bornias in confusion.

"Well, Megan's been acting weird since we went to this sword shop. When we were outside Pocky's, she knew which was the right door to get inside, and then when we got inside, she knew which door you and Pocky were waiting behind. She also knew the answer to the riddle before everyone else."

Bornias mulled this over. "I've been wondering why Pocky wouldn't let you help with the clues." He leaned towards Megan. "Look at me, Megan."

She did so, and Bornias studied her face. "She doesn't seem to be under any enchantment," he said. "You must be mistaken, Ainsley."

"Maybe he's not," said Megan. "When I disappeared, I went to a room with all these mirrors, and a fairy gave me this." She pulled the necklace out from under her tunic and held it up so that the trinket dangled in the air, the minute pearl inside rolling in circles around the base of the bottle.

Everyone at the table, except for Rayne, leaned in for a closer look.

"You say a fairy gave this to you, Megan?" asked Bornias. "Did she say anything to you?"

"Yes," she said, almost choking as Ainsley pulled the necklace towards him to inspect the tiny bottle. "She said 'Seek the truth and hold it fast. It will not betray you.'"

"Fascinating," said Bornias, staring at the pearl.

"So, is this necklace special or something, Bornias?" she asked, wrenching the necklace free of Ainsley's grasp.

"It is indeed," he said. "As special as the wearer, you might say," he said with a smile.

"What do you mean?" she asked, looking down at the bottled pearl.

"This is a fairy pearl," Bornias explained. "From what you and Ainsley have told me, it appears to be a Pearl of

Truth. They are very rare and only granted to those who justly deserve them. You should feel very privileged that this gift has been bestowed upon you. Pearls of Truth are rarer even than Pearls of Wisdom."

Megan looked at the tiny gem with a newfound respect.

"If they're so rare, why did the fairies give her one?" asked Ainsley, a bit jealous that Megan should be given her own magic when she didn't even care about it.

"There must have been an area in Megan's life where she was being gravely misled. The fairy gave her this pearl to help her see the truth."

"But that's just a little pearl," said Ainsley. "It couldn't have done much of anything."

"As I've told you before, sometimes it takes just a little to make all the difference in the world," said Bornias. He looked up at Megan. "Does any of this make sense?"

Megan fingered the necklace and nodded, too overwhelmed by emotion to speak.

"Let me try it on," begged Ainsley.

"It won't work for you," Bornias told him. "It only works for whom it was created."

Roderick returned to their table, a rough-looking towel in one hand and a pitcher of water in the other.

"Do you suppose you could get him out of here soon?" He gestured to Rayne. "I can't afford to lose too much more business."

"We'll leave as soon as we get him cleaned up," promised Bornias, taking the pitcher and towel from him.

He did a quick but thorough job of washing Rayne's face and used the remaining water in the pitcher to smooth down what hair Rayne had left.

"Let's get going," said Frieden, pulling Rayne to his feet as he rose from his own seat. Rayne grabbed for the table, upending it and sending the pitcher of water and mug of warm beer spilling onto the ground. The glass table-top shattered as it hit the floor.

"I must wait here for my master!" Rayne yelped, swinging feebly at Frieden. "He must return to punish me!"

Bornias balled up the wet towel and stuffed it into Rayne's mouth. He twisted his grandson's hands behind his back.

"Frieden, give me your belt," he commanded, struggling to keep Rayne under control.

Frieden removed his belt and helped Bornias tie Rayne's wrists together. Rayne choked and sputtered on the towel, finally managing to spit it out.

"My master must punish me, and then he shall punish you," Rayne growled.

The other customers in the tavern were all watching Rayne now, and Roderick was looking around nervously.

"Oy, Quinn, free round of ales for everyone!" he called to another man who had taken his place behind the bar.

The customers cheered and returned to their own business.

"It may cost a lot of money, but if it'll keep them from leaving, so be it," Roderick told Bornias glumly. Bornias reached into his cloak pocket and pulled out a fat roll of bills. "This should cover any inconveniences." He clapped it into Roderick's hand before turning to help Frieden with the struggling Rayne.

"Megan, Ainsley, let's go," said Bornias.

Megan climbed out of her chair and almost slipped on the wet floor, but Ainsley caught her and pulled her to her feet.

"Thanks," she said. "This floor's really slippery."

Bornias glanced down at Rayne's spilt beer and did a double take. "What's this?" he asked, letting go of Rayne.

"Ainsley, help me, won't you?" gasped Frieden as he struggled to keep Rayne under control.

Bornias bent over and ran his fingers through the pool of beer. They became coated with an oil-like substance and he touched one of his fingers to his tongue.

"Oh, thank heavens!" he said with a sigh.

Megan, Ainsley, and Frieden exchanged curious looks.

"What did you find?" asked Frieden.

"It's ninayet," Bornias told him, straightening with a smile on his face. "Rayne's been drinking ninayet."

"That certainly *is* a relief," said Frieden in agreement. "And it explains quite a bit."

"Hello," said Ainsley impatiently, "Megan and I are still in the dark here. What's ninayet?"

"It's a mind-controlling drug," said Frieden. "It allows the person who serves the drink to control the drinker's actions."

"Which means Rayne hasn't been acting under his own free will," said Bornias happily. "So he's not a traitor."

"The problem remains though," said Frieden, as Rayne fidgeted in his binds, "that one of the main ingredients, soulfire, is impossible to find. So where did our mastermind get his?"

"It's not impossible to find," said Bornias, wiping his fingers on his robes. "It's just difficult. I only know one person who sells it."

"Nick," said Ainsley. Frieden and Bornias looked at him in surprise.

"Yes, that's right. How did you know?"

"He told us," said Megan. "He said one of the reasons he was going out was to get more soulfire."

"Nick keeps a ledger of all the people he sells soulfire to," said Bornias, "in case something just like this should ever happen. We can ride back to Amdor, get an antidote for Rayne, and check Nick's ledger."

———

"Megan, this woman you saw. What did she look like?" asked Bornias as they walked behind Frieden and Ainsley. They were headed back toward Eastride Avenue, still tow-ing along a begrudging Rayne. The crowd in the street, though much sparser since it had gotten dark, was giving the group a wide berth.

Rayne had managed to remove the towel from his mouth again and was shrieking and snapping at everyone they passed. It had been very difficult to convince the town guards to let them keep Rayne in their custody. Bornias had insisted they would "dispose" of Rayne once they were outside the city limits, and only then were they allowed to continue on their path.

"Well," said Megan, reflecting on the picture she had seen, "she had dark hair and eyes, and an evil smile."

"Any distinguishing features?" asked Bornias.

Megan shook her head. "None that I can recall."

"Maybe Rayne can lead us to her," suggested Frieden.

"I doubt that," said Bornias. "I'm sure if this woman stole the Quatrys, she has already fled the city."

The closer the party got to the outskirts of town, the more Rayne wriggled and dragged his feet, until Frieden and Ainsley had to carry him while Bornias and Megan retrieved the horses from the stable.

The guard at the entrance eyed the group as they stepped onto the platform. "Is this all of you?" he asked, watching Frieden and Ainsley lift Rayne onto the platform with great effort.

"Yes," said Bornias. "Just the five of us."

"Are you sure you folks are going to be okay with that one?" The guard pointed at Rayne. "He seems a bit off his knack."

"We'll be fine," said Bornias, "but I appreciate your concern."

"No problem," said the guard, "It's my job. Right, down you go then."

He mashed a button on a post by his elbow and a hiss sounded from the ground as the flow of air against the air-pad subsided.

"Thank you for visiting Pontsford," the guard said by way of a farewell, and he slowly disappeared from sight as they were lowered back to the ground.

"Maybe we should have left Rayne up in the town," said Ainsley as he tried to help Frieden get Rayne on a horse. Rayne looked terrified and sweat had begun to trickle down his face.

"My Master has returned!" he roared into the night. Then his eyes rolled into the back of his head and he fainted. Frieden and Ainsley dropped him on the ground.

"Well, at least he'll be easier to handle now," said Ainsley.

"Yes, but why do I feel as though we've walked into a trap?" Frieden reached beneath his cloak and withdrew his sword, scanning the valley apprehensively.

It was dark enough outside the city for someone to be lurking in the thick, tall grass, and the wind's direction carried their scent to anyone who might be tracking them.

Bornias reached into *his* cloak and clutched the Staff of Lexiam tightly.

"Are you really going to use that?" whispered Megan, her fingers closing around the hilt of her own sword.

"I never like to use it," he said, "but if someone is coming after us, I won't hesitate."

They all strained their ears for odd rustles in the brush and looked for any strange shadow cast by the moonlight.

Then, the wind that had been whispering through the tall grass silenced itself, and the creatures that lived between its blades ceased their chirping and singing. The only noise came from the city above, and that too seemed downplayed in the darkness.

Megan could hear nothing but her heart beating in her ears, and Ainsley knelt beside her, clenching and un-clenching his hand around the Quatrys in his pocket.

"Bornias, there *is* something out there," whispered Frieden. "We must return to town."

Suddenly, a dark silhouette leapt out of the grass and rammed into Bornias. He grunted and tumbled from his horse, which reared in fright and galloped away.

A blinding brilliance, like sunlight reflected off snow, painted the evening sky, and Ainsley and Megan were forced to turn away, their faces pressed into their arms. Something tackled them both to the ground, and they heard Frieden say, "Stay down!"

Then the light faded, eclipsed by the night, and the sounds of the plain's nocturnal inhabitants returned. Ainsley and Megan raised their heads slowly, and as their eyes adjusted to the darkness, they watched Frieden dart about in the grass, calling out to Bornias.

A few minutes later, he returned to them with sagging shoulders made more prominent by his heavy breathing.

"Bornias is gone."

Return to Amdor

"Back so soon?" asked the guard as the party, now minus Bornias, stepped onto the platform outside Pontsford once more. Ainsley and Frieden supported Rayne between them while Megan held the reins of the horses.

"We need to see about making a trade for these animals," said Frieden. "We've had a little trouble."

The guard grunted in satisfaction. "I told you that fellow was no good, didn't I?" He pointed to a barn near the barracks. "The stable manager is the man you need to talk to about animal trades. If you want to leave that fellow with me," he gestured to Rayne, "I'll watch him until you get back."

"Thank you," said Frieden. "That may be best."

They led the horses to the shack and Frieden instructed Ainsley and Megan to wait outside while he spoke with the stable manager. He returned a moment later with a pudgy, beetle-browed man who looked the horses over and made Frieden an offer.

"I'd give you more, but these horses look like they've been through a lot."

"You have been more than reasonable," said Frieden. "I wish to apply that money to a few zippers if you have any."

The stable manager raised his eyebrows. "Of course we've got zippers, but they won't come cheap."

"What's your price?" Frieden asked without hesitation. "We'll need two."

The stable manager looked as though he had just discovered a goldmine. He quoted a price, and his face lit up when Frieden removed two gold bars from one of the saddlebags.

The stable manager bit each gold bar to ensure its authenticity before calling out to the stable boy. "Garner! Get out here!"

Megan made a gurgling sound in her throat and turned ten shades of red.

"Oh, boy," murmured Ainsley as Garner emerged from the stables holding a pitchfork. When he saw Megan and Ainsley, he grinned broadly at them.

"Look who it is," he said.

"Garner, take these horses inside and transfer the saddles to two of our zippers," said the stable manager.

Garner nodded and threw the pitchfork into a bale of hay as if it were a spear. It sunk in past the tines, the handle vibrating like a tuning fork.

"I saw you at Blades and Baubles earlier today," he said, reaching to take the reins from Megan. "I'm sorry we didn't get a chance to talk."

"No worries," said Megan, looking him in the eye. "We only came to town for the day. Besides, you looked as if you already had enough company."

"I suppose." Garner leaned close to Megan, and she felt a thrill in her stomach as he whispered in her ear. "If you consider the stable manager's arrogant daughters company." He led the horses away, and Megan stared after him, unsure what to think of his response.

It took no more than a few minutes for Garner to return, pulling the reins of two zippers, both of which sported smooth lustrous coats and shining golden hooves.

"This is Sparks." He handed the reins of a powdery white mare with a gray mane to Frieden. "And this is my favorite, Girt." He patted a whinnying dapple-gray zipper and held his hand out to Megan.

"Do you need help getting up?"

Megan shook her head. "I can manage, thanks."

Ainsley noticed that Garner looked disappointed as he saw Megan step into the stirrup and hoist herself onto her mount.

"Well, it was nice seeing you again," she told him.

"Yeah, thanks, Garner," said Ainsley. "We'll see you around."

Garner nodded and looked as if he wanted to say more, but the stable manager called him away. Megan believed it was the last time she would see Garner, the stableboy.

———

"Let's get Rayne onto the front of the white zipper," said Frieden, dragging the comatose man off the platform and onto the grass. "The sooner we get out of here, the better."

"But what about Bornias?" asked Ainsley.

Frieden shook his head. "There is nothing we can do for him here. We need to probe Rayne's memory to see how much he can tell us, and we'll have to get the supplies at Nick's."

"Can't we just buy them here?" asked Megan.

Frieden shook his head as Ainsley helped him toss Rayne over Sparks's back like a sack of flour. "They don't sell knacks in Pontsford after nightfall. Besides, we need to get back to Kaelin's so he can watch over Rayne while I search for Bornias."

Frieden climbed in front of Rayne on Sparks, and Ainsley climbed in front of Megan on Girt.

"Hang on tight," Frieden directed as the zippers pawed at the grass, tossing their manes in anticipation.

"Our mounts look eager, and from what I've seen, they run quite fast."

Frieden nudged Sparks, and the horse lunged directly into a gallop, as if he had no understanding of anything slower. Frieden almost toppled backwards out of the saddle as Sparks shot across the grass, which waved wildly in his wake.

Megan squeezed Ainsley around the middle, digging in her nails.

"Ouch, Megan! Grab onto the saddle pommel, not my stomach!" She obliged and gripped the pommel until her knuckles turned white.

Ainsley bent low and gave Girt a slight nudge in the sides. With an excited whinny, Girt's hooves left the ground as one as she leapt forward like a pouncing jaguar. When her hooves hit the grass again, Ainsley and Megan felt themselves propelled forward at a speed that was alarming at first but became enjoyable when they saw how easily Girt cleared any obstacle in her path.

There was no experience comparable to riding a zipper. Girt's stride was so smooth, it felt as though they were gliding low over the plains. They moved so fast that everything around them was a blur and the cool night wind stung their cheeks.

They caught up quickly with Frieden, and rode through the night and into the morning, feeling the warmth of the rising sun against their backs. It was a hard ride, but one that had passed without incident, and soon they were cresting the hill that overlooked Amdor.

As they passed under the entrance, their bodies tingled from the no-magic borders, which even the zippers seemed to feel as they shivered and tossed their heads. Kaelin, who had been reading a book on his porch, waved at them as they approached, but his accompanying smile faded at their harried state.

"What's happened to Rayne?" he asked, setting his book down and rising from his seat. "And where's Bornias?"

Frieden reined in his zipper, which snorted and neighed, as if reluctant to halt its grueling pace. "Rayne was attacked by an unknown woman, who he claims is his master, and Bornias has been abducted, possibly by the same woman." He dismounted and pulled Rayne off Sparks's back.

Kaelin hurried down the steps to assist him. "Unknown woman? Who? Is she working for Evren?"

"We're not sure of any of that. We're going to try some memory extraction on Rayne."

Kaelin released his hold on the crown prince, and Frieden struggled to hold the limp form. "Are you serious? Frieden, I don't think that's wise. Memory extraction can be very dangerous."

"What other choice have we?" grunted Frieden, hefting Rayne over his shoulder. "We need the information now. We cannot wait for Rayne to come around on his own."

He walked away but didn't head in the direction of Kaelin's cottage.

"Where are you going?" Kaelin called after him.

"I think we should attempt this at Nick's. Rayne will probably start screaming when the extraction begins. I may actually need your assistance."

"But what about us?" asked Ainsley as he and Megan dismounted.

"Sasha went out hunting, but she should be back soon," said Kaelin. "She can look after you while you rest." He turned to Frieden. "I'll stable the horses and join you at Nick's."

"Come on, Megan," Ainsley said with a yawn. "Let's get some sleep."

Too tired to protest anything, she nodded and trudged after him up the cottage steps.

Meeting Evil

"Don't hurt me!"

Megan gasped and sat up straight, sleep-blurred eyes darting around Kaelin's living room in confusion. A harsh scream had invaded her dreams, ripping her from slumber. She strained her ears, and a chill coursed up her spine as the scream pierced the air again.

"Ainsley!" She jostled his shoulder, staring at the front door uneasily.

"Ugh, Megan, you have got to stop waking me like that," he grumbled, rolling away and pulling a pillow over his head.

Megan grabbed the cushion from him and hugged it to her. "Ainsley, there's something outside. I think it just attacked Sasha."

"What?" He turned to look into Megan's terrified, bloodshot eyes.

"There is something outside," she repeated, on the verge of hysterics. "I thought I heard Sasha's voice, and then there was this terrible wailing sound. What should we do?"

Ainsley rolled to his feet and looked out the living room window. "I can't see anything out there," he said, squinting into the darkness. "I don't think there's anything to worry about, though."

As if to prove him wrong, a loud squealing erupted from outside, followed by a series of frantic screeches.

"See?" Megan hurried to the door and bolted it. "Help me barricade the entrance," she said, grabbing a chair from the kitchen.

Ainsley barred her path. "No, Megan. We can't just hide in here." He pulled the poker from the fireplace and slid back the bolt. "Run and get Frieden, and I'll see if anyone's in trouble. If it's Sasha, she could be caught in a trap or something."

Megan regarded Ainsley dubiously, then dropped her chair. "All right, but don't leave the boundaries of Amdor," she warned him.

"Don't worry. There's plenty of neighbors around . . . I'll be fine." Ainsley opened the door once more and peered around the front porch. "Go," he whispered to her, brandishing the poker in front of him like a sword. Megan hurried down the porch steps and darted across the lawns to Nick's where she began hammering on the door.

"Sasha?" Ainsley called out into the night. "Are you out there?"

From somewhere ahead, a moan answered, and he crept across Kaelin's property, his eyes sweeping the ground for any clues. Something shone wetly on the grass in front of him, and when he bent to see what it was, his breath caught in his throat—blood.

Gripping his poker a little tighter, he followed the foreboding trail where it pooled around a limp form.

"Sasha!" Ainsley crouched in the grass beside her. She lay on her side, her breathing labored and her fur matted with the same blood that dotted the grass. Sasha raised her head at the sound of Ainsley's voice, and her eyes widened in fear.

"Ainsley!" she wheezed. "Get back in the house! He's here!"

"Who—who's here?" asked Ainsley in confusion. From what Megan had said, he thought they were after a woman.

"The man who did this to me." She rolled onto her stomach with a strained effort. "The man who's after the Staff of Lexiam. Evren!"

Sasha's words fell like a lead weight on Ainsley's stomach. "Where is he now?"

"He headed towards Nicodemus's shop."

"What?" Ainsley looked at her in horror. "Megan's over there!"

"No, I'm here," said Megan from behind him.

He flinched in surprise and turned to face her, his grim expression haunting in the pale moonlight.

"Kaelin and Frieden aren't answering the door," she added. "What happened to Sasha?"

The injured woman-turned-mountain-lion yowled in pain again. Megan stroked her head soothingly, but Sasha jerked out of reach.

"Please, leave me! He'll come after you, too!" Sasha beseeched them.

"Who's 'he'?" Megan looked up at Ainsley. "I thought we were looking for a woman."

Ainsley dropped his fire poker and shook his head. "I don't know, but we can't leave Sasha here. She'll be safer inside Kaelin's cottage. Come on, help me."

Megan crouched with Ainsley and they both wrapped their arms around each of Sasha's forelegs.

"Pull!" instructed Ainsley. He tugged on Sasha's left leg as Megan pulled on her right, but Sasha slid forward no more than a few inches.

"I need to get a better hold," said Megan, crawling forward to regrip Sasha above her elbow joint.

Megan felt the strange tingling in her body that meant she had just crossed outside Amdor's boundaries, but thought nothing of it . . . until the downy fur she had been clutching suddenly turned to human flesh. She looked up at Sasha curiously and choked back a gasp.

Gone was the furry feline head that had been there moments before. In its place was the face of a woman, whose dark hair was flecked with gray, the skin wrinkled with age. She looked familiar, but Megan couldn't quite remember where she had seen Sasha in human form before.

Then Sasha met Megan's gaze, her green eyes flashing, and the corners of her mouth curled into an evil smile. Megan released Sasha's arms.

"Ainsley, let go of her and back away," she said, tugging at his tunic.

"Why?" Ainsley shot Megan a confused look that contorted into one of immense pain. Sasha buried her claws in his arm and dragged him toward her, her talons ripping open his flesh.

Frozen to the spot with terror, Megan held her face in trembling hands as Ainsley screamed in agony.

"What are you doing?" he cried as the blood streamed down his arms.

"I told you that you should have run away, didn't I?" taunted Sasha. She bared her teeth at him, which were slowly diminishing to that of a human's, still tinged a dirty yellow. Her paws transformed into human hands, the claws becoming curled black fingernails tipped with the scarlet of Ainsley's blood.

Ainsley paled. "Who are you?"

"She's the one that's been using Rayne!" exclaimed Megan.

As if this truth had shattered the fear that held her, Megan raised her sword and thrust it at Sasha's stomach, but inches before it made contact, the blade melted into a silvery puddle. Megan gaped at her useless weapon, which gave Sasha the opportunity to wrap her fingers around Megan's wrist, constricting until Megan crumbled to her knees.

"I'm curious as to how you know that," growled Sasha, her gentle nature transformed along with her body.

"It's . . . just the way Rayne described you," lied Megan, trying to tuck her necklace beneath her tunic with her free hand.

Sasha released her grip on Ainsley and grabbed the bottle holding the Pearl of Truth. "So, it doesn't have anything to do with *this*?"

She yanked, snapping the delicate chain, and dropped Megan's necklace into a drawstring pouch around her neck.

"Give that back!" cried Megan. She pinched Sasha hard on the arm, and Sasha screamed, pulling Megan's hair. While the two tussled, Ainsley backed away, reaching into his pocket.

"Stop right there, boy," growled Sasha, clamping a hand around Megan's throat. "Hand me the Quatrys or she dies."

"Don't, Ainsley," Megan croaked. She tried to shake her head, but Sasha held her too firmly.

Ainsley hesitated, torn between saving Megan and keeping the Quatrys—not from Sasha but for himself. He knew what had to be done, however, and, feeling as if he was surrendering a member of his own family, he held out the Quatrys of Air. Megan groaned and sagged against Sasha who flashed her wicked grin.

"Excellent. Drop it in the pouch," she said, shaking the bag at him. "Then cinch it."

Ainsley did as he was told with fumbling fingers.

"You're a fool," Sasha said with a smirk, taking her hand from Megan's throat and gripping Ainsley's arm once more. "I never would have known you had the Quatrys if you hadn't brought it out to use it."

"What do you even want with it?" gasped Megan, her throat burning in the chill night air.

"Well, the Staff of Lexiam doesn't work as well without the Quatrys, does it?" asked Sasha.

"I don't understand how you're even involved," said Ainsley. He held his cloak to his arms to staunch the bloodflow. "Evren was the one who asked Rayne to steal the staff for him. Are you working for him or something?"

"Evren?" Sasha spat on the ground. "I would *never* work for such filth! His kind defiles the name of a wizard."

Ainsley furrowed his eyebrows. "But the busboy in Guevan saw Rayne talking to—"

"You!" Megan pointed at Sasha, eyes wide. "You're . . . you're a shape-shifter, and you pretended to be Evren!"

Sasha's lip curled into a sneer. "You're very clever . . . even without your little necklace."

"But why Evren?" asked Ainsley, glancing down the path towards Nick's cottage. He was stalling for time, wondering how much longer Frieden and Kaelin might be. "Why not a complete nobody that couldn't be traced?"

"You've obviously never met Evren," said Sasha. "It wouldn't hurt him to be brought down a notch or two, and this way, I was able to accomplish two tasks at once. I've cleared myself of any involvement with the Staff of Lexiam, and when word spreads of 'his' nefarious deed, he'll never become Master Mage or be able to secure a position in the community."

"None of this explains why you need the staff, though," said Megan. She had caught Ainsley looking towards Nick's and understood what he was doing.

"My needs are my own," said Sasha, "and unfortunately for you, you won't be around long enough to figure them out."

All strategizing left Megan's brain. "You're going to kill us?" she squeaked.

Sasha rested her head on Megan's in mock tenderness. "There, there. You *will* die. But for now I think I'll dangle your lives over King Bornias's head. It seems his majesty isn't too willing to part with that staff of his," Sasha smiled sweetly down at them, but her tone suggested she was none too happy with this fact. "Therefore, I've decided to give him a little incentive . . . actually *two* little incentives," she corrected herself, squeezing their arms even more tightly. "He's quite fond of both of you, is he not?"

"Not really," said Ainsley, trying to wrench his bleeding arm free of Sasha's vise-like grip. "He can't stand us."

"I'm sure," said Sasha with a knowing smile reminiscent of her feline form. "Well, we've wasted enough time making idle chatter," she said. "Shall we go now?"

For a moment, she appeared to be transforming back into a cat, but then a pair of enormous feathery wings sprouted from her back. Her hands changed, too, into enormous taloned bird's claws, but it appeared that the transformation was taking its toll upon Sasha. Her breathing was labored and sweat trickled down her face, which appeared more wrinkled and aged than it had moments before.

"This will have to do," she wheezed, looking down at her semi-transformed body and flapping her broad wings. "Don't struggle or I may drop you," she warned as their feet lifted from the ground.

They climbed into the night sky, higher and higher with each beat of Sasha's great wings, Ainsley and Megan dangling from Sasha's talons in an awkward fashion. The moon shone down upon the trio, and they cast a grotesque, deformed shadow on the ground, like some immense flying monster.

"Where are you taking us?" Megan shouted over the rustling of Sasha's wings.

"The Swamp of Sheiran."

The Unity

Of all the modes of travel they had used, flying was by far the swiftest. They soared over sleepy villages and acres of planting fields, rivers that sparkled in the moonlight and abundant groves of trees.

As they drifted over a particularly large forest, Megan noticed their altitude was beginning to decrease, but it didn't really bother her until they fell low enough that her toes were skimming the treetops. She glanced up at Sasha who wore a strained expression, as if it were taking every ounce of her strength to keep them airborne.

Ainsley had seen it, too. "Are you okay?" he asked as he lifted his legs so his feet were no longer pruning the trees.

"I'm fine," snapped Sasha. "I'm just a little . . . tired."

She flapped her wings with renewed strength, and the trio rose higher into the sky.

Ainsley nudged Megan's arm. "I think she's a little too old to be doing this. The way you described her, I thought she was a lot younger," he said, nodding up at Sasha.

"Well, she *did* look young when Rayne talked about her," Megan whispered back. "I think she's making herself age faster when she transforms. Remember what Bornias told us about that?"

"Oh, yeah. I wonder how many times she—hey! We're getting close to the swamp." Ainsley pointed at a break in the trees.

For whatever reason, these words seemed to be the end of Sasha. With a stomach-turning jerk, the trio dropped the height they had just gained.

"Woah!" cried Megan, as she felt Sasha's grip loosen on her arms. She clamped her free hand around Sasha's wrist and looked up at their captor. Sasha's eyelids fluttered as if she were dropping off to sleep. Her wings were still outstretched, but she was no longer moving them.

"Sasha?" Megan waved at the bird-woman and was almost jerked free of Sasha's grip by a tree branch that snagged her breeches.

"Sasha!" Megan pinched her under the arm, but Sasha didn't respond, and they continued to lose altitude.

"At least we're past all the trees," said Ainsley as he, too, clung to Sasha, wincing as one of his legs contacted with a thick branch.

"I'm not worried about the trees," said Megan. "It's smashing into the ground that bothers me. I wish we had some extra wind to slow our descent."

"Extra wind?" An idea came to Ainsley, and he slapped the heel of his hand to his forehead. "If I can get the Quatrys . . ." He reached towards Sasha's neck with his right hand, his fingertips brushing the leather bag.

"Ainsley, hurry!" entreated Megan.

Megan glanced down at the marsh, now less than ten feet below. "It's too late!" she squeaked. "We're gonna hit the swamp!"

They plowed into the marsh water, sending up a miniature tidal wave that unsettled a swarm of angry, buzzing mosquitoes from the swamp's fetid surface.

Megan coughed and sputtered as she staggered upright, lily pads plastered to her sodden clothes. She helped Ainsley to his feet and swept her dripping hair out of her face, staring at Sasha's limp body, which floated facedown in the sludgy water.

"Is she dead?" she asked quietly, nudging Sasha with the toe of her boot.

Ainsley rolled Sasha onto her back, a difficult task due to her broad wings. Sasha coughed up a mouthful of water, but her eyes remained closed.

"I think she'll make it, but I'm not sure she deserves to. Let's prop her up over there." He pointed to an island in the marsh where a lone, stump of a tree managed to thrive.

They dragged Sasha ashore, the porridge-like consistency of the swamp floor doing its best to suck the boots off their feet. When they finally arrived at their destination, sweat was trickling down their backs, and a smell more pungent than the stagnant swamp water assaulted their nostrils.

"This must be a mossfur tree," said Megan, gagging and wrinkling her nose as they lowered Sasha to the ground.

"Just breathing this stuff may be enough to revive Sasha," agreed Ainsley. He propped her against the tree, and her head lolled to one side. "We don't want to forget this." He removed the pouch from around Sasha's neck and poured the contents into his palm. Out rolled the purple Quatrys and . . . the shattered remains of Megan's necklace.

"Uh-oh," he said, looking back at Megan. She let out a small cry and plucked the Pearl of Truth from the shards of glass.

"That evil witch broke it!" she sobbed, massive tears sliding down her cheeks. She dropped to her knees and buried her head in her hands.

"It's all right, Megan," said Ainsley, sitting down beside her. "We can get you a new bottle and chain for the pearl."

Megan shook her head, tucking the pearl into her left breast pocket. "It's not just that," she sniffled. "I'm trapped on an island that smells like a dog kennel with a bird woman and my worst enemy . . . and I think there's something wriggling in my boot!"

She yanked it off and flung it at Sasha, and a slimy lungfish skittered out. "See?"

But Ainsley hadn't taken his eyes off Megan. "After all we've been through, you still think of me as your enemy? Your *worst* enemy?"

"What?" Megan looked up at him through her tangles of hair, surprised at the wounded look on his face. "Well, probably not the worst. She's the worst," Megan pointed at Sasha.

"But I thought we were over the past," said Ainsley. "You know, I forgive you for trying to control my life, and you forgive me for . . . whatever you think I did."

Megan rolled her eyes. "See? *That's* why we can't get along. We could if you weren't so cruel all the time." Ainsley's frown deepened and Megan hurried to correct herself. "I mean you're not that bad all of the time. Some of the time you're funny."

Ainsley didn't say anything. He poked at the ground with a stick, jamming it into the mud.

"Look," continued Megan, retrieving her boot. "I shouldn't have said you're my enemy. I should have just said you . . . could be difficult to get along with."

"No, you're right. I've been kind of a jerk," said Ainsley, snapping his stick in half. "I'm sorry."

Megan raised her eyebrows. "What's this? The Great Ainsley is saying 'I'm sorry' and it's not followed by the words 'that you exist'?"

Ainsley looked up at the impish grin on her face and smiled. "Let's not make a big deal out of this."

"But this is the second time you've apologized in what . . . two weeks? I think you've just bested your own record."

She laughed, but Ainsley didn't join her. "Do you hear something?" he asked, getting to his feet.

Megan cocked her head to one side. "Yeah, it sounds like rocks in a tin can. Where is it coming from?" She stood beside Ainsley.

"All around us. Look." He pointed at the water, which rippled towards them from the left, the right, and directly ahead.

"I have a feeling we're about to be outnumbered," said Ainsley softly.

Bonemaster

Ainsley and Megan watched the marsh reeds around them with increasing trepidation. The plants waved in various directions that no wind could have caused, and they could hear heavy splashes like bodies wading towards them through the water.

Then, the cattails shifted aside and the first figure came into view.

Megan screamed and stumbled backwards, collapsing in the mud as more of the figures appeared. Ainsley could make no motion to help her; the shock at what he had seen held him rooted to the ground.

Fleshless skeletons marched toward the island like macabre marionettes, their bones rattling with every ominous step. Rusting metal helms covered their hairless skulls and tattered cloaks adorned their backs, which were nothing but rib bones. Each animated corpse wielded a crude buckler in one hand and a spear held aloft in the other. They marched across the sludgy swamp floor as easily as if it had been dry ground until they encircled Ainsley and Megan.

Megan scrambled to her feet and stood with her back to Ainsley's. "What do we do now?"

One of the skeletons turned its head at the sound of Megan's voice, granting a frontal view of its helmet. "They're Silvan Sentry," Ainsley said in disbelief. "The insignia on those helmets—I recognize it from when we were in Raklund."

Megan's eyes widened as the skeletons stood at ease. "Are these the same soldiers that came to find Losen all those years ago?"

"I think so," said Ainsley, stepping in front of Megan and taking a defensive stance. "Stand back. I'll fight them off."

"Um . . . Captain Courageous," Megan tried to push his arms down, "I'm not sure that's such a brilliant idea. There are a lot of them, and they haven't even attacked *us*. We don't want to provoke them."

"We need to get them before they get us," said Ainsley, shrugging her off. "Besides, they're just skeletons. Just bones. This'll be easy."

As he stepped towards one of the soldiers, it raised its spear defensively. Ainsley punched at the skeleton with his right fist, but the skeleton raised its shield to block the blow, and Ainsley's fist clashed with solid steel.

"Shit!" Ainsley retracted his arm and clenched his throbbing hand. He aimed a kick at the skeletal soldier, but it dropped its shield and grabbed his leg. Ainsley tried another punch, but the soldier released its spear and grasped Ainsley's fist, twisting his wrist slightly. "Ow, ow, ow!"

Megan tapped Ainsley on the shoulder. "Um, this doesn't seem to be going well," she whispered.

"Brilliant observation. How about being productive and helping me?" he asked as he fought to release himself from the skeleton's grasp.

"But they're just bones, Ainsley," Megan mimicked him. "Surely a martial arts champ like yourself can take them all."

"You're really putting a damper on our friendship, you know," said Ainsley as another soldier approached from the rear, pointing a spear at the back of his neck. The soldier that Ainsley had been attacking released Ainsley's wrist and dropped his leg into the water with a splash.

"I hate to suggest this," said Megan as she felt a spear-point part her hair, "but maybe you should use the Quatrys."

"Of course," said Ainsley, reaching into his pocket.

"What do you want, my friend?" whispered the familiar voice in his mind. *"How can I use my power?"*

Ainsley hesitated for a moment. He wasn't sure if he imagined it, but the voice seemed less subservient than before, as if the Quatrys now thought itself his equal.

"Ainsley, if you're going to do something, do it quick," urged Megan, the spearpoint pricking the nape of her neck.

I need a mighty gust of wind, requested Ainsley. The familiar ringing filled the air, and the water rippled, bowing the cattails. Nothing appeared to be happening to the soldiers, however.

"What's going on?" Megan asked. "Why weren't they blown away?"

"I don't know. It's like they're invincible," said Ainsley. He popped the Quatrys into his mouth and gulped. As it slid down his throat, it felt warm, like he had just taken a swig of firepot.

"What did you . . . did you just swallow the Quatrys?" asked Megan, narrowing her eyes.

"I had to. If anyone wants it, they're going to have to kill me first."

"I'm not sure if that's stupid or brilliant," said Megan as a second spear was aimed at her jugular.

"Well, I'm guessing there's a reason they haven't killed us yet. Maybe they're friends of Sasha's."

As if in answer, the crowd of skeletons around them parted, and two skeletons wearing tattered green cloaks stepped forward with a makeshift stretcher between them. They gingerly rolled Sasha onto it and carried her away.

One of the Silvan Sentry skeletons nudged Ainsley in the back with its shield, causing him to lurch forward.

"Shall we go then?" he asked the skeleton, shooting it a nasty look.

Ainsley and Megan stumbled through the mud, flanked by the skeletons. After wading through the slop for close to an hour, they reached solid ground, stopping just outside a foul-smelling clump of mossfur trees planted around a mud-covered shanty. An enormous ball of fire was floating in front of the crude structure, and next to it stood a twenty-something-year-old man in black robes.

He towered over them at six feet tall. His hair was akin to an oil spill, both in color and in texture, and his skin was as pale as a sheet of parchment. Emerald green eyes glared back at them from a face that at one time must have been quite handsome but looked as if it had not had cause to smile for many years.

The man was carrying a staff with a skull perched atop it, and he stroked it absentmindedly as he watched the procession approach.

"I hope he's not looking for a skull to replace that one," Megan whispered to Ainsley.

"I heard that," said the young man, staring stonily at Megan. "Trust me. What I have in store for you is far worse than being a head propped on my staff."

He waved his staff and the skeletons crumpled into dusty piles of bones. Then he reached into his robes and extracted a small glittering object. He opened his palm to reveal the Quatrys of Land and rolled it from one knuckle to the next, as a magician would a coin. Hypnotized, Ainsley followed the Quatrys intently with his eyes, unaware of the vines pushing through the earth around him until they had wound their way up his legs.

Megan, too, was ensnared and tried to pull free from her vines, but the harder she pulled, the more they constricted.

"Careful," said the young man without a hint of concern. "You might cut off your circulation."

Ainsley relaxed in his own bindings to keep them loose. "I assume you're the one Sasha was taking us to meet?" he asked.

"Yes. And *what* did you do to my mother?" asked the young man in an abrasive voice. "Why did you hurt her?"

"We didn't hurt Sasha," said Ainsley. "She did that to herself."

"Wait a minute," said Megan, shaking her head. "Sasha's your mother? You're Losen?"

"In the flesh," the pale man said with a flourish, his skull-topped staff bowing with him.

"I thought you were dead," said Megan.

Losen leaned almost casually upon his staff. "That's what my mother wanted people to believe, and it's worked quite well for me. The only people who know the truth are my mother, my uncle, and my father."

"Kaelin knows about you?" asked Ainsley.

"You have a father?" asked Megan at the same time.

"I won't answer your question because it's far too moronic," Losen pointed to Megan and then turned to Ainsley, "but in answer to your question, yes, my uncle has known from the beginning. When he saw the path that I had chosen, he disowned me. I was dead to him."

"What path could you have chosen that would have made him hate you so much?" asked Ainsley.

Losen stroked the skull on his staff. "I decided to follow in my father's footsteps and become a necromancer."

Megan leaned towards Ainsley. "A what?"

Losen stepped between them, his face in Megan's. "A necromancer. A wizard with power over death and disease."

"Oh." Megan fidgeted in her bindings. "Well, that's an understandable reason to hate you."

"Mmm . . . yes, that's the way my mother felt, too," said Losen with a perverse smile. "That's why she tried to change me. At first, she thought it was just a phase, but when she realized I was serious, she tried to forcibly separate me from my father. *That* was a big mistake." Losen indicated the pile of bones that had been former Raklund soldiers.

"That's when the Silvan Sentry came in, isn't it?" asked Megan.

"My, my, that thing on your shoulders is good for something after all," said Losen, leaning forward and rapping her on the head. "They came, we attacked, and they all died. Kaelin gave up on me and convinced my mother to accept things as they were. My father and I lived happily together in the swamp. He taught me everything he could until . . . he caught The Illness."

For a moment, Losen seemed less sure of himself, as if speaking of his father's infirmity drained him of confidence, but it didn't take long for the venom to return to his speech. "He shouldn't have died. *Your* people let him, though."

"Our people?" asked Ainsley.

Losen paced before Ainsley and Megan in tight squares. "I asked for help in finding the cure, but your people refused to help us," said Losen, his voice shaking with anger. "Because we're *different*."

"I'm sure it probably had something to do with the fact that you and your father are cold-blooded killers," said Megan icily.

"Are we?" Losen stepped up to Megan, peering down into her eyes until she squirmed. "Or are *you*? Isn't it rather cold-blooded to try and separate a father from his son? Isn't it cold-blooded to reject a man in society and then let that same man die when you could have helped him?" Losen's nostrils flared and his lip trembled as he blinked back angry tears.

"By the time I found the cure, it was too late," he continued, turning away.

"So, what do you need the Staff of Lexiam for?" asked Ainsley.

Losen turned to face them again. "When I found the cure, I also found a way to bring my father's soul back. The staff is the answer." Losen removed the Quatrys of Fire from his robes. "So it seems that we both have something the other wants. I need the Staff of Lexiam and the remaining Quatrys and you, I believe, are looking for him." Losen waved his hand, and the globe of flame became transparent to reveal Bornias suspended in the air, his body limp.

"What did you do to him?" gasped Megan.

"Your precious king is fine," drawled Losen, rolling his eyes. "He's just asleep . . . and very difficult to get along with, I might add. He refuses to separate himself from the staff and he's cast a binding spell on it so I can't take it. I need you to make him give it to me." Losen said this in a casual tone, as if he were asking for nothing more than a glass of water.

"Forget it," said Ainsley flatly.

Losen scowled at him and waved his staff in Bornias's direction. Bornias shook his head groggily and opened his eyes. "Megan? Ainsley?" he called upon seeing them. "Are you all right?"

"For now," Losen told Bornias. "If you don't hand over that staff, however, I will kill them." He studied both teenagers, then tilted Ainsley's chin back with the end of his staff. "I think I'll start with him first."

Bornias pressed himself against the wall of the globe. "Please, let them go," he implored.

"I'll release them if you give me the staff," bargained Losen.

Bornias gazed at Ainsley and Megan and his eyes watered with tears. "He plans to do more with the staff than restore his father's life. I'm . . . I'm sorry, but I cannot let him have it."

Bornias turned his back to them, and Losen frowned. "I was hoping I wouldn't have to do this," he turned to Ainsley and Megan, "but you two have outlasted your usefulness." He raised the Quatrys of Fire in his hand. "Good-bye."

Losen hurled a fistful of fire at Ainsley's heart. The next sixty seconds crawled by in slow motion, as Ainsley did his best to back away, but the vines around his legs held him fast. With a panicked shout, Megan dove at him and knocked him to the ground. The vines around Ainsley's legs finally snapped, but Megan had placed herself in danger. The flames struck her in the chest, knocking her backwards and jerking her free of the vines as well.

If her clothes hadn't still been wet from wading through the swamp, they would have most certainly caught fire. At any rate, the flames were still hot enough to eat through her tunic, leaving a blackened hole in their wake and Megan clutching her chest in pain.

"Megan!" The world around them returned to normal speed. Ainsley knelt beside Megan and raised her head into his lap. Losen didn't try to stop him. If it was possible, the young necromancer looked even paler.

Ainsley attempted to pull Megan's hand from her chest so he could inspect the damage, but she shrugged him away, tears spilling freely down her cheeks.

"Ainsley. You have to . . . bring Losen . . . down and free Bornias." Megan's speech was sporadic, punctuated by gasps as she clutched at her heart. "Save Raklund . . . and go home."

Then, the pained expression on Megan's face relaxed and her eyes glazed over; her hands fell to her side and her eyelids slid shut.

Showdown

"Megan?" Ainsley slapped her across the face, but she didn't respond. His throat tightened, and fought back tears as he shook her by the shoulders, her head flopping around like a rag doll's. He pressed his fingers to her neck and was relieved to find that she still had a pulse.

"I warned you," said Losen. His hair was matted with sweat and he licked his lips nervously. Ainsley glared at him.

"What's the matter? Never tried to kill someone so innocent before? Not too eager to follow in daddy's footsteps now?"

Losen's eyes flashed in anger before his lips curved into a sneer. "Actually, I quite enjoyed watching her squirm in pain. I think I might do it again . . . but this time *you'll* do the writhing."

"Bornias!" Ainsley shouted, keeping his eyes trained on Losen. "I need your help to get Megan out of here!"

Bornias tried to stand, but whatever Losen had done to him appeared to have drained his strength. He raised his staff before him and tried to invoke the magic within it, but it fizzled, sending off a shower of sparks.

"I'm sorry, Ainsley," he murmured. "You'll have to defeat Losen on your own. But perhaps if you—"

Bornias didn't have the chance to finish his sentence, for Losen enclosed him once more in the fiery prison. Ainsley lowered his head, feeling defeated for the first time since he had come to Arylon.

"Cheer up, now." Losen interrupted his thoughts, nudging him with a muddy boot. "I want to see you smiling when I send you to meet your maker. Then, when I'm done with you, I think I'll revive your little girlfriend," he gestured to Megan's comatose form, "and make her my personal slave."

Losen cackled as he towered over Megan, and Ainsley felt an insurmountable rage building within him. Head still lowered, he raised hate-filled eyes to meet Losen's.

"*He must pay,*" the voice whispered in his mind. "*Let me kill him.*"

"You hurt my friends," Ainsley said with an almost primeval growl. "You put thousands of lives in danger for your own selfish interests. You really are a cold-blooded killer."

Something stirred inside Ainsley, a minor twitch that spread into a massive wave, washing over his entire body and causing every hair on his scalp to stand on end. The power of the Quatrys was awakening inside him, eager to unleash their full potential.

Lightning flashed across the sky as dark clouds rolled in to block the sunlight. An intense wind swept through the trees, sending leaves and branches flitting across the ground, and causing Losen's shack to creak ominously, as if it were on the verge of collapse.

Ainsley's sudden burst of force seemed to have intimidated Losen, but he didn't back down from the challenge. Losen held the Quatrys of Land and the Quatrys of Fire in one hand, clenching them in his fist. The ground quaked and the mossfur trees ignited around Ainsley and Losen.

"The Staff of Lexiam will be mine," said Losen, raising his hand in the air. Something crackled and splintered behind Ainsley, and he turned in time to see one of the flaming mossfur trees fracture at the base, falling towards him. Ainsley thrust his hands forward, using wind to hold the tree upright until he could get out of its path. He let it fall with a crash, sending red-hot embers spilling across the ground.

"You can't win, Losen," he said. "Give up."

"Not a chance," the necromancer snarled through clenched teeth. He dropped his hand to his side and gestured at the ground beneath Ainsley's feet. The damp soil crumbled and split, opening a gaping fissure beneath Ainsley's boots. Ainsley swung his arms in wide circles like an off-kilter acrobat and was able to avoid plummeting into chasm. Losen used this break in Ainsley's concentration to launch another surge of fire at him, but Ainsley recovered in time to roll out of the way.

"Have I worn you out yet, hero?" taunted Losen as Ainsley stood to face him once more. "Or shall I place a few more obstacles in your path?"

"It's too bad you're afraid to fight me without the Quatrys," said Ainsley, trying to keep his breathing even. "Are you so weak that you can't fight me without magic?"

Losen sealed the ground between him and Ainsley and stepped forward until they were nose-to-nose. "I could crush you with my magic," scoffed Losen, "but I'm going to enjoy this so much more."

Losen tucked his Quatrys into his pocket and tossed his staff aside. Ainsley took a step backward, sizing Losen up in anticipation of the first blow.

Losen swung at Ainsley with his right fist. Ainsley blocked with his own right hand and jabbed Losen in the stomach with his left. Losen grunted but didn't double over. "Is that the best you can do, strong man?" he jeered.

Ainsley foolishly allowed his anger to get the best of him and kicked out at Losen with his right leg. Losen grabbed

Ainsley's leg inches before it reached his chest and wrenched it to the right. Ainsley screamed with pain and did a spinning kick, lifting his other leg off the ground and connecting solidly with the side of Losen's head. Losen released Ainsley, and both of them fell to the ground, Ainsley on his stomach and Losen on his back.

"Not bad," said Losen as they both got to their feet. A trickle of blood ran from his temple and down his cheek like an evil teardrop. "I may have underestimated you."

"Thank you for the vote of . . . confidence." Ainsley grimaced as he popped his leg back into place.

In one fluid movement, Losen picked up a fallen tree limb that was as thick as Ainsley's arm. He twirled it like a baton in front of him, toying with Ainsley, who was trying to follow Losen's movements, waiting for the strike. Losen whipped the branch sideways, catching Ainsley in the ribs. Ainsley gasped in pain, but grabbed the branch and jabbed it into Losen's chest, knocking him backwards.

A ringing echoed in his ears, but Ainsley didn't recognize the sound soon enough. The ground rumbled again and he was caught off balance. Losen tackled him to the dirt and tried to punch him in the face, but Ainsley blocked him. Losen may have been bigger, but Ainsley was faster.

"You just used the Quatrys of Land. I thought you agreed you wouldn't resort to magic," said Ainsley, barely dodging a cuff to his right ear.

"I never actually said I wouldn't," said Losen, landing a solid punch to Ainsley's cheek. "I could beat on you for hours, but I just don't have that kind of time to spare."

"*I can defeat him for you,*" the voice said to Ainsley. "*Give me control.*"

"No, I won't," said Ainsley aloud, hoping this would strengthen his resolve. Between Losen and the voice of the Quatrys in his mind, he felt as though he were fighting two battles and was emerging the victor in neither.

The dark clouds overhead began to leak droplets of rain that hissed and fizzled as they hit the burning trees. Ainsley watched a particularly fat drop splash onto an ember that had fallen on the grass. The ember made a spitting noise as it became saturated, and an idea came to Ainsley.

He grabbed a handful of embers, the flesh on his hand blistering from the heat, and tossed them into Losen's face.

Losen yelped and jumped to his feet, brushing the hot ash from his eyes and off his clothes. Taking advantage of Losen's preoccupation, Ainsley reached into his pocket and pulled out a small tube. Removing the top, he lobbed it at the flaming ball that held Bornias. As the tube spun through the air, its contents dripped onto the ground, leaving frozen patches of earth in its wake.

Losen tackled Ainsley to the ground once more, but Ainsley didn't take his eyes off the tube.

Please, he begged silently, *just one drop.*

The glass tube shattered the moment it made impact with the blazing heat from the fire. Its contents splattered to the ground, and Ainsley groaned.

Losen grabbed Ainsley by the throat and began to squeeze. Ainsley pushed at Losen with his legs and pried at Losen's hands with his own fingers, feeling dizzy from the pressure around his neck.

A loud crackling and popping startled both of them, and Losen released his grip on Ainsley's throat.

"What did you do?" he asked in disbelief as he looked over his shoulder.

Ainsley followed Losen's gaze and could barely suppress a grin of relief. The globe of fire that held Bornias had frozen into an enormous crystalline ball. "It's Instant Ice," he answered.

"It looks like your plan to thaw out your old friend backfired," said Losen. He tightened his grip around Ainsley's throat once more.

Ainsley swallowed hard but made no effort to fight Losen. Letting his arms fall by his sides, he closed his eyes.

"Given up, have you?" gloated Losen. "I can't blame you. Don't worry. Your life will be over in a matter of seconds."

Ainsley's eyelids flew open and he whispered, "Not if I can help it."

Ainsley's ears rang as the frozen globe of ice behind Losen shuddered and creaked, protesting against the wind that was pushing it. Ainsley felt the resistance fade, and he grinned at Losen as the frozen globe of ice flew rapidly towards them.

"Good-bye," said Ainsley.

The weight of Losen's body lifted off him as the globe of ice smashed into Losen and knocked him away. Ainsley rolled to his feet, panting from the effort of using his Quatrys.

Losen lay in a crumpled heap beneath one of the scorched mossfur trees, half-burned in an enormous pile of melting ice-shards. Bornias, too, lay against the tree, but he was awake and smiling weakly at Ainsley.

"Well done, Ainsley. Now, if you don't mind going through our friend's pockets and getting the Quatrys, I would be most appreciative. Take away his staff while you're at it and tie him up with those vines," Bornias added as an afterthought.

"What about Megan?" asked Ainsley, pulling open Losen's robes and transferring the three remaining Quatrys to his own breast pocket.

"Can you carry her to me?" asked Bornias as Ainsley tossed Losen's staff to him.

"I think so," said Ainsley, scooping Megan into his arms and lifting her experimentally. He staggered over to Bornias and lowered Megan to the ground with a soft grunt. Then, he began binding Losen's hands behind him. "Explain to me why you drank the potion Losen gave you."

"I didn't drink anything. I was stabbed in the rear with a poisoned dart." Bornias rubbed his posterior and winced. "It still hurts a bit, but don't worry. I'll take an antidote when we get back to Amdor."

"So, do we wait here for someone to rescue us?" asked Ainsley.

"No, we need to get you and Megan back to Kaelin's, and we need to hand Losen over to the Silvan Sentry."

"Won't everyone be looking for us, though?" asked Ainsley. "Shouldn't we stay put?"

"I'm sure they have already discovered the truth, but I'll get a message to Frieden. I have a feeling that Kaelin stayed in Amdor to watch over Rayne."

"What'll we do about Sasha?" asked Ainsley. "I think she's in that shack."

"We'll leave her to the authorities as well," said Bornias. He reached into his robes and removed the Staff of Lexiam. "Here. Place the Quatrys in their slots," he said, indicating four grooves on one end of the staff.

Ainsley clicked the red, blue, and green Quatrys into place.

"Where's the purple one?" asked Bornias.

"I swallowed it," said Ainsley, blushing. "I didn't want anyone to take it from me."

Bornias groaned and rubbed his forehead, leaving a smear of ash behind.

"Will the staff not work now?" asked Ainsley nervously.

Bornias shook his head. "I'm not sure if it's good for your health, but the Quatrys of Air should be able to transfer its energy through your body."

Ainsley handed the staff back to Bornias. "What happens now?" he asked.

"I'll need you to place your hand on the tip of the staff where the Quatrys are," said Bornias.

"I hope this works," said Ainsley, resting his hand over the Quatrys.

Bornias closed his eyes and spoke in a lilting voice, his incantations like the verses of a song. "*Krida doshin pres siosfra.*"

The staff began to glow, the light casting a circle around Ainsley, Bornias, Megan, and Losen. The light changed from red to green to blue. Ainsley felt warmth spread from his chest, down his arm to the hand resting on the staff. As the warmth reached his hand, the staff glowed purple.

"*Cufan Amdor xesh e nopshi.*"

Bornias opened his eyelids halfway. "It has been set in motion. Sit and rest, letting your thoughts be of Amdor."

Ainsley lowered himself beside Bornias and concentrated on Amdor. The purple light grew brighter, almost blindingly so, before it faded away, replaced by a softer golden light. Ainsley closed his eyes and let himself be bathed in the glow.

The ground melted away below him, but he didn't experience a sensation of falling as he had when they first came to Arylon. Instead, he floated languidly through the air, as if drifting on an invisible sea. The wind didn't whip around him, but rather it tickled his face, tugging on the ends of his hair so that his scalp tingled.

Exhaustion was setting in, and he decided that he would nap for a few days once they got back to wherever it was they were going.

Amdor, he reminded himself. They were going to Amdor, and they would be heroes when they got back.

Megan and I will be famous, he thought. But for what he couldn't remember.

I'm going to be famous for something I can't remember, he thought, and laughed aloud, as if this were the funniest thing he had ever heard. Opening his eyes, he blinked lazily, as if it were almost too much trouble to raise his eyelids. To his left, he saw an old man floating beside him, but Ainsley couldn't recall where he had seen him.

Behind the old man were a girl and a younger man, both lying on their sides. They didn't look familiar either, but they seemed to have the right idea. He lay back and closed his eyes, letting sleep take him.

The End is the Beginning

Megan opened her eyes, a slight pain over her heart drawing her from the deepest slumber.

She recognized her surroundings as the inside of Kaelin's cottage, and she could hear voices outside on the front porch. The sunlight filtering through the living room window told her it was late morning, but she was unsure of how many days had past. She vaguely remembered Bornias waking her to take a medicine tasting of vomit, but she had slept through everything else.

She glanced around and saw Ainsley curled into a tight ball on the floor beside her, still lost to sleep. Not wanting to wake him, Megan crept out the front door where Bornias, Frieden, Rayne, and Kaelin greeted her. They were eating fried doo-dah, and the gurgling in her stomach made her realize she hadn't had any real food in days.

"Well, look who's awake!" said Kaelin with a smile. "Rayne just woke up today himself." He offered a piece of doo-dah to Megan who settled on the porch stoop and began to devour her drumstick.

"You're looking much better," she told Rayne between bites, trying not to let her eyes stray to his head, which had been shaven smooth.

"Don't let her fool you," Frieden teased Rayne. "You looked much better when you were under Sasha's influence."

Rayne ran a hand over the stubble on his scalp. "What a nightmare that was."

"Maybe that'll teach you not to drink firepots with strangers," his grandfather admonished him, licking the doo-dah grease off his fingers.

"She looked like Evren," said Rayne in his own defense. "I thought it was him trying to make up for the past. How was I supposed to know he, or rather *she,* was going to slip something in my drink?"

"Well, at least you learned from the experience," said Bornias. "I hope."

Megan listened to their conversation with rapt attention. So far, no one had mentioned how she, Ainsley, and

Bornias had made it back to Amdor, and they hadn't brought up her near-death experience either.

"What happened after I passed out?" she finally asked Bornias when Kaelin stepped inside with the dirty dishes.

Frieden and Rayne, who hadn't been in the Sheiran Swamp, sat quietly while Bornias recounted the story of Ainsley's defeat over Losen.

"It was quite ingenious, really," said Bornias. "I have to admit I did not give you two enough credit."

"Where is Sasha now?" asked Megan. "Is she okay?"

"She's recovering at a no-magic prison in Raklund," said Bornias, "along with her son, who has been quite humbled by his defeat."

Megan pulled her knees up to her chest and wrapped her arms around them.

"I know it sounds strange, but I can't help feeling a little sorry for Losen. I can see how he'd be upset that someone tried to take him from his father."

"I still find it hard to believe he was alive all this time," said Bornias as Kaelin came back outside. Bornias snorted at him. "And I can't believe you never told anyone."

Kaelin wordlessly pulled a pipe from his pocket, banged it against his palm, and packed it with tobacco. "What would I have said, Bornias?" he asked after he had lit his pipe and puffed on it for a moment. "How could I have told the people of Raklund that their husbands and fathers died trying to save a boy that didn't want to be saved?"

He exhaled a smoke ring and shook his head. "I couldn't live among the people knowing that, and I certainly wasn't fit to remain governor."

"So you knew all along that Losen was living with his father?" asked Megan.

"Yes, after Farris, Losen's father, had to leave the Protectors, he wasn't a very good influence. I felt, as did Sasha, that he would be better off in a more . . . civilized environment."

Megan couldn't believe what she was hearing. "Losen's father was a Protector?"

"Yes, but Evren had him ousted for performing dark magic," said Frieden. "Granted, Evren is no better."

"So that's why Sasha hates Evren so much," said Megan, waving her drumstick bone.

"Luckily, Losen's started to come to terms with his father's death," said Bornias, "and he actually apologized for trying to kill you."

"I can't believe I survived that," said Megan, shaking her head. "I mean, the fireball came straight for my heart."

"You were very lucky," said Bornias. "You sustained mild burns and bruising; your pearl took the brunt of the damage."

"My pearl!" exclaimed Megan, searching her pockets. "Where is it?"

Frieden and Rayne looked at Bornias who coughed uncomfortably.

"It's some place you'll never lose it," he assured her. "Close to your heart."

"What do you mean?" Megan put her hand to her chest and felt a bump under her skin. "It couldn't have?" She pulled on her tunic front and looked inside her top. The smooth, white Pearl of Truth was half-imbedded in her flesh amidst an ugly purple bruise.

"It's in my skin!" she squeaked.

Frieden nodded. "We tried to dislodge it, but it doesn't seem to want to leave."

Megan continued to stare at the pearl until its image became blurred by her tears. "This is so cool," she said, her breath catching in her throat. "It's like . . . like the Pearl of Truth and I are inseparable now, isn't it?" She looked up at Bornias, who nodded.

"This may make things more difficult for you in the future, however," he warned. "Because the truth is so near to your heart, you'll feel pain with every lie you hear or any deceit that occurs near you."

"And there's plenty of deceit out there," said Rayne. "I should know."

Everyone laughed except Kaelin, who was quietly sobbing into a kerchief.

"Kaelin? What's the matter?" asked Bornias.

Kaelin shook his head. "You were right, old friend. This whole thing is my fault. If not for me, all those people would still be alive and Sasha would never have gone after the staff."

He sat on the porch bench cradling his pipe in one hand. Bornias sat beside him and patted Kaelin on the shoulder.

"You mustn't blame yourself for all those deaths. Those men were sent into the swamps on a mission. You couldn't have predicted their failure."

"It's my fault they went in the first place. I knew Losen hadn't been kidnapped, that he was living happily with his father, but I didn't want anyone to know I was associated with Farris. I deceived everyone for my own selfish gain."

"Many people have dark secrets that they would sooner forget," said Frieden, sitting on Kaelin's other side. "And you tried to make amends by offering Losen a better life than being a swamp rat."

"Frieden's right," said Bornias, offering Kaelin another kerchief into which Kaelin blew. "And it's certainly not your fault that Sasha went after the staff. You didn't convince her to go after it, did you?"

"No, but I as good as did. She would have never known the staff had regenerative capabilities if she hadn't seen that book."

Bornias took his hand off Kaelin's shoulder. "What book?"

"It was a book of magical artifacts," said Kaelin, gesturing with his pipe. "*The Tondex*, I think it was called. When I was tracking Evren, I followed him to Poloi's bookstore and saw him reading it. When he left, I borrowed the book to see what Evren had been studying, and one of the sections of the book talked about the Staff of Lexiam. I left the book on the kitchen table, and she must have found it."

"So, you assumed Evren was studying it to find out about the Staff of Lexiam," Bornias thought aloud, "but we know that it wasn't really Evren who was interested in the staff. So what was Evren looking for?" Bornias turned to Kaelin. "Can you retrieve *The Tondex* for me?"

"Of course," said Kaelin. "I'll ask Poloi if I can borrow it." He hurried down the porch steps towards Nick's cottage.

Bornias stood and faced Frieden and Rayne. "When Kaelin returns with the book, I want the three of you to study it and see what you can come up with. I'll wake Ainsley so I can get him and Megan home."

Bornias had said the words Megan longed to hear for weeks. She felt like singing, but when she looked at Frieden, a lump rose in her throat as if she'd swallowed a chicken bone whole.

"Come here," said Frieden with a sad smile. He opened his arms and Megan ran to him, tears spilling down her cheeks.

She buried her face in his cloak and breathed deep the earthy smell of wood smoke and horses.

"I want to go home," she said in a muffled voice, "but I'm going to miss everyone."

"You can always come and visit," said Frieden, stroking her hair. "Bornias can bring you back."

"You live in Pontsford, don't you Megan?" asked Rayne. Megan released Frieden and looked at Rayne. He appeared confused by Megan's sadness, and she remembered that he hadn't yet learned about access to other dimensions.

"Yeah, but it feels like I live worlds away," she said, sharing a secretive smile with Frieden.

"Is Bornias still trying to wake Ainsley?" Kaelin trudged back onto the porch carrying a battered, gray book under his arm. He moved to the door, but it swung open before he could reach it, and Bornias appeared in the doorway. He had a troubled look in his eyes and a frown that made his lower lip protrude.

"Having trouble waking him?" asked Kaelin. "I have some smelling salts in the pantry." He tried to elbow his way inside, but Bornias blocked his path.

"You mustn't touch him," said Bornias. His tone was anxious, not angry. "I don't want you to catch it."

"Catch what?" asked Kaelin confusedly.

"Just step back and stay out of the cottage," said Bornias, shooing Kaelin with his hand.

Kaelin backed away, and as Bornias stepped into the light, Megan saw how pale his face was, the sweat on his brow.

"Wh-what's wrong with Ainsley?" she asked nervously. Megan tried to push past him into the cottage, but Frieden grabbed her by the arms.

"I'll need to do some more research first to confirm it's what I think it is, but it doesn't look good," said Bornias.

"What's wrong with Ainsley?" she shrieked, trying to wrestle free of Frieden. She managed to slip out of his grasp and hurried to the living room window.

She pressed her forehead against the pane to look into the room and saw Ainsley propped up against some floor cushions with his back to her.

"Ainsley!" she shouted, pounding on the glass.

Bornias stepped away from the door. "Megan, you don't want—"

Ainsley turned his head to look at her, and Megan let out a bloodcurdling scream.

"It's impossible," whispered Frieden, looking through the window.

"What's wrong with his eyes?" asked Rayne, looking at Ainsley from the doorway. "They're not green anymore. They're—"

"Red," said Bornias with a nod. "If it's what I fear, Ainsley has been infected with The Illness."

"No," whispered Megan.

Ainsley's crimson eyes locked with her brown ones, and for the briefest moment, their minds seemed to meet as well.

Don't leave me, he pleaded.

Megan pressed her forehead to the glass. "If I never see my family again," she whispered, "if I have to die a thousand deaths, I'll find a way to save you. I swear it."

This ends the first book in
"The Escape from Arylon" trilogy

Where would you like to go?